HENRY OF LANCASTER WHO IN 1399 AS HENRY IV BECAME ENGLAND'S KING IN
THE STEAD OF THE WEAK, WICKED, AND TREACHEROUS RICHARD II

MEN OF IRON

BY

HOWARD PYLE

AUTHOR OF

"THE WONDER CLOCK" "PEPPER AND SALT"
"THE ROSE OF PARADISE" ETC.

Illustrated

NEW YORK AND LONDON
HARPER & BROTHERS PUBLISHERS

3109

TO

MY FRIEND AND CRITIC

J. HENRY HARPER

𝕴𝖘 𝕴𝖓𝖘𝖈𝖗𝖎𝖇𝖊𝖉

ALL THAT MAY BE OF WORTH

IN THIS VOLUME

H. P.

ILLUSTRATIONS.

INTRODUCTION

THE year 1400 opened with more than usual peacefulness in England. Only a few months before, Richard II.—weak, wicked, and treacherous—had been dethroned, and Henry IV. declared King in his stead. But it was only a seeming peacefulness, lasting but for a little while; for though King Henry proved himself a just and a merciful man—as justice and mercy went with the men of iron of those days—and though he did not care to shed blood needlessly, there were many noble families who had been benefited by King Richard during his reign, and who had lost somewhat of their power and prestige from the coming in of the new King.

Among these were a number of great lords—the Dukes of Albemarle, Surrey, and Exeter, the

1

Marquis of Dorset, the Earl of Gloucester, and others—who had been degraded to their former titles and estates, from which King Richard had lifted them. These and others brewed a secret plot to take King Henry's life, which plot might have succeeded had not one of their own number betrayed them.

Their plan had been to fall upon the King and his adherents, and to massacre them during a great tournament, to be held at Oxford. But Henry did not appear at the lists; whereupon, knowing that he had been lodging at Windsor with only a few attendants, the conspirators marched thither against him. In the mean time the King had been warned of the plot, so that, instead of finding him in the royal castle, they discovered through their scouts that he had hurried to London, whence he was even then marching against them at the head of a considerable army. So nothing was left them but flight. Some betook themselves one way, some another; some sought sanctuary here, some there; but one and another, they were all of them caught and killed.

The Earl of Kent—one time Duke of Surrey—and the Earl of Salisbury were beheaded in the market-place at Cirencester; Lord Le Despencer—once the Earl of Gloucester—and Lord Lumley met the same fate at Bristol; the Earl of Huntingdon was taken in the Essex fens, carried to the castle of the Duke of Gloucester, whom he had betrayed to his death in King Richard's time, and was there killed by the castle people. Those few who found friends faithful and bold enough to afford them shelter, dragged those friends down in their own ruin.

Just such a case was that of the father of the boy hero of this story, the blind Lord Gilbert Reginald Falworth, Baron of Falworth and Easterbridge, who, though having no part in the plot, suffered through it ruin, utter and complete.

He had been a faithful counsellor and adviser to King Richard, and perhaps it was this, as much and more than his roundabout connection with the plot, that brought upon him the punishment he suffered.

CHAPTER I.

MYLES FALWORTH was but eight years of age at that time, and it was only afterwards, and when he grew old enough to know more of the ins and outs of the matter, that he could remember by bits and pieces the things that afterwards happened; how one evening a knight came clattering into the court-yard upon a horse, red-nostrilled and smeared with the sweat and foam of a desperate ride—Sir John Dale, a dear friend of the blind Lord.

Even though so young, Myles knew that something very serious had happened to make Sir John so pale and haggard, and he dimly remembered leaning against the 'knight's iron-covered knees, looking up into his gloomy face, and asking him if he was sick to look so strange. Thereupon those who had been too troubled before to notice him, bethought themselves of him, and sent him to bed, rebellious at having to go so early.

He remembered how the next morning, look-ing out of a window high up under the eaves, he saw a great troop of horsemen come riding into the court-yard beneath, where a powdering of snow had whitened everything, and of how the leader, a knight clad in black armor, dismounted and entered the great hall door-way below, fol-lowed by several of the band.

He remembered how some of the castle wom-en were standing in a frightened group upon the landing of the stairs, talking together in low voices about a matter he did not understand, excepting that the armed men who had ridden into the court-yard had come for Sir John Dale. None of the women paid any attention to him; so, shunning their notice, he ran off down the winding stairs, expecting every moment to be called back again by some one of them.

A crowd of castle people, all very serious and quiet, were gathered in the hall, where a num-ber of strange men-at-arms lounged upon the benches, while two billmen in steel caps and leathern jacks stood guarding the great door, the butts of their weapons resting upon the ground, and the staves crossed, barring the door-way.

In the anteroom was the knight in black ar-mor whom Myles had seen from the window. He was sitting at the table, his great helmet lying upon the bench beside him, and a quart beaker of spiced wine at his elbow. A clerk sat at the other end of the same table, with inkhorn in one hand and pen in the other, and a parchment spread in front of him.

Master Robert, the castle steward, stood before the knight, who every now and then put to him a question, which the other would answer, and the clerk write the answer down upon the parchment.

His father stood with his back to the fireplace, looking down upon the floor with his blind eyes, his brows drawn moodily together, and the scar of the great wound that he had received at the tournament at York—the wound that had made him blind—showing red across his forehead, as it always did when he was angered or troubled.

There was something about it all that frightened Myles, who crept to his father's side, and slid his little hand into the palm that hung limp and inert. In answer to the touch, his father grasped the hand tightly, but did not seem otherwise to notice that he was there. Neither did the black knight pay any attention to him, but continued putting his questions to Master Robert.

Then, suddenly, there was a commotion in the hall without, loud voices, and a hurrying here and there. The black knight half arose, grasping a heavy iron mace that lay upon the bench beside him, and the next moment Sir John Dale himself, as pale as death, walked into the ante-chamber. He stopped in the very middle of the room. "I yield me to my Lord's grace and mercy," said he to the black knight, and they were the last words he ever uttered in this world.

The black knight shouted out some words of command, and swinging up the iron mace in his hand, strode forward clanking towards Sir John, who raised his arm as though to shield himself from the blow. Two or three of those who stood in the hall without came running into the room with drawn swords and bills, and little Myles, crying out with terror, hid his face in his father's long gown.

The next instant came the sound of a heavy blow and of a groan, then another blow and the sound of one falling upon the ground. Then the clashing of steel, and in the midst Lord Falworth crying, in a dreadful voice, "Thou traitor! thou coward! thou murderer!"

Master Robert snatched Myles away from his father, and bore him out of the room in spite of his screams and struggles, and he remembered just one instant's sight of Sir John lying still and silent upon his face, and of the black knight standing above him, with the terrible mace in his hand stained a dreadful red.

It was the next day that Lord and Lady Falworth and little Myles, together with three of the more faithful of their people, left the castle.

His memory of past things held a picture for Myles of old Diccon Bowman standing over him in the silence of midnight with a lighted lamp in his hand, and with it a recollection of being bidden to hush when he would have spoken, and of being dressed by Diccon and one of the women, bewildered with sleep, shuddering and chattering with cold.

He remembered being wrapped in the sheepskin that lay at the foot of his bed, and of being carried in Diccon Bowman's arms down the silent darkness of the winding stair-way, with the great black giant shadows swaying and flickering upon the stone wall as the dull flame of the lamp swayed and flickered in the cold breathing of the night air.

Below were his father and mother and two or three others. A stranger stood warming his hands at a newly-made fire, and little Myles, as he peeped from out the warm sheepskin, saw that he was in riding-boots and was covered with mud. He did not know till long years afterwards that the stranger was a messenger sent by a friend at the King's court, bidding his father fly for safety.

They who stood there by the red blaze of the

fire were all very still, talking in whispers and walking on tiptoes, and Myles's mother hugged him in her arms, sheepskin and all, kissing him, with the tears streaming down her cheeks, and whispering to him, as though he could understand their trouble, that they were about to leave their home forever.

Then Diccon Bowman carried him out into the strangeness of the winter midnight.

Outside, beyond the frozen moat, where the osiers stood stark and stiff in their winter nakedness, was a group of dark figures waiting for them with horses. In the pallid moonlight Myles recognized the well-known face of Father Edward, the Prior of St. Mary's.

After that came a long ride through that silent night upon the saddle-bow in front of Diccon Bowman; then a deep, heavy sleep, that fell upon him in spite of the galloping of the horses.

When next he woke the sun was shining, and his home and his whole life were changed.

CHAPTER II.

FROM the time the family escaped from Falworth Castle that midwinter night to the time Myles was sixteen years old he knew nothing of the great world beyond Crosbey-Dale. A fair was held twice in a twelvemonth at the market-town of Wisebey, and three times in the seven years old Diccon Bowman took the lad to see the sights at that place. Beyond these three glimpses of the outer world he lived almost as secluded a life as one of the neighboring monks of St. Mary's Priory.

Crosbey - Holt, their new home, was different enough from Falworth or Easterbridge Castle, the former baronial seats of Lord Falworth. It was a long, low, straw-thatched farm-house, once, when the church lands were divided into two holdings, one of the bailiff's houses. All around were the fruitful farms of the priory, tilled by well-to-do tenant holders, and rich with fields of waving grain, and meadow-lands where sheep and cattle grazed in flocks and herds; for in those days the church lands were under church rule, and were governed by church laws, and there, when war and famine and waste and sloth blighted the outside world, harvests flourished and were gathered, and sheep were sheared and cows were milked in peace and quietness.

The Prior of St. Mary's owed much if not all of the church's prosperity to the blind Lord Falworth, and now he was paying it back with a haven of refuge from the ruin that his former patron had brought upon himself by giving shelter to Sir John Dale.

I fancy that most boys do not love the grinding of school life — the lessons to be conned, the close application during study hours. It is not often pleasant to brisk, lively lads to be so cooped up. I wonder what the boys of to-day would have thought of Myles's training. With him that training was not only of the mind, but of the body as well, and for seven years it was almost unremitting. "Thou hast thine own way to make in the world, sirrah," his father said more than once when the boy complained of the grinding hardness of his life, and to make one's way in those days meant a thousand times more than it does now; it meant not only a heart to feel and a brain to think, but a hand quick and

strong to strike in battle, and a body tough to
endure the wounds and blows in return. And so
it was that Myles's body as well as his mind had
to be trained to meet the needs of the dark age
in which he lived.

Every morning, winter or summer, rain or
shine, he tramped away six long miles to the
priory school, and in the evenings his mother
taught him French.

Myles, being prejudiced in the school of
thought of his day, rebelled not a little at that
last branch of his studies. " Why must I learn
that vile tongue?" said he.

" Call it not vile," said the blind old Lord,
grimly; " belike, when thou art grown a man,
thou'lt have to seek thy fortune in France land,
for England is haply no place for such as be of
Falworth blood." And in after-years, true to his
father's prediction, the " vile tongue " served him
well.

As for his physical training, that pretty well
filled up the hours between his morning studies
at the monastery and his evening studies at home.
Then it was that old Diccon Bowman took him
in hand, than whom none could be better fitted
to shape his young body to strength and his
hands to skill in arms. The old bowman had
served with Lord Falworth's father under the

Black Prince both in France and Spain, and in long years of war had gained a practical knowledge of arms that few could surpass. Besides the use of the broadsword, the short sword, the quarter-staff, and the cudgel, he taught Myles to shoot so skilfully with the long-bow and the cross-bow that not a lad in the country-side was his match at the village butts. Attack and defence with the lance, and throwing the knife and dagger were also part of his training.

Then, in addition to this more regular part of his physical training, Myles was taught in another branch not so often included in the military education of the day—the art of wrestling. It happened that a fellow lived in Crosbey village, by name Ralph-the-Smith, who was the greatest wrestler in the country-side, and had worn the champion belt for three years. Every Sunday afternoon, in fair weather, he came to teach Myles the art, and being wonderfully adept in bodily feats, he soon grew so quick and active and firm-footed that he could cast any lad under twenty years of age living within a range of five miles.

" It is main ungentle armscraft that he learneth," said Lord Falworth one day to Prior Edward. " Saving only the broadsword, the dagger, and the lance, there is but little that a gentleman of his strain may use. Neth'less, he gaineth quickness and suppleness, and if he hath true blood in his veins he will acquire knightly arts shrewdly quick when the time cometh to learn them."

But hard and grinding as Myles's life was, it was not entirely without pleasures. There were many boys living in Crosbey-Dale and the village; yeomen's and farmers' sons, to be sure, but, nevertheless, lads of his own age, and that, after all, is the main requirement for friendship in boyhood's world. Then there was the river to bathe in; there were the hills and valleys to roam over, and the wold and woodland, with their wealth of nuts and birds'-nests and what not of boyhood's treasures.

Once he gained a triumph that for many a day was very sweet under the tongue of his memory. As was said before, he had been three times to the market-town at fair-time, and upon the last of these occasions he had fought a bout of quarter-staff with a young fellow of twenty, and had been the conqueror. He was then only a little over fourteen years old.

Old Diccon, who had gone with him to the fair, had met some cronies of his own, with whom he had sat gossiping in the ale-booth, leaving Myles for the nonce to shift for himself. By-and-by the old man had noticed a crowd gathered at one part of the fair-ground, and, snuffing a fight, had gone running, ale-pot in hand. Then, peering over the shoulders of the crowd, he had seen his young master, stripped to the waist, fighting like a gladiator with a fellow a head taller than himself. Diccon was about to force his way through the crowd and drag them asunder, but a second look had showed his practised eye that Myles was not only holding his own, but was in the way of winning the victory. So he had stood with the others looking on, withholding himself from any interference and whatever upbraiding might be necessary until the fight had been brought to a triumphant close. Lord Falworth never heard directly of the redoubtable affair, but old Diccon was not so silent with the common folk of Crosbey-Dale, and so no doubt the father had some inkling of what had happened. It was shortly after this notable event that Myles was formally initiated into squirehood. His father and mother, as was the custom, stood sponsors for him. By them, each bearing a lighted taper, he was escorted to the altar. It was at St. Mary's Priory, and Prior Edward blessed the sword and girded it to the lad's side. No one was present but the four, and when the good Prior had given the benediction and had signed the cross upon his forehead, Myles's mother stooped and kissed his brow just where the priest's finger had drawn the holy sign. Her eyes brimmed bright with tears as she did so. Poor lady! perhaps she only then and for the first time realized how big her fledgling was growing for his nest. Henceforth Myles had the right to wear a sword.

Myles had ended his fifteenth year. He was a bonny lad, with brown face, curling hair, a square, strong chin, and a pair of merry laughing blue eyes; his shoulders were broad; his chest was thick of girth; his muscles and thews were as tough as oak.

The day upon which he was sixteen years old, as he came whistling home from the monastery school he was met by Diccon Bowman.

" Master Myles," said the old man, with a snuffle in his voice—" Master Myles, thy father would see thee in his chamber, and bade me send thee to him as soon as thou didst come home. Oh, Master Myles, I fear me that belike thou art going to leave home to-morrow day."

Myles stopped short. " To leave home!" he cried.

" Aye," said old Diccon, " belike thou goest to some grand castle to live there, and be a page there and what not, and then, haply, a gentleman-at-arms in some great lord's pay."

" What coil is this about castles and lords and gentlemen-at-arms?" said Myles. " What talkest thou of, Diccon? Art thou jesting?"

" Nay," said Diccon, " I am not jesting. But go to thy father, and then thou wilt presently know all. Only this I do say, that it is like thou leavest us to-morrow day."

And so it was as Diccon had said; Myles was to leave home the very next morning. He found his father and mother and Prior Edward together, waiting for his coming.

" We three have been talking it over this morning," said his father, " and so think each one that the time hath come for thee to quit this poor home of ours. An thou stay here ten years longer, thou'lt be no more fit to go then than now. To-morrow I will give thee a letter to my kinsman, the Earl of Mackworth. He has thriven in these days and I have fallen away, but time was that he and I were true sworn companions, and plighted together in friendship never to be sundered. Methinks, as I remember him, he will abide by his plighted troth, and will give thee his aid to rise in the world. So, as I said, to-morrow morning thou shalt set forth with Diccon Bowman, and shall go to Castle Devlen, and there deliver this letter, which prayeth him to give thee a place in his household. Thou mayst have this afternoon to thyself to make ready such things as thou shalt take with thee. And bid me Diccon to take the gray horse to the village and have it shod."

Prior Edward had been standing looking out of the window. As Lord Falworth ended he turned.

"And, Myles," said he, "thou wilt need some money, so I will give thee as a loan forty shillings, which some day thou mayst return to me an thou wilt. For this know, Myles, a man cannot do in the world without money. Thy father hath it ready for thee in the chest, and will give it thee to-morrow ere thou goest."

Lord Falworth had the grim strength of manhood's hard sense to upbear him in sending his son into the world, but the poor lady mother had nothing of that to uphold her. No doubt it was as hard then as it is now for the mother to see the nestling thrust from the nest to shift for itself. What tears were shed, what words of love were spoken to the only man-child, none but the mother and the son ever knew.

The next morning Myles and the old bowman rode away, and no doubt to the boy himself the dark shadows of leave-taking were lost in the golden light of hope as he rode out into the great world to seek his fortune.

CHAPTER III.

WHAT Myles remembered of Falworth loomed great and grand and big, as things do in the memory of childhood, but even memory could not make Falworth the equal of Devlen Castle, when, as he and Diccon Bowman rode out of Devlen-town across the great, rude stone bridge that spanned the river, he first saw, rising above the crowns of the trees, those huge hoary walls, and the steep roofs and chimneys clustered thickly together, like the roofs and chimneys of a town.

The castle was built upon a plateau-like rise of ground, which was enclosed by the outer wall. It was surrounded on three sides by a loop-like bend of the river, and on the fourth was protected by a deep, broad, artificial moat, almost as wide as the stream from which it was fed. The road from the town wound for a little distance along by the edge of this moat. As Myles and the old bowman galloped by, with the answering

19

echo of their horses' hoof-beats rattling back from the smooth stone face of the walls, the lad looked up, wondering at the height and strength of the great ancient fortress. In his air-castle building Myles had pictured the Earl receiving him as the son of his one-time comrade in arms —receiving him, perhaps, with somewhat of the rustic warmth that he knew at Crosbey-Dale; but now, as he stared at those massive walls from below, and realized his own insignificance and the greatness of this great Earl, he felt the first keen, helpless ache of homesickness shoot through his breast, and his heart yearned for Crosbey-Holt again.

Then they thundered across the bridge that spanned the moat, and through the dark shadows of the great gaping gate-way, and Diccon, bidding him stay for a moment, rode forward to bespeak the gate-keeper.

The gate-keeper gave the two in charge of one of the men-at-arms who were lounging upon a bench in the archway, who in turn gave them into the care of one of the house-servants in the outer court-yard. So, having been passed from one to another, and having answered many questions, Myles in due time found himself in the outer waiting-room sitting beside Diccon Bowman upon a wooden bench that stood along the wall under the great arch of a glazed window.

For a while the poor country lad sat stupidly bewildered. He was aware of people coming and going; he was aware of talk and laughter sounding around him; but he thought of nothing but his aching homesickness and the oppression of his utter littleness in the busy life of this great castle.

Meantime old Diccon Bowman was staring about him with huge interest, every now and then nudging his young master, calling his attention now to this and now to that, until at last the lad began to awaken somewhat from his despondency to the things around. Besides those servants and others who came and went, and a knot of six or eight men-at-arms with bills and pole-axes, who stood at the farther door-way talking together in low tones, now and then broken by a stifled laugh, was a group of four young squires, who lounged upon a bench beside a door way hidden by an arras, and upon them Myles's eyes lit with a sudden interest. Three of the four were about his own age, one was a year or two older, and all four were dressed in the black-and-yellow uniform of the house of Beaumont.

Myles plucked the bowman by the sleeve. " Be

they squires, Diccon?" said he, nodding towards the door.

"Eh?" said Diccon. "Aye; they be squires."

"And will my station be with them?" asked the boy.

"Aye; an the Earl take thee to service, thou'lt haply be taken as squire."

Myles stared at them, and then of a sudden was aware that the young men were talking of him. He knew it by the way they eyed him askance, and spoke now and then in one another's ears. One of the four, a gay young fellow, with long riding-boots laced with green laces, said a few words, the others gave a laugh, and poor Myles, knowing how ungainly he must seem to them, felt the blood rush to his cheeks, and shyly turned his head.

Suddenly, as though stirred by an impulse, the same lad who had just created the laugh arose from the bench, and came directly across the room to where Myles and the bowman sat.

"Give thee good-den," said he. "What be'st thy name and whence comest thou, an I may make bold so to ask?"

"My name is Myles Falworth," said Myles; "and I come from Crosbey-Dale bearing a letter to my Lord."

"Never did I hear of Crosbey-Dale," said the

squire. "But what seekest here, if so be I may ask that much?"

"I come seeking service," said Myles, "and would enter as an esquire such as ye be in my Lord's household."

Myles's new acquaintance grinned. "Thou'lt make a droll squire to wait in a Lord's household," said he. "Hast ever been in such service?"

"Nay," said Myles, "I have only been at school, and learned Latin and French and what not. But Diccon Bowman here hath taught me use of arms."

The young squire laughed outright. "By 'r Lady, thy talk doth tickle me, friend Myles," said he. "Think'st thou such matters will gain thee footing here? But stay! Thou didst say anon that thou hadst a letter to my Lord. From whom is it?"

"It is from my father," said Myles. "He is of noble blood, but fallen in estate. He is a kinsman of my Lord's, and one time his comrade in arms."

"Sayst so?" said the other. "Then mayhap thy chances are not so ill, after all." Then, after a moment, he added: "My name is Francis Gascoyne, and I will stand thy friend in this matter. Get thy letter ready, for my Lord and his Grace of York are within, and come forth anon. The Archbishop is on his way to Dalworth, and my Lord escorts him so far as Uppingham. I and those others are to go along. Dost thou know my Lord by sight?"

" Nay," said Myles, "I know him not."

" Then I will tell thee when he cometh. Listen!" said he, as a confused clattering sounded in the court-yard without. " Yonder are the horses now. They come presently. Busk thee with thy letter, friend Myles."

The attendants who passed through the anteroom now came and went more hurriedly, and Myles knew that the Earl must be about to come forth. He had hardly time to untie his pouch, take out the letter, and tie the strings again when the arras at the door-way was thrust suddenly aside, and a tall thin squire of about twenty came forth, said some words to the young men upon the bench, and then withdrew again. Instantly the squires arose and took their station beside the door-way. A sudden hush fell upon all in the room, and the men-at-arms stood in a line against the wall, stiff and erect as though all at once transformed to figures of iron. Once more the arras was drawn back, and in the hush Myles heard voices in the other room.

" My Lord cometh," whispered Gascoyne in

his ear, and Myles felt his heart leap in answer.

The next moment two noblemen came into the anteroom, followed by a crowd of gentlemen, squires, and pages. One of the two was a dignitary of the Church; the other Myles instantly singled out as the Earl of Mackworth.

CHAPTER IV.

He was a tall man, taller even than Myles's father. He had a thin face, deep-set bushy eyebrows, and a hawk nose. His upper lip was clean shaven, but from his chin a flowing beard of iron-gray hung nearly to his waist. He was clad in a riding-gown of black velvet that hung a little lower than the knee, trimmed with otter fur and embroidered with silver goshawks—the crest of the family of Beaumont.

A light shirt of link mail showed beneath the gown as he walked, and a pair of soft undressed leather riding-boots were laced as high as the knee, protecting his scarlet hose from mud and dirt. Over his shoulders he wore a collar of enamelled gold, from which hung a magnificent jewelled pendant, and upon his fist he carried a beautiful Iceland falcon.

As Myles stood staring, he suddenly heard Gascoyne's voice whisper in his ear, "Yon is my Lord; go forward and give him thy letter."

Scarcely knowing what he did, he walked towards the Earl like a machine, his heart pounding within him and a great humming in his ears. As he drew near, the nobleman stopped for a moment and stared at him, and Myles, as in a dream, kneeled, and presented the letter. The Earl took it in his hand, turned it this way and that, looked first at the bearer, then at the packet, and then at the bearer again.

"Who art thou?" said he; "and what is the matter thou wouldst have of me?"

"I am Myles Falworth," said the lad, in a low voice; "and I come seeking service with you."

The Earl drew his thick eyebrows quickly together, and shot a keen look at the lad. "Falworth?" said he, sharply—"Falworth? I know no Falworth!"

"The letter will tell you," said Myles. "It is rom one once dear to you."

The Earl took the letter, and handing it to a gentleman who stood near, bade him break the seal. "Thou mayst stand," said he to Myles; "needst not kneel there forever." Then, taking the opened parchment again, he glanced first at the face and then at the back, and, seeing its length, looked vexed. Then he read for an earnest moment or two, skipping from line to line. Presently he folded the letter and thrust it into

the pouch at his side. " So it is, your Grace,"
said he to the lordly prelate, "that we who have
luck to rise in the world must ever suffer by being plagued at all times and seasons. Here is
one I chanced to know a dozen years ago, who
thinks he hath a claim upon me, and saddles me
with his son. I must e'en take the lad, too, for
the sake of peace and quietness." He glanced
around, and seeing Gascoyne, who had drawn
near, beckoned to him. " Take me this fellow,"
said he, " to the buttery, and see him fed ; and
then to Sir James Lee, and have his name entered in the castle books. And stay, sirrah," he
added ; " bid me Sir James, if it may be so done,
to enter him as a squire-at-arms. Methinks he
will be better serving so than in the household,
for he appeareth a soothly rough cub for a
page."

Myles did look rustic enough, standing clad
in frieze in the midst of that gay company, and
a murmur of laughter sounded around, though
he was too bewildered to fully understand that
he was the cause of the merriment. Then some
hand drew him back—it was Gascoyne's—there
was a bustle of people passing, and the next minute they were gone, and Myles and old Diccon
Bowman and the young squire were left alone in
the anteroom.

Gascoyne looked very sour and put out. "Murrain upon it!" said he; "here is good sport spoiled for me to see thee fed. I wish no ill to thee, friend, but I would thou hadst come this afternoon or to-morrow."

"Methinks I bring trouble and dole to every one," said Myles, somewhat bitterly. "It would have been better had I never come to this place, methinks."

His words and tone softened Gascoyne a little. "Ne'er mind," said the squire; "it was not thy fault, and is past mending now. So come and fill thy stomach, in Heaven's name."

Perhaps not the least hard part of the whole trying day for Myles was his parting with Diccon. Gascoyne and he had accompanied the old retainer to the outer gate, in the archway of which they now stood; for without a permit they could go no farther The old bowman led by the bridle-rein the horse upon which Myles had ridden that morning. His own nag, a vicious brute, was restive to be gone, but Diccon held him in with tight rein. He reached down, and took Myles's sturdy brown hand in his crooked, knotted grasp.

"Farewell, young master," he croaked, tremulously, with a watery glimmer in his pale eyes. "Thou wilt not forget me when I am gone?"

"Nay," said Myles; "I will not forget thee."

"Aye, aye," said the old man, looking down at him, and shaking his head slowly from side to side; "thou art a great tall sturdy fellow now, yet have I held thee on my knee many and many's the time, and dandled thee when thou wert only a little weeny babe. Be still, thou devil's limb!" he suddenly broke off, reining back his restive raw-boned steed, which began again to caper and prance. Myles was not sorry for the interruption; he felt awkward and abashed at the parting, and at the old man's reminiscences, knowing that Gascoyne's eyes were resting amusedly upon the scene, and that the men-at-arms were looking on. Certainly old Diccon did look droll as he struggled vainly with his vicious high-necked nag "Nay, a murrain on thee! an' thou wilt go, go!" cried he at last, with a savage dig of his heels into the animal's ribs, and away they clattered, the led-horse kicking up its heels as a final parting, setting Gascoyne fairly alaughing. At the bend of the road the old man turned and nodded his head; the next moment he had disappeared around the angle of the wall, and it seemed to Myles, as he stood looking after him, as though the last thread that bound him to his old life had snapped and broken. As he turned he saw that Gascoyne was looking at him.

"Dost feel downhearted?" said the young squire, curiously.

"Nay," said Myles, brusquely. Nevertheless his throat was tight and dry, and the word came huskily in spite of himself.

CHAPTER V.

THE Earl of Mackworth, as was customary among the great lords in those days, maintained a small army of knights, gentlemen, men-at-arms, and retainers, who were expected to serve him upon all occasions of need, and from whom were supplied his quota of recruits to fill such levies as might be made upon him by the King in time of war.

The knights and gentlemen of this little army of horse and foot soldiers were largely recruited from the company of squires and bachelors, as the young novitiate soldiers of the castle were called.

This company of esquires consisted of from eighty to ninety lads, ranging in age from eight to twenty years. Those under fourteen years were termed pages, and served chiefly the Countess and her waiting gentlewomen, in whose company they acquired the graces and polish of the times, such as they were. After reaching the age

"Myles, as in a dream, kneeled and presented the letter"

of fourteen the lads were entitled to the name of esquire or squire.

In most of the great houses of the time the esquires were the especial attendants upon the Lord and Lady of the house, holding such positions as body-squires, cup-bearers, carvers, and sometimes the office of chamberlain. But Devlen, like some other of the princely castles of the greatest nobles, was more like a military post or a fortress than an ordinary household. Only comparatively few of the esquires could be used in personal attendance upon the Earl; the others were trained more strictly in arms, and served rather in the capacity of a sort of body-guard than as ordinary squires. For, as the Earl rose in power and influence, and as it so became well worth while for the lower nobility and gentry to enter their sons in his family, the body of squires became almost cumbersomely large. Accordingly, that part which comprised the squires proper, as separate from the younger pages, was divided into three classes — first, squires of the body, who were those just past pagehood, and who waited upon the Earl in personal service; second, squires of the household, who, having regular hours assigned for exercise in the manual of arms, were relieved from personal service excepting upon especial occasions; and thirdly and last-ly, at the head of the whole body of lads, a class called bachelors—young men ranging from eighteen to twenty years of age. This class was supposed to exercise a sort of government over the other and younger squires—to keep them in order as much as possible, to marshal them upon occasions of importance, to see that their arms and equipments were kept in good order, to call the roll for chapel in the morning, and to see that those not upon duty in the house were present at the daily exercise at arms. Orders to the squires were generally transmitted through the bachelors, and the head of that body was expected to make weekly reports of affairs in their quarters to the chief captain of the body.

From this overlordship of the bachelors there had gradually risen a system of fagging, such as is or was practised in the great English public schools — enforced services exacted from the younger lads—which at the time Myles came to Devlen had, in the five or six years it had been in practice, grown to be an absolute though unwritten law of the body—a law supported by all the prestige of long-continued usage. At that time the bachelors numbered but thirteen, yet they exercised over the rest of the sixty-four squires and pages a rule of iron, and were taskmasters, hard, exacting, and oftentimes cruel.

34

The whole company of squires and pages was under the supreme command of a certain one-eyed knight, by name Sir James Lee; a soldier seasoned by the fire of a dozen battles, bearing a score of wounds won in fight and tourney, and withered by hardship and labor to a leather-like toughness. He had fought upon the King's side in all the late wars, and had at Shrewsbury received a wound that unfitted him for active service, so that now he was fallen to the post of Captain of Esquires at Devlen Castle — a man disappointed in life, and with a temper imbittered by that failure as well as by cankering pain.

Yet perhaps no one could have been better fitted for the place he held than Sir James Lee. The lads under his charge were a rude, rough, unruly set, quick, like their elders, to quarrel, and to quarrel fiercely, even to the drawing of sword or dagger. But there was a cold, iron sternness about the grim old man that quelled them, as the trainer with a lash of steel might quell a den of young wolves. The apartments in which he was lodged, with his clerk, were next the dormitory of the lads, and even in the midst of the most excited brawlings the distant sound of his harsh voice, "Silence, messieurs!" would bring an instant hush to the loudest uproar.

It was into his grim presence that Myles was

introduced by Gascoyne. Sir James was in his office, a room bare of ornament or adornment or superfluous comfort of any sort—without even so much as a mat of rushes upon the cold stone pavement to make it less cheerless. The old one-eyed knight sat gnawing his bristling mustaches. To any one who knew him it would have been apparent that, as the castle phrase went, " the devil sat astride of his neck," which meant that some one of his blind wounds was aching more sorely than usual.

His clerk sat beside him, with account-books and parchment spread upon the table, and the head squire, Walter Blunt, a lad some three or four years older than Myles, and half a head taller, black-browed, powerfully built, and with cheek and chin darkened by the soft budding of his adolescent beard, stood making his report.

Sir James listened in grim silence while Gascoyne told his errand.

" So, then, pardee, I am bid to take another one of ye, am I?" he snarled. " As though ye caused me not trouble enow; and this one a cub, looking a very boor in carriage and breeding. Mayhap the Earl thinketh I am to train boys to his dilly-dally household service as well as to use of arms."

" Sir," said Gascoyne, timidly, "my Lord sayeth he would have this one entered direct as a squire of the body, so that he need not serve in the household."

"Sayest so?" cried Sir James, harshly. "Then take thou my message back again to thy Lord. Not for Mackworth—no, nor a better man than he—will I make any changes in my government. An I be set to rule a pack of boys, I will rule them as I list, and not according to any man's bidding. Tell him, sirrah, that I will enter no lad as squire of the body without first testing an he be fit at arms to hold that place." He sat for a while glowering at Myles and gnawing his mustaches, and for the time no one dared to break the grim silence. "What is thy name?" said he, suddenly. And then, almost before Myles could answer, he asked the head squire whether he could find a place to lodge him.

"There is Gillis Whitlock's cot empty," said Blunt. "He is in the infirmary, and belike goeth home again when he cometh thence. The fever hath gotten into his bones, and—"

"That will do," said the knight, interrupting him impatiently. "Let him take that place, or any other that thou hast. And thou, Jerome," said he to his clerk, "thou mayst enter him upon the roll, though whether it be as page or squire or bachelor shall be as I please, and not as Mackworth biddeth me. Now get ye gone."

"Old Bruin's wound smarteth him sore," Gascoyne observed, as the two lads walked across the armory court. He had good-naturedly offered to show the new-comer the many sights of interest around the castle, and in the hour or so of ramble that followed, the two grew from acquaintances to friends with a quickness that boyhood alone can bring about. They visited the armory, the chapel, the stables, the great hall, the Painted Chamber, the guard-house, the mess-room, and even the scullery and the kitchen, with its great range of boilers and furnaces and ovens. Last of all Myles's new friend introduced him to the armor-smithy.

"My Lord hath sent a piece of Milan armor thither to be repaired," said he. "Belike thou would like to see it."

"Aye," said Myles, eagerly, "that would I."

The smith was a gruff, good-natured fellow, and showed the piece of armor to Myles readily and willingly enough. It was a beautiful bascinet of inlaid workmanship, and was edged with a rim of gold. Myles scarcely dared touch it; he gazed at it with an unconcealed delight that warmed the smith's honest heart.

"I have another piece of Milan here," said he, "Did I ever show thee my dagger, Master Gascoyne?"

38

"Nay," said the squire.

The smith unlocked a great oaken chest in the corner of the shop, lifted the lid, and brought thence a beautiful dagger with a handle of ebony and silver-gilt, and a sheath of Spanish leather, embossed and gilt. The keen, well-tempered blade was beautifully engraved and inlaid with niello-work, representing a group of figures in a then popular subject—the dance of Death. It was a weapon at once unique and beautiful, and even Gascoyne showed an admiration scarcely less keen than Myles's openly-expressed delight.

"To whom doth it belong?" said he, trying the point upon his thumb nail.

"There," said the smith, "is the jest of the whole, for it belongeth to me. Sir William Beauclerk bade me order the weapon through Master Gildersworthy, of London town, and by the time it came hither, lo! he had died, and so it fell to my hands. No one here payeth the price for the trinket, and so I must e'en keep it myself, though I be but a poor man."

"How much dost thou hold it for?" said Gascoyne.

"Seventeen shillings buyeth it," said the armorer, carelessly.

"Aye, aye," said Gascoyne, with a sigh; "so it is to be poor, and not be able to have such things as one loveth and would fain possess. Seventeen shillings is nigh as much by half again as all my yearly wage."

Then a sudden thought came to Myles, and as it came his cheeks glowed as hot as fire "Master Gascoyne," said he, with gruff awkwardness, "thou hast been a very good, true friend to me since I have come to this place, and hast befriended me in all ways thou mightest do, and I, as well I know, but a poor rustic clod. Now I have forty shillings by me which I may spend as I list, and so I do beseech thee that thou wilt take yon dagger of me as a love-gift, and have and hold it for thy very own."

Gascoyne stared open-mouthed at Myles. "Dost mean it?" said he, at last.

"Aye," said Myles, "I do mean it. Master Smith, give him the blade."

At first the smith grinned, thinking it all a jest; but he soon saw that Myles was serious enough, and when the seventeen shillings were produced and counted down upon the anvil, he took off his cap and made Myles a low bow as he swept them into his pouch. "Now, by my faith and troth," quoth he, "that I do call a true lordly gift. Is it not so, Master Gascoyne?"

"Aye," said Gascoyne, with a gulp, "it is, in soothly earnest." And thereupon, to Myles's great wonderment, he suddenly flung his arms about his neck, and, giving him a great hug, kissed him upon the cheek. " Dear Myles," said he, " I tell thee truly and of a verity I did feel warm towards thee from the very first time I saw thee sitting like a poor oaf upon the bench up yonder in the anteroom, and now of a sooth I give thee assurance that I do love thee as my own brother. Yea, I will take the dagger, and will stand by thee as a true friend from this time forth. Mayhap thou mayst need a true friend in this place ere thou livest long with us, for some of us esquires be soothly rough, and knocks are more plenty here than broad pennies, so that one new come is like to have a hard time gaining a footing."

" I thank thee," said Myles, " for thy offer of love and friendship, and do tell thee, upon my part, that I also of all the world would like best to have thee for my friend."

Such was the manner in which Myles formed the first great friendship of his life, a friendship that was destined to last him through many years to come. As the two walked back across the great quadrangle, upon which fronted the main buildings of the castle, their arms were wound across one another's shoulders, after the manner, as a certain great writer says, of boys and lovers.

CHAPTER VI.

A BOY's life is of a very flexible sort. It takes
but a little while for it to shape itself to any new
surroundings in which it may be thrown, to make
itself new friends, to settle itself to new habits;
and so it was that Myles fell directly into the
ways of the lads of Devlen. On his first morning,
as he washed his face and hands with the other
squires and pages in a great tank of water in the
armory court-yard, he presently found himself
splashing and dashing with the others, laughing
and shouting as loud as any, and calling some by
their Christian names as though he had known
them for years instead of overnight. During
chapel he watched with sympathetic delight the
covert pranks of the youngsters during the half-
hour that Father Emmanuel droned his Latin, and
with his dagger point he carved his own name
among the many cut deep into the back of the
bench before him. When, after breakfast, the
squires poured like school-boys into the great

armory to answer to the roll-call for daily exercise, he came storming in with the rest, beating the lad in front of him with his cap.

Boys are very keen to feel the influence of a forceful character. A lad with a strong will is quick to reach his proper level as a greater or lesser leader among the others, and Myles was of just the masterful nature to make his individuality felt among the Devlen squires. He was quick enough to yield obedience upon all occasions to proper authority, but would never bend an inch to the usurpation of tyranny. In the school at St. Mary's Priory at Crosbey-Dale he would submit without a murmur or offer of resistance to chastisement by old Father Ambrose, the regular teacher; but once, when the fat old monk was sick, and a great long-legged strapping young friar, who had temporarily taken his place, undertook to administer punishment, Myles, with a wrestling trip, flung him sprawling backward over a bench into the midst of a shoal of small boys amid a hubbub of riotous confusion. He had been flogged soundly for it under the supervision of Prior Edward himself; but so soon as his punishment was over, he assured the prior very seriously that should like occasion again happen he would act in the same manner, flogging or no flogging.

It was this bold, outspoken spirit that gained

him at once friends and enemies at Devlen, and though it first showed itself in what was but a little matter, nevertheless it set a mark upon him that singled him out from the rest, and, although he did not suspect it at the time, called to him the attention of Sir James Lee himself, who regarded him as a lad of free and frank spirit.

The first morning after the roll-call in the armory, as Walter Blunt, the head bachelor, rolled up the slip of parchment, and the temporary silence burst forth into redoubled noise and confusion, each lad arming himself from a row of racks that stood along the wall, he beckoned Myles to him.

"My Lord himself hath spoken to Sir James Lee concerning thee," said he. "Sir James maintaineth that he will not enter thee into the body till thou hast first practised for a while at the pels, and shown what thou canst do at broadsword. Hast ever fought at the pel?"

"Aye," answered Myles, "and that every day of my life sin I became esquire four years ago, saving only Sundays and holy days."

"With shield and broadsword?"

"Sometimes," said Myles, "and sometimes with the short sword."

"Sir James would have thee come to the tilt-yard this morn; he himself will take thee in hand to try what thou canst do. Thou mayst take the arms upon yonder rack, and use them until otherwise bidden. Thou seest that the number painted above it on the wall is seventeen; that will be thy number for the nonce."

So Myles armed himself from his rack as the others were doing from theirs. The armor was rude and heavy, used to accustom the body to the weight of the iron plates rather than for any defence. It consisted of a cuirass, or breastplate of iron, opening at the side with hinges, and latching with hooks and eyes *epauliers*, or shoulder-plates; arm-plates and leg-pieces; and a bascinet, or open-faced helmet. A great triangular shield covered with leather and studded with bosses of iron, and a heavy broadsword, pointed and dulled at the edges, completed the equipment.

The practice at the pels which Myles was bidden to attend comprised the chief exercise of the day with the esquires of young cadet soldiers of that time, and in it they learned not only all the strokes, cuts, and thrusts of sword-play then in vogue, but also toughness, endurance, and elastic quickness. The pels themselves consisted of upright posts of ash or oak, about five feet six inches in height, and in girth somewhat thicker than a man's thigh. They were firmly planted in the

45

ground, and upon them the strokes of the broad-sword were directed.

At Devlen the pels stood just back of the open and covered tilting courts and the archery ranges, and thither those lads not upon household duty were marched every morning except ing Fridays and Sundays, and were there exercised under the direction of Sir James Lee and two assistants. The whole company was divided into two, sometimes into three parties, each of which took its turn at the exercise, delivering at the word of command the various strokes, feints, attacks, and retreats as the instructors ordered.

After five minutes of this mock battle the perspiration began to pour down the faces, and the breath to come thick and short; but it was not until the lads could absolutely endure no more that the order was given to rest, and they were allowed to fling themselves panting upon the ground, while another company took its place at the triple row of posts.

As Myles struck and hacked at the pel assigned to him, Sir James Lee stood beside him watching him in grim silence. The lad did his best to show the knight all that he knew of upper cut, under cut, thrust, and back-hand stroke, but it did not seem to him that Sir James was very well satisfied with his skill.

"Thou fightest like a clodpole," said the old man. "Ha, that stroke was but ill-recovered. Strike me it again, and get thou in guard more quickly."

Myles repeated the stroke.

"Pest!" cried Sir James. "Thou art too slow by a week. Here, strike thou the blow at me."

Myles hesitated. Sir James held a stout staff in his hand, but otherwise he was unarmed.

"Strike, I say!" said Sir James. "What stayest thou for? Art afeard?"

It was Myles's answer that set the seal of individuality upon him. "Nay," said he, boldly, "I am not afeard. I fear not thee nor any man!" So saying, he delivered the stroke at Sir James with might and main. It was met with a jarring blow that made his wrist and arm tingle, and the next instant he received a stroke upon the bascinet that caused his ears to ring and the sparks to dance and fly before his eyes.

"Pardee!" said Sir James, grimly. "An I had had a mace in my hand, I would have knocked thy cockerel brains out that time. Thou mayst take that blow for answering me so pertly. And now we are quits. Now strike me the stroke again an thou art not afeard."

Myles's eyes watered in spite of himself, and he shut the lids tight to wink the dimness away.

Nevertheless he spoke up undauntedly as before. "Aye, marry, will I strike it again," said he; and this time he was able to recover guard quickly enough to turn Sir James's blow with his shield, instead of receiving it upon his head.

"So!" said Sir James. "Now mind thee of this, that when thou strikest that lower cut at the legs, recover thyself more quickly. Now, then, strike me it at the pel."

Gascoyne and other of the lads who were just then lying stretched out upon the grass beneath a tree at the edge of the open court where stood the pels, were interested spectators of the whole scene. Not one of them in their memory had heard Sir James so answered face to face as Myles had answered him; and, after all, perhaps the lad himself would not have done so had he been longer a resident in the squires' quarters at Devlen.

"By 'r Lady! thou art a cool blade, Myles," said Gascoyne, as they marched back to the armory again. "Never heard I one bespeak Sir James as thou hast done this day."

"And, after all," said another of the young squires, "old Bruin was not so ill-pleased, methinks. That was a shrewd blow he fetched thee on the crown, Falworth. Marry, I would not have had it on my own skull for a silver penny."

"*When thou strikest that lower cut at the legs, recover thyself more quickly*"

CHAPTER VII.

So little does it take to make a body's reputation.

That night all the squires' quarters buzzed with the story of how the new boy, Falworth, had answered Sir James Lee to his face without fear, and had exchanged blows with him hand to hand. Walter Blunt himself was moved to some show of interest.

" What said he to thee, Falworth?" asked he.

"He said naught," said Myles, brusquely. "He only sought to show me how to recover from the under cut."

" It is passing strange that he should take so much notice of thee as to exchange blows with thee with his own hand. Haply thou art either very quick or parlous slow at arms."

" It is quick that he is," said Gascoyne, speaking up in his friend's behalf. " For the second time that Falworth delivered the stroke, Sir James could not reach him to return; so I saw with mine own eyes."

But that very sterling independence that had brought Myles so creditably through this adventure was certain to embroil him with the rude, half-savage lads about him, some of whom, especially among the bachelors, were his superiors as well in age as in skill and training. As said before, the bachelors had enforced from the younger boys a fagging sort of attendance on their various personal needs, and it was upon this point that Myles first came to grief. As it chanced, several days passed before any demand was made upon him for service to the heads of the squirehood, but when that demand was made, the bachelors were very quick to see that the boy who was bold enough to speak up to Sir James Lee was not likely to be a willing fag for them.

"I tell thee, Francis," he said, as Gascoyne and he talked over the matter one day—"I tell thee I will never serve them. Prithee, what shame can be fouler than to do such menial service, saving for one's rightful Lord?"

"Marry!" quoth Gascoyne; "I reason not of shame at this or that. All I know is that others serve them who are haply as good and maybe better than I be, and that if I do not serve them I get knocked i' th' head therefore, which same goeth soothly against my stomach."

"I judge not for thee," said Myles. "Thou art used to these castle ways, but only I know that I will not serve them, though they be thirty against me instead of thirteen."

"Then thou art a fool," said Gascoyne, dryly.

Now in this matter of service there was one thing above all others that stirred Myles Falworth's ill-liking. The winter before he had come to Devlen, Walter Blunt, who was somewhat of a Sybarite in his way, and who had a repugnance to bathing in the general tank in the open armory court in frosty weather, had had Dick Carpenter build a trough in the corner of the dormitory for the use of the bachelors, and every morning it was the duty of two of the younger squires to bring three pails of water to fill this private tank for the use of the head esquires. It was seeing two of his fellow-esquires fetching and carrying this water that Myles disliked so heartily, and every morning his bile was stirred anew at the sight.

"Sooner would I die than yield to such vile service," said he.

He did not know how soon his protestations would be put to the test.

One night—it was a week or two after Myles had come to Devlen—Blunt was called to attend the Earl at livery. The livery was the last meal

of the day, and was served with great pomp
and ceremony about nine o'clock at night to
the head of the house as he lay in bed. Curfew
had not yet rung, and the lads in the squires'
quarters were still wrestling and sparring and
romping boisterously in and out around the long
row of rude cots in the great dormitory as they
made ready for the night. Six or eight flaring
links in wrought-iron brackets that stood out
from the wall threw a great ruddy glare through
the barrack-like room—a light of all others to
romp by. Myles and Gascoyne were engaged
in defending the passage-way between their two
cots against the attack of three other lads, and
Myles held his sheepskin coverlet rolled up into
a ball and balanced in his hand, ready for launch-
ing at the head of one of the others so soon as
it should rise from behind the shelter of a cot.
Just then Walter Blunt, dressed with more than
usual care, passed by on his way to the Earl's
house. He stopped for a moment and said,

"Mayhap I will not be in until late to-night.
Thou and Falworth, Gascoyne, may fetch water
to-morrow."

Then he was gone. Myles stood staring after
his retreating figure with eyes open and mouth
agape, still holding the ball of sheepskin balanced
in his hand. Gascoyne burst into a helpless laugh

at his blank, stupefied face, but the next moment he laid his hand on his friend's shoulder.

"Myles," said he, "thou wilt not make trouble, wilt thou?"

Myles made no answer. He flung down his sheepskin and sat him gloomily down upon the side of the cot.

"I said that I would sooner die than fetch water for them," said he.

"Aye, aye," said Gascoyne; "but that was spoken in haste."

Myles said nothing, but shook his head.

But, after all, circumstances shape themselves. The next morning when he rose up through the dark waters of sleep it was to feel some one shaking him violently by the shoulder.

"Come!" cried Gascoyne, as Myles opened his eyes—"come, time passeth, and we are late."

Myles, bewildered with his sudden awakening, and still fuddled with the fumes of sleep, huddled into his doublet and hose, hardly knowing what he was doing; tying a point here and a point there, and slipping his feet into his shoes. Then he hurried after Gascoyne, frowzy, half-dressed, and even yet only half-awake. It was not until he was fairly out into the fresh air and saw Gascoyne filling the three leathern buckets at the tank, that he fully awakened to the fact that he was actually doing that hateful service for the bachelors which he had protested he would sooner die than render.

The sun was just rising, gilding the crown of the donjon-keep with a flame of ruddy light. Below, among the lesser buildings, the day was still gray and misty. Only an occasional noise broke the silence of the early morning: a cough from one of the rooms; the rattle of a pot or a pan, stirred by some sleepy scullion; the clapping of a door or a shutter, and now and then the crowing of a cock back of the long row of stables—all sounding loud and startling in the fresh dewy stillness.

"Thou hast betrayed me," said Myles, harshly, breaking the silence at last. "I knew not what I was doing, or else I would never have come hither. Ne'theless, even though I be come, I will not carry the water for them."

"So be it," said Gascoyne, tartly. "An thou canst not stomach it, let be, and I will e'en carry all three myself. It will make me two journeys, but, thank Heaven, I am not so proud as to wish to get me hard knocks for naught." So saying, he picked up two of the buckets and started away across the court for the dormitory.

Then Myles, with a lowering face, snatched up the third, and, hurrying after, gave him his hand with the extra pail. So it was that he came to do service, after all.

"Why tarried ye so long?" said one of the older bachelors, roughly, as the two lads emptied the water into the wooden trough. He sat on the edge of the cot, blowzed and untrussed, with his long hair tumbled and disordered.

His dictatorial tone stung Myles to fury. "We tarried no longer than need be," answered he, savagely. "Have we wings to fly withal at your bidding?"

He spoke so loudly that all in the room heard him; the younger squires who were dressing stared in blank amazement, and Blunt sat up suddenly in his cot.

"Why, how now?" he cried. "Answerest thou back thy betters so pertly, sirrah? By my soul, I have a mind to crack thy head with this clog for thy unruly talk."

He glared at Myles as he spoke, and Myles glared back again with right good-will. Matters might have come to a crisis, only that Gascoyne and Wilkes dragged their friend away before he had opportunity to answer.

"An ill-conditioned knave as ever I did see," growled Blunt, glaring after him.

"Myles, Myles," said Gascoyne, almost despairingly, "why wilt thou breed such mischief for thyself? Seest thou not thou hast got thee the ill-will of every one of the bachelors, from Wat Blunt to Robin de Ramsey?"

"I care not," said Myles, fiercely, recurring to his grievance. "Heard ye not how the dogs upbraided me before the whole room? That Blunt called me an ill-conditioned knave."

"Marry!" said Gascoyne, laughing, "and so thou art."

Thus it is that boldness may breed one enemies as well as gain one friends. My own notion is that one's enemies are more quick to act than one's friends.

"At last they had the poor boy down"

CHAPTER VIII.

EVERY one knows the disagreeable, lurking discomfort that follows a quarrel—a discomfort that imbitters the very taste of life for the time being. Such was the dull distaste that Myles felt that morning after what had passed in the dormitory. Every one in the proximity of such an open quarrel feels a reflected constraint, and in Myles's mind was a disagreeable doubt whether that constraint meant disapproval of him or of his late enemies.

It seemed to him that Gascoyne added the last bitter twang to his unpleasant feelings when, half an hour later, they marched with the others to chapel.

"Why dost thou breed such trouble for thyself, Myles?" said he, recurring to what he had already said. "Is it not foolish for thee to come hither to this place, and then not submit to the ways thereof, as the rest of us do?"

"Thou talkest not like a true friend to chide

me thus," said Myles, sullenly; and he withdrew his arm from his friend's.

"Marry, come up!" said Gascoyne; "an I were not thy friend, I would let thee jog thine own way. It aches not my bones to have thine drubbed."

Just then they entered the chapel, and words that might have led to a quarrel were brought to a close.

Myles was not slow to see that he had the ill will of the head of their company. That morning in the armory he had occasion to ask some question of Blunt; the head squire stared coldly at him for a moment, gave him a short, gruff answer, and then, turning his back abruptly, began talking with one of the other bachelors. Myles flushed hot at the other's insulting manner, and looked quickly around to see if any of the others had observed what had passed. It was a comfort to him to see that all were too busy arming themselves to think of anything else; nevertheless, his face was very lowering as he turned away.

"Some day I will show him that I am as good a man as he," he muttered to himself. "An evil-hearted dog to put shame upon me!"

The storm was brewing and ready to break.

That day was exceptionally hot and close, and permission had been asked by and granted to those squires not on duty to go down to the river for a bath after exercise at the pels. But as Myles replaced his arms in the rack, a little page came with a bidding to come to Sir James in his office.

"Look, now," said Myles, "here is just my ill-fortune. Why might he not have waited an hour longer rather than cause me to miss going with ye?"

"Nay," said Gascoyne, "let not that grieve thee, Myles. Wilkes and I will wait for thee in the dormitory—will we not, Edmund? Make thou haste and go to Sir James."

Sir James was sitting at the table studying over a scroll of parchment, when Myles entered his office and stood before him at the table.

"Well, boy," said he, laying aside the parchment and looking up at the lad, "I have tried thee fairly for these few days, and may say that I have found thee worthy to be entered upon the rolls as esquire of the body."

"I give thee thanks, sir," said Myles.

The knight nodded his head in acknowledgment, but did not at once give the word of dismissal that Myles had expected. "Dost mean to write thee a letter home soon?" said he, suddenly.

"Aye," said Myles, gaping in great wonderment at the strangeness of the question.

"Then when thou dost so write," said Sir James, "give thou my deep regards to thy father." Then he continued, after a brief pause, " Him did I know well in times gone by, and we were right true friends in hearty love, and for his sake I would befriend thee—that is, in so much as is fitting."

"Sir," said Myles; but Sir James held up his hand, and he stopped short in his thanks.

"But, boy," said he, "that which I sent for thee for to tell thee was of more import than these. Dost thou know that thy father is an attainted outlaw?"

"Nay," cried Myles, his cheeks blazing up as red as fire; "who sayeth that of him lieth in his teeth."

" Thou dost mistake me," said Sir James, quietly. " It is sometimes no shame to be outlawed and banned. Had it been so, I would not have told thee thereof, nor have bidden thee send my true love to thy father, as I did but now. But, boy, certes he standest continually in great danger—greater than thou wottest of. Were it known where he lieth hid, it might be to his undoing and utter ruin. Methought that belike thou mightest not know that; and so I sent for thee for to tell thee that it behoovest thee to say not one single word concerning him to any of these new friends of thine, nor who he is, nor what he is."

"But how came my father to be so banned?"
said Myles, in a constrained and husky voice, and
after a long time of silence.

"That I may not tell thee just now," said the
old knight, "only this—that I have been bidden
to make it known to thee that thy father hath an
enemy full as powerful as my Lord the Earl himself, and that through that enemy all his ill-fortune—his blindness and everything—hath come.
Moreover, did this enemy know where thy father
lieth, he would slay him right speedily."

"Sir," cried Myles, violently smiting his open
palm upon the table, "tell me who this man is,
and I will kill him!"

Sir James smiled grimly. "Thou talkest like
a boy," said he. "Wait until thou art grown to
be a man. Mayhap then thou mayst repent thee
of these bold words, for one time this enemy of
thy father's was reckoned the foremost knight in
England, and he is now the King's dear friend
and a great lord."

"But," said Myles, after another long time of
heavy silence, "will not my Lord then befriend
me for the sake of my father, who was one time
his dear comrade?"

Sir James shook his head. "It may not be,"
said he. "Neither thou nor thy father must look
for open favor from the Earl. An he befriended

Falworth, and it came to be known that he had given him aid or succor, it might belike be to his own undoing. No, boy; thou must not even look to be taken into the household to serve with gentlemen as the other squires do serve, but must even live thine own life here and fight thine own way."

Myles's eyes blazed. "Then," cried he, fiercely, "it is shame and attaint upon my Lord the Earl, and cowardice as well, and never will I ask favor of him who is so untrue a friend as to turn his back upon a comrade in trouble as he turneth his back upon my father."

"Thou art a foolish boy," said Sir James with a bitter smile, "and knowest naught of the world. An thou wouldst look for man to befriend man to his own danger, thou must look elsewhere than on this earth. Was I not one time Mackworth's dear friend as well as thy father? It could cost him naught to honor me, and here am I fallen to be a teacher of boys. Go to! thou art a fool."

Then, after a little pause of brooding silence, he went on to say that the Earl was no better or worse than the rest of the world. That men of his position had many jealous enemies, ever seeking their ruin, and that such must look first of all each to himself, or else be certainly ruined, and drag down others in that ruin. Myles was silenced, but the bitterness had entered his heart, and abided with him for many a day afterwards.

Perhaps Sir James read his feelings in his frank face, for he sat looking curiously at him, twirling his grizzled mustache the while. " Thou art like to have hard knocks of it, lad, ere thou hast gotten thee safe through the world," said he, with more kindness in his harsh voice than was usual. " But get thee not into fights before thy time." Then he charged the boy very seriously to live at peace with his fellow-squires, and for his father's sake as well as his own to enter into none of the broils that were so frequent in their quarters.

It was with this special admonition against brawling that Myles was dismissed, to enter, before five minutes had passed, into the first really great fight of his life.

Besides Gascoyne and Wilkes, he found gathered in the dormitory six or eight of the company of squires who were to serve that day upon household duty; among others, Walter Blunt and three other bachelors, who were changing their coarse service clothes for others more fit for the household.

"Why didst thou tarry so long, Myles?" said Gascoyne, as he entered. "Methought thou wert never coming."

"Where goest thou, Falworth?" called Blunt from the other end of the room, where he was lacing his doublet.

Just now Myles had no heart in the swimming or sport of any sort, but he answered, shortly, "I go to the river to swim."

"Nay," said Blunt, "thou goest not forth from the castle to-day. Hast thou forgot how thou didst answer me back about fetching the water this morning? This day thou must do penance, so go thou straight to the armory and scour thou up my breastplate."

From the time he had arisen that morning everything had gone wrong with Myles. He had felt himself already outraged in rendering service to the bachelors, he had quarrelled with the head of the squires, he had nearly quarrelled with Gascoyne, and then had come the bitterest and worst of all, the knowledge that his father was an outlaw, and that the Earl would not stretch out a hand to aid him or to give him any countenance. Blunt's words brought the last bitter cut to his heart, and they stung him to fury. For a while he could not answer, but stood glaring with a face fairly convulsed with passion at the young man, who continued his toilet, unconscious of the wrath of the new recruit.

Gascoyne and Wilkes, accepting Myles's punishment as a thing of course, were about to leave the dormitory when Myles checked them.

"Stop, Francis!" he cried, hoarsely. "Thinkest thou that I will stay behind to do yon dog's dirty work? No; I go with ye."

A moment or two of dumb, silent amazement followed his bold words; then Blunt cried, "Art thou mad?"

"Nay," answered Myles in the same hoarse voice, "I am not mad. I tell thee a better man than thou shouldst not stay me from going an I list to go."

"I will break thy cockerel head for that speech," said Blunt, furiously. He stooped as he spoke, and picked up a heavy clog that lay at his feet.

It was no insignificant weapon either. The shoes of those days were sometimes made of cloth, and had long pointed toes stuffed with tow or wool. In muddy weather thick heavy clogs or wooden soles were strapped, like a skate, to the bottom of the foot. That clog which Blunt had seized was perhaps eighteen or twenty inches long, two or two and a half inches thick at the heel, tapering to a point at the toe. As the older lad advanced, Gascoyne stepped between him and his victim.

"Do not harm him, Blunt," he pleaded. "Bear thou in mind how new-come he is among us. He knoweth not our ways as yet."

"Stand thou back, Gascoyne," said Blunt, harshly, as he thrust him aside. "I will teach him our ways so that he will not soon forget them."

Close to Myles's feet was another clog like that one which Blunt held. He snatched it up, and set his back against the wall, with a white face and a heart beating heavily and tumultuously, but with courage steeled to meet the coming encounter. There was a hard, grim look in his blue eyes that, for a moment perhaps, quelled the elder lad. He hesitated. "Tom! Wat! Ned!" he called to the other bachelors, "come hither, and lend me a hand with this knave."

"An ye come nigh me," panted Myles, "I will brain the first within reach."

Then Gascoyne dodged behind the others, and, without being seen, slipped out of the room for help.

The battle that followed was quick, sharp, and short. As Blunt strode forward, Myles struck, and struck with might and main, but he was too excited to deliver his blow with calculation. Blunt parried it with the clog he held, and the next instant, dropping his weapon, gripped Myles tight about the body, pinning his arms to his sides.

66

Myles also dropped the clog he held, and, wrenching out his right arm with a sudden heave, struck Blunt full in the face, and then with another blow sent him staggering back. It all passed in an instant; the next the three other bachelors were upon him, catching him by the body, the arms, the legs. For a moment or two they swayed and stumbled hither and thither, and then down they fell in a struggling heap.

Myles fought like a wild-cat, kicking, struggling, scratching; striking with elbows and fists. He caught one of the three by his collar, and tore his jacket open from the neck to the waist; he drove his foot into the pit of the stomach of another, and knocked him breathless. The other lads not in the fight stood upon the benches and the beds around, but such was the awe inspired by the prestige of the bachelors that not one of them dared to lend hand to help him, and so Myles fought his fierce battle alone.

But four to one were odds too great, and though Myles struggled as fiercely as ever, by-and-by it was with less and less resistance.

Blunt had picked up the clog he had dropped when he first attacked the lad, and now stood over the struggling heap, white with rage, the blood running from his lip, cut and puffed where Myles had struck him, and murder looking out from his face, if ever it looked out of the face of any mortal being.

"Hold him a little," said he, fiercely, "and I will still him for you."

Even yet it was no easy matter for the others to do his bidding, but presently he got his chance and struck a heavy, cruel blow at Myles's head. Myles only partly warded it with his arm. Hitherto he had fought in silence; now he gave a harsh cry.

"Holy Saints!" cried Edmund Wilkes. "They will kill him."

Blunt struck two more blows, both of them upon the body, and then at last they had the poor boy down, with his face upon the ground and his arms pinned to his sides; and Blunt, bracing himself for the stroke, with a grin of rage raised a heavy clog for one terrible blow that should finish the fight.

CHAPTER IX.

" How now, messieurs?" said a harsh voice,
that fell upon the turmoil like a thunder·clap,
and there stood Sir James Lee. Instantly the
struggle ceased, and the combatants scrambled
to their feet.

The older lads stood silent before their chief,
but Myles was deaf and blind and mad with
passion; he knew not where he stood or what
he said or did. White as death, he stood for a
while glaring about him, catching his breath convulsively. Then he screamed hoarsely

" Who struck me? Who struck me when I
was down? I will have his blood that struck
me!" He caught sight of Blunt. " It was he
that struck me!" he cried. " Thou foul traitor!
thou coward!" and thereupon leaped at his enemy like a wild-cat.

" Stop!" cried Sir James Lee, clutching him
by the arm

Myles was too blinded by his fury to see who

it was that held him. "I will not stop!" he cried, struggling and striking at the knight. "Let me go! I will have his life that struck me when I was down!"

The next moment he found himself pinned close against the wall, and then, as though his sight came back, he saw the grim face of the old one-eyed knight looking into his.

"Dost thou know who I am?" said a stern, harsh voice.

Instantly Myles ceased struggling, and his arms fell at his side. "Aye," he said, in a gasping voice, "I know thee." He swallowed spasmodically for a moment or two, and then, in the sudden revulsion of feeling, burst out sobbing convulsively.

Sir James marched the two off to his office, he himself walking between them, holding an arm of each, the other lads following behind, awe-struck and silent. Entering the office, Sir James shut the door behind him, leaving the group of squires clustered outside about the stone steps, speculating in whispers as to what would be the outcome of the matter.

After Sir James had seated himself, the two standing facing him, he regarded them for a while in silence. "How now, Walter Blunt," said he at last, "what is to do?"

"Why, this," said Blunt, wiping his bleeding lip. "That fellow, Myles Falworth, hath been breeding mutiny and revolt ever sin he came hither among us, and because he was thus mutinous I would punish him therefor."

"In that thou liest!" burst out Myles. "Never have I been mutinous in my life."

"Be silent, sir," said Sir James, sternly. "I will hear thee anon."

"Nay," said Myles, with his lips twitching and writhing, "I will not be silent. I am friendless here, and ye are all against me, but I will not be silent, and brook to have lies spoken of me."

Even Blunt stood aghast at Myles's boldness. Never had he heard any one so speak to Sir James before. He did not dare for the moment even to look up. Second after second of dead stillness passed, while Sir James sat looking at Myles with a stern, terrifying calmness that chilled him in spite of the heat of his passion.

"Sir," said the old man at last, in a hard, quiet voice, "thou dost know naught of rules and laws of such a place as this. Nevertheless, it is time for thee to learn them. So I will tell thee now that if thou openest thy lips to say only one single word more except at my bidding, I will send thee to the black vault of the donjon to cool thy hot spirits on bread and water for a week."

There was something in the measured quietness of the old knight's tone that quelled Myles utterly and entirely. A little space of silence followed. "Now, then, Blunt," said Sir James, turning to the bachelor, "tell me all the ins and outs of this business without any more underdealing."

This time Blunt's story, though naturally prejudiced in his own favor, was fairly true. Then Myles told his side of the case, the old knight listening attentively.

"Why, how now, Blunt," said Sir James, when Myles had ended, "I myself gave the lads leave to go to the river to bathe. Wherefore shouldst thou forbid one of them?"

"I did it but to punish this fellow for his mutiny," said the bachelor. "Methought we at their head were to have oversight concerning them."

"So ye are," said the knight; "but only to a degree. Ere ye take it upon ye to gainsay any of my orders or permits, come ye first to me. Dost thou understand?"

"Aye," answered Blunt, sullenly.

"So be it, and now get thee gone," said the knight; "and let me hear no more of beating out brains with wooden clogs. An ye fight your battles, let there not be murder in them. This is twice that the like hath happed; gin I hear more of such doings—" He did utter his threat, but stopped short, and fixed his one eye sternly upon the head squire. " Now shake hands, and be ye friends," said he, abruptly.

Blunt made a motion to obey, but Myles put his hand behind him.

" Nay, I shake not hands with any one who struck me while I was down."

" So be it," said the knight, grimly. " Now thou mayst go, Blunt. Thou, Falworth, stay; I would bespeak thee further."

" Tell me," said he, when the elder lad had left them, " why wilt thou not serve these bachelors as the other squires do ? Such is the custom here. Why wilt thou not obey it ?"

" Because," said Myles, " I cannot stomach it, and they shall not make me serve them. An thou bid me do it, sir, I will do it; but not at their command."

" Nay," said the knight, " I do not bid thee do them service. That lieth with thee, to render or not, as thou seest fit. But how canst thou hope to fight single-handed against the commands of a dozen lads all older and mightier than thou ?"

" I know not," said Myles; " but were they an hundred, instead of thirteen, they should not make me serve them."

" Thou art a fool !" said the old knight, smiling faintly, "for that be'st not courage, but folly. When one setteth about righting a wrong, one driveth not full head against it, for in so doing one getteth naught but hard knocks. Nay, go deftly about it, and then, when the time is ripe, strike the blow. Now our beloved King Henry, when he was the Earl of Derby, what could he have gained had he stood so against the old King Richard, brooking the King face to face? I tell thee he would have been knocked on the head as thou wert like to have been this day. Now were I thee, and had to fight a fight against odds, I would first get me friends behind me, and then—" He stopped short, but Myles understood him well enough.

"Sir," said he, with a gulp, 'I do thank thee for thy friendship, and ask thy pardon for doing as I did anon."

"I grant thee pardon," said the knight, "but tell thee plainly, an thou dost face me so again, I will truly send thee to the black cell for a week. Now get thee away."

All the other lads were gone when Myles came forth, save only the faithful Gascoyne, who sacrificed his bath that day to stay with his friend; and perhaps that little act of self-denial moved Myles more than many a great thing might have done.

"It was right kind of thee, Francis," said he, laying his hand affectionately on his friend's shoulder. "I know not why thou lovest me so."

"Why, for one thing, this matter," answered his friend; "because methinks thou art the best fighter and the bravest one of all of us squires."

Myles laughed. Nevertheless Gascoyne's words were a soothing balm for much that had happened that day. "I will fight me no more just now," said he; and then he told his friend all that Sir James had advised about biding his time.

Gascoyne blew a long whistle. "Beshrew me!" quoth he, "but methinks old Bruin is on thy side of the quarrel, Myles. An that be so, I am with thee also, and others that I can name as well."

"So be it," said Myles. "Then am I content to abide the time when we may become strong enough to stand against them."

CHAPTER X.

PERHAPS there is nothing more delightful in the romance of boyhood than the finding of some secret hiding-place whither a body may creep away from the bustle of the world's life, to nestle in quietness for an hour or two. More especially is such delightful if it happen that, by peeping from out it, one may look down upon the bustling matters of busy every-day life, while one lies snugly hidden away unseen by any, as though one were in some strange invisible world of one's own.

Such a hiding-place as would have filled the heart of almost any boy with sweet delight Myles and Gascoyne found one summer afternoon. They called it their Eyry, and the name suited well for the roosting-place of the young hawks that rested in its windy stillness, looking down upon the shifting castle life in the courts below.

Behind the north stable, a great, long, rambling building, thick-walled, and black with age, lay an older part of the castle than that peopled by the better class of life—a cluster of great thick walls, rudely but strongly built, now the dwelling-place of stable-lads and hinds, swine and poultry. From one part of these ancient walls, and fronting an inner court of the castle, arose a tall, circular, heavy-buttressed tower, considerably higher than the other buildings, and so mantled with a dense growth of aged ivy as to stand a shaft of solid green. Above its crumbling crown circled hundreds of pigeons, white and pied, clapping and clattering in noisy flight through the sunny air. Several windows, some closed with shutters, peeped here and there from out the leaves, and near the top of the pile was a row of arched openings, as though of a balcony or an airy gallery.

Myles had more than once felt an idle curiosity about this tower, and one day, as he and Gascoyne sat together, he pointed his finger and said, "What is yon place?"

"That," answered Gascoyne, looking over his shoulder—"that they call Brutus Tower, for why they do say that Brutus he built it when he came hither to Britain. I believe not the tale mine own self; ne'theless, it is marvellous ancient, and old Robin-the-Fletcher telleth me that there be stair-ways built in the wall and passage-ways, and a maze wherein a body may get lost, an he know not the way aright, and never see the blessed light of day again."

"Marry," said Myles, "those same be strange sayings. Who liveth there now?"

"No one liveth there," said Gascoyne, "saving only some of the stable villains, and that half-witted goose-herd who flung stones at us yesterday when we mocked him down in the paddock. He and his wife and those others dwell in the vaults beneath, like rabbits in any warren. No one else hath lived there since Earl Robert's day, which belike was an hundred years agone. The story goeth that Earl Robert's brother—or step-brother—was murdered there, and some men say by the Earl himself. Sin that day it hath been tight shut."

Myles stared at the tower for a while in silence. "It is a strange-seeming place from without," said he, at last, "and mayhap it may be even more strange inside. Hast ever been within, Francis?"

"Nay," said Gascoyne; "said I not it hath been fast locked since Earl Robert's day?"

"By 'r Lady," said Myles, "an I had lived here in this place so long as thou, I wot I would have been within it ere this."

"Beshrew me," said Gascoyne, "but I have never thought of such a matter." He turned and looked at the tall crown rising into the warm sunlight with a new interest, for the thought of entering it smacked pleasantly of adventure. " How wouldst thou set about getting within ?" said he, presently.

" Why, look," said Myles; "seest thou not yon hole in the ivy branches? Methinks there is a window at that place. An I mistake not, it is in reach of the stable eaves. A body might come up by the fagot pile to the roof of the hen-house, and then by the long stable to the north stable, and so to that hole."

Gascoyne looked thoughtfully at the Brutus Tower, and then suddenly inquired, " Wouldst go there ?"

" Aye," said Myles, briefly.

" So be it. Lead thou the way in the venture, I will follow after thee," said Gascoyne.

As Myles had said, the climbing from roof to roof was a matter easy enough to an active pair of lads like themselves; but when, by-and-by, they reached the wall of the tower itself, they found the hidden window much higher from the roof than they had judged from below—perhaps ten or twelve feet—and it was, besides, beyond the eaves and out of their reach.

Myles looked up and looked down. Above was the bushy thickness of the ivy, the branches

73

as thick as a woman's wrist, knotted and inter-twined; below was the stone pavement of a narrow inner court between two of the stable buildings.

"Methinks I can climb to yon place," said he.

"Thou'lt break thy neck an thou tryest," said Gascoyne, hastily.

"Nay," quoth Myles, "I trust not; but break or make, we get not there without trying. So here goeth for the venture."

"Thou art a hare-brained knave as ever drew breath of life," quoth Gascoyne, "and will cause me to come to grief some of these fine days. Ne'theless, an thou be Jack Fool and lead the way, go, and I will be Tom Fool and follow anon. If thy neck is worth so little, mine is worth no more."

It was indeed a perilous climb, but that special providence which guards reckless lads befriended them, as it has thousands of their kind before and since. So, by climbing from one knotted, clinging stem to another, they were presently seated snugly in the ivied niche in the window. It was barred from within by a crumbling shutter, the rusty fastening of which, after some little effort upon the part of the two, gave way, and entering the narrow opening, they found themselves in a small triangular passage-way, from which a steep flight of stone steps led down through a hollow in the massive wall to the room below.

At the bottom of the steps was a heavy oaken door, which stood ajar, hanging upon a single rusty hinge, and from the room within a dull, gray light glimmered faintly. Myles pushed the door farther open; it creaked and grated horribly on its rusty hinge, and, as in instant answer to the discordant shriek, came a faint piping squeaking, a rustling and a pattering of soft footsteps.

" The ghosts !" cried Gascoyne, in a quavering whisper, and for a moment Myles felt the chill of goose-flesh creep up and down his spine. But the next moment he laughed.

" Nay," said he, " they be rats. Look at yon fellow, Francis ! Be'st as big as Mother Joan's kitten. Give me that stone." He flung it at the rat, and it flew clattering across the floor. There was another pattering rustle of hundreds of feet, and then a breathless silence.

The boys stood looking around them, and a strange enough sight it was. The room was a perfect circle of about twenty feet across, and was piled high with an indistinguishable mass of lumber—rude tables, ruder chairs, ancient chests, bits and remnants of cloth and sacking and leather, old helmets and pieces of armor of a by-gone time, broken spears and pole-axes, pots and pans and kitchen furniture of all sorts and kinds.

A straight beam of sunlight fell through a broken shutter like a bar of gold, and fell upon the floor in a long streak of dazzling light that illuminated the whole room with a yellow glow.

" By 'r Lady !" said Gascoyne at last, in a hushed voice, " here is Father Time's garret for sure. Didst ever see the like, Myles ? Look at yon arbalist; sure Brutus himself used such an one !"

" Nay," said Myles; " but look at this saddle Marry, here be'st a rat's nest in it."

Clouds of dust rose as they rummaged among the mouldering mass, setting them coughing and sneezing. Now and then a great gray rat would shoot out beneath their very feet, and disappear. like a sudden shadow, into some hole or cranny in the wall.

" Come," said Myles at last, brushing the dust from his jacket, " an we tarry here longer we will have chance to see no other sights; the sun is falling low."

An arched stair-way upon the opposite side of the room from which they had entered wound upward through the wall, the stone steps being lighted by narrow slits of windows cut through the massive masonry. Above the room they had just left was another of the same shape and size, but with an oak floor, sagging and rising into hollows and hills, where the joist had rotted away beneath. It was bare and empty, and not even a rat was to be seen. Above was another room; above that, another; all the passages and stair-ways which connected the one story with the other being built in the wall, which was, where solid, perhaps fifteen feet thick.

From the third floor a straight flight of steps led upward to a closed door, from the other side of which shone the dazzling brightness of sun-light, and whence came a strange noise—a soft rustling, a melodious murmur. The boys put their shoulders against the door, which was fastened, and pushed with might and main—once, twice; suddenly the lock gave way, and out they pitched headlong into a blaze of sunlight. A deafening clapping and uproar sounded in their ears, and scores of pigeons, suddenly disturbed, rose in stormy flight.

They sat up and looked around them in silent wonder. They were in a bower of leafy green. It was the top story of the tower, the roof of which had crumbled and toppled in, leaving it open to the sky, with only here and there a slanting beam or two supporting a portion of the tiled roof, affording shelter for the nests of the pigeons crowded closely together. Over everything the ivy had grown in a mantling sheet —a net-work of shimmering green, through which the sunlight fell flickering.

"This passeth wonder," said Gascoyne, at last, breaking the silence.

"Aye," said Myles, "I did never see the like in all my life." Then, "Look, yonder is a room beyond; let us see what it is, Francis."

Entering an arched door-way, the two found themselves in a beautiful little vaulted chapel, about eighteen feet long and twelve or fifteen wide. It comprised the crown of one of the large massive buttresses, and from it opened the row of arched windows which could be seen from below through the green shimmering of the ivy leaves. The boys pushed aside the trailing tendrils and looked out and down. The whole castle lay spread below them, with the busy people unconsciously intent upon the matters of their daily work. They could see the gardener, with bowed back, patiently working among the flowers in the garden, the stable-boys below grooming the horses, a bevy of ladies in the privy garden playing at shuttlecock with battledoors of wood, a group of gentlemen walking up and down in front of the Earl's house. They could see the household servants hurrying hither and thither, two little scullions at fisticuffs, and a kitchen girl standing in the door-way scratching her frowzy head.

It was all like a puppetshow of real life, each acting unconsciously a part in the play. The cool wind came in through the rustling leaves and fanned their cheeks, hot with the climb up the winding stair-way.

"We will call it our Eyry," said Gascoyne, "and we will be the hawks that live here." And that was how it got its name.

The next day Myles had the armorer make him a score of large spikes, which he and Gascoyne drove between the ivy branches and into the cement of the wall, and so made a safe passage-way by which to reach the window niche in the wall.

CHAPTER XI.

THE two friends kept the secret of the Eyry to themselves for a little while, now and then visiting the old tower to rummage among the lumber stored in the lower room, or to loiter away the afternoon in the windy solitudes of the upper heights. And in that little time, when the ancient keep was to them a small world unknown to any but themselves—a world far away above all the dull matters of every-day life—they talked of many things that might else never have been known to one another. Mostly they spoke the crude romantic thoughts and desires of boyhood's time—chaff thrown to the wind, in which, however, lay a few stray seeds, fated to fall to good earth, and to ripen to fruition in manhood's day.

In the intimate talks of that time Myles imparted something of his honest solidity to Gascoyne's somewhat weathercock nature, and to Myles's ruder and more uncouth character Gas-

coyne lent a tone of his gentler manners, learned
in his pagehood service as attendant upon the
Countess and her ladies.

In other things, also, the character and experience of the one lad helped to supply what was
lacking in the other. Myles was replete with
old Latin gestes, fables, and sermons picked up
during his school life, in those intervals of his
more serious studies when Prior Edward had
permitted him to browse in the greener pastures
of the *Gesta Romanorum* and the *Disciplina
Clericalis* of the monastery library, and Gascoyne
was never weary of hearing him tell those marvellous stories culled from the crabbed Latin of
the old manuscript volumes.

Upon his part Gascoyne was full of the lore
of the waiting-room and the antechamber, and
Myles, who in all his life had never known a
lady, young or old, excepting his mother, was
never tired of lying silently listening to Gascoyne's chatter of the gay doings of the castle
gentle-life, in which he had taken part so often
in the merry days of his pagehood.

" I do wonder," said Myles, quaintly, " that thou
couldst ever find the courage to bespeak a young
maid, Francis. Never did I do so, nor ever could.
Rather would I face three strong men than one
young damsel."

Whereupon Gascoyne burst out laughing. "Marry!" quoth he, "they be no such terrible things, but gentle and pleasant spoken, and soft and smooth as any cat."

"No matter for that," said Myles; "I would not face one such for worlds."

It was during the short time when, so to speak, the two owned the solitude of the Brutus Tower, that Myles told his friend of his father's outlawry and of the peril in which the family stood. And thus it was.

"I do marvel," said Gascoyne one day, as the two lay stretched in the Eyry, looking down into the castle court-yard below—"I do marvel, now that thou art 'stablished here this month and more, that my Lord doth never have thee called to service upon household duty. Canst thou riddle me why it is so, Myles?"

The subject was a very sore one with Myles. Until Sir James had told him of the matter in his office that day he had never known that his father was attainted and outlawed. He had accepted the change from their earlier state and the bald poverty of their life at Crosbey-Holt with the easy carelessness of boyhood, and Sir James's words were the first to awaken him to a realization of the misfortunes of the house of Falworth. His was a brooding nature, and in the

"Myles pushed the door farther open"

three or four weeks that passed he had meditated
so much over what had been told him, that by
and-by it almost seemed as if a shadow of shame
rested upon his father's fair fame, even though
the attaint set upon him was unrighteous and
unjust, as Myles knew it must be. He had felt
angry and resentful at the Earl's neglect, and as
days passed and he was not noticed in any way,
his heart was at times very bitter.

So now Gascoyne's innocent question touched
a sore spot, and Myles spoke with a sharp, angry
pain in his voice that made the other look quickly up. "Sooner would my Lord have yonder
swine-herd serve him in the household than me,"
said he.

"Why may that be, Myles?" said Gascoyne.

"Because," answered Myles, with the same angry bitterness in his voice, "either the Earl is a
coward that feareth to befriend me, or else he is
a caitiff, ashamed of his own flesh and blood, and
of me, the son of his one-time comrade."

Gascoyne raised himself upon his elbow, and
opened his eyes wide in wonder. "Afeard of
thee, Myles!" quoth he. "Why should he be
afeared to befriend thee? Who art thou that
the Earl should fear thee?"

Myles hesitated for a moment or two; wisdom
bade him remain silent upon the dangerous topic,

but his heart yearned for sympathy and companionship in his trouble. "I will tell thee," said he, suddenly, and therewith poured out all of the story, so far as he knew it, to his listening, wondering friend, and his heart felt lighter to be thus eased of its burden. "And now," said he, as he concluded, "is not this Earl a mean-hearted caitiff to leave me, the son of his one-time friend and kinsman, thus to stand or to fall alone among strangers and in a strange place without once stretching me a helping hand?" He waited, and Gascoyne knew that he expected an answer.

"I know not that he is a mean-hearted caitiff, Myles," said he at last, hesitatingly. "The Earl hath many enemies, and I have heard that he hath stood more than once in peril, having been accused of dealings with the King's foes. He was cousin to the Earl of Kent, and I do remember hearing that he had a narrow escape at that time from ruin. There be more reasons than thou wottest of why he should not have dealings with thy father."

"I had not thought," said Myles, bitterly, after a little pause, "that thou wouldst stand up for him and against me in this quarrel, Gascoyne. Him will I never forgive so long as I may live, and I had thought that thou wouldst have stood by me."

"So I do," said Gascoyne, hastily, "and do love thee more than any one in all the world, Myles; but I had thought that it would make thee feel more easy to think that the Earl was not against thee. And, indeed, from all thou has told me, I do soothly think that he and Sir James mean to befriend thee and hold thee privily in kind regard."

"Then why doth he not stand forth like a man and befriend me and my father openly, even if it be to his own peril?" said Myles, reverting stubbornly to what he had first spoken.

Gascoyne did not answer, but lay for a long while in silence. "Knowest thou," he suddenly asked, after a while, "who is this great enemy of whom Sir James speaketh, and who seeketh so to drive thy father to ruin?"

"Nay," said Myles, "I know not, for my father hath never spoken of these things, and Sir James would not tell me. But this I know," said he, suddenly, grinding his teeth together, "an I do not hunt him out some day and slay him like a dog—" He stopped abruptly, and Gascoyne, looking askance at him, saw that his eyes were full of tears, whereupon he turned his looks away again quickly, and fell to shooting pebbles out through the open window with his finger and thumb.

"Thou wilt tell no one of these things that I have said?" said Myles, after a while.

"Not I," said Gascoyne. "Thinkest thou I could do such a thing?"

"Nay," said Myles, briefly.

Perhaps this talk more than anything else that had ever passed between them knit the two friends the closer together, for, as I have said, Myles felt easier now that he had poured out his bitter thoughts and words; and as for Gascoyne, I think that there is nothing so flattering to one's soul as to be made the confidant of a stronger nature.

But the old tower served another purpose than that of a spot in which to pass away a few idle hours, or in which to indulge the confidences of friendship, for it was there that Myles gathered a backing of strength for resistance against the tyranny of the bachelors, and it is for that more than for any other reason that it has been told how they found the place and of what they did there, feeling secure against interruption.

Myles Falworth was not of a kind that forgets or neglects a thing upon which the mind has once been set. Perhaps his chief objective since the talk with Sir James following his fight in the dormitory had been successful resistance to the exactions of the head of the body of squires. He was now (more than a month had passed) looked upon by nearly if not all of the younger lads as an acknowledged leader in his own class. So one day he broached a matter to Gascoyne that had for some time been digesting in his mind. It was the formation of a secret order, calling themselves the " Knights of the Rose," their meeting-place to be the chapel of the Brutus Tower, and their object to be the righting of wrongs, " as they," said Myles, " of Arthur his Round-table did right wrongs."

" But, prithee, what wrongs are there to right in this place?" quoth Gascoyne, after listening intently to the plan which Myles set forth.

" Why, first of all, this," said Myles, clinching his fists, as he had a habit of doing when anything stirred him deeply, " that we set those vile bachelors to their right place; and that is, that they be no longer our masters, but our fellows."

Gascoyne shook his head. He hated clashing and conflict above all things, and was for peace. Why should they thus rush to thrust themselves into trouble? Let matters abide as they were a little longer; surely life was pleasant enough without turning it all topsy-turvy. Then, with a sort of indignation, why should Myles, who had only come among them a month, take such service more to heart than they who had endured it for years? And, finally, with the hopefulness of so many of the rest of us, he advised Myles to let matters alone, and they would right themselves in time.

But Myles's mind was determined; his active spirit could not brook resting passively under a wrong; he would endure no longer, and now or never they must make their stand.

"But look thee, Myles Falworth," said Gascoyne, "all this is not to be done withouten fighting shrewdly. Wilt thou take that fighting upon thine own self? As for me, I tell thee I love it not."

"Why, aye," said Myles; "I ask no man to do what I will not do myself."

Gascoyne shrugged his shoulders. "So be it," said he. "An thou hast appetite to run thy head against hard knocks, do it i' mercy's name! I for one will stand thee back while thou art taking thy raps."

There was a spirit of drollery in Gascoyne's speech that rubbed against Myles's earnestness.

"Out upon it!" cried he, his patience giving way. "Seest not that I am in serious earnest? Why then dost thou still jest like Mad Noll, my Lord's fool? An thou wilt not lend me thine aid in this matter, say so and ha' done with it, and I will bethink me of somewhere else to turn."

94.

Then Gascoyne yielded at once, as he always did when his friend lost his temper, and having once assented to it, entered into the scheme heart and soul. Three other lads—one of them that tall thin squire Edmund Wilkes, before spoken of— were sounded upon the subject. They also en. tered into the plan of the secret organization with an enthusiasm which might perhaps not have been quite so glowing had they realized how very soon Myles designed embarking upon active practical operations One day Myles and Gascoyne showed them the strange things that they had discovered in the old tower—the inner staircases, the winding passage-ways, the queer niches and cupboard, and the black shaft of a well that pierced down into the solid wall, and whence, perhaps, the old castle folk had one time drawn their supply of water in time of siege, and with every new wonder of the marvellous place the enthusiasm of the three recruits rose higher and higher. They rummaged through the lumber pile in the great circular room as Myles and Gascoyne had done, and at last, tired out, they ascended to the airy chapel, and there sat cooling themselves in the rustling freshness of the breeze that came blowing briskly in through the arched windows.

It was then and there that the five discussed and finally determined upon the detailed plans of their organization, canvassing the names of the squirehood, and selecting from it a sufficient number of bold and daring spirits to make up a roll of twenty names in all.

Gascoyne had, as I said, entered into the matter with spirit, and perhaps it was owing more to him than to any other that the project caught its delightful flavor of romance.

"Perchance," said he, as the five lads lay in the rustling stillness through which sounded the monotonous and ceaseless cooing of the pigeons— "perchance there may be dwarfs and giants and dragons and enchanters and evil knights and what not even nowadays. And who knows but that if we Knights of the Rose hold together we may go forth into the world, and do battle with them, and save beautiful ladies, and have tales and gestes written about us as they are writ about the Seven Champions and Arthur his Round-table."

Perhaps Myles, who lay silently listening to all that was said, was the only one who looked upon the scheme at all in the light of real utility, but I think that even with him the fun of the matter outweighed the serious part of the business.

So it was that the Sacred Order of the Twenty Knights of the Rose came to be initiated. They appointed a code of secret passwords and countersigns which were very difficult to remember, and which were only used when they might excite the curiosity of the other and uninitiated boys by their mysterious sound. They elected Myles as their Grand High Commander, and held secret meetings in the ancient tower, where many mysteries were soberly enacted.

Of course in a day or two all the body of squires knew nearly everything concerning the Knights of the Rose, and of their secret meetings in the old tower. The lucky twenty were the objects of envy of all not so fortunate as to be included in this number, and there was a marked air of secrecy about everything they did that appealed to every romantic notion of the youngsters looking on. What was the stormy outcome of it all is now presently to be told.

CHAPTER XII.

THUS it was that Myles, with an eye to open war with the bachelors, gathered a following to his support. It was some little while before matters were brought to a crisis—a week or ten days. Perhaps even Myles had no great desire to hasten matters. He knew that whenever war was declared, he himself would have to bear the brunt of the battle, and even the bravest man hesitates before deliberately thrusting himself into a fight.

One morning Myles and Gascoyne and Wilkes sat under the shade of two trees, between which was a board nailed to the trunks, making a rude bench—always a favorite lounging-place for the lads in idle moments. Myles was polishing his bascinet with lard and wood-ashes, rubbing the metal with a piece of leather, and wiping it clean with a fustian rag. The other two, who had just been relieved from household duty, lay at length idly looking on.

Just then one of the smaller pages, a boy of twelve or thirteen, by name Robin Ingoldsby, crossed the court. He had been crying; his face was red and blubbered, and his body was still shaken with convulsive sniffs.

Myles looked up. "Come hither, Robin," he called from where he sat. "What is to do?"

The little fellow came slowly up to where the three rested in the shade. "Mowbray beat me with a strap," said he, rubbing his sleeve across his eyes, and catching his breath at the recollection.

"Beat thee, didst say?" said Myles, drawing his brows together. "Why did he beat thee?"

"Because," said Robin, "I tarried overlong in fetching a pot of beer from the buttery for him and Wyatt." Then, with a boy's sudden and easy quickness in forgetting past troubles, "Tell me, Falworth," said he, "when wilt thou give me that knife thou promised me — the one thou break the blade of yesterday?"

"I know not," said Myles, bluntly, vexed that the boy did not take the disgrace of his beating more to heart. "Some time soon, mayhap. Methinks thou shouldst think more of thy beating than of a broken knife. Now get thee gone to thy business."

The youngster lingered for a moment or two

99

watching Myles at his work. "What is that on the leather scrap, Falworth?" said he, curiously.

"Lard and ashes," said Myles, testily. "Get thee gone, I say, or I will crack thy head for thee;" and he picked up a block of wood, with a threatening gesture.

The youngster made a hideous grimace, and then scurried away, ducking his head, lest in spite of Myles's well-known good-nature the block should come whizzing after him.

"Hear ye that now!" cried Myles, flinging down the block again and turning to his two friends. "Beaten with straps because, forsooth, he would not fetch and carry quickly enough to please the haste of these bachelors. Oh, this passeth patience, and I for one will bear it no longer"

"Nay, Myles," said Gascoyne, soothingly, "the little imp is as lazy as a dormouse and as mischievous as a monkey I'll warrant the hiding was his due, and that more of the like would do him good."

"Why, how dost thou talk, Francis!" said Myles, turning upon him indignantly "Thou knowest that thou likest to see the boy beaten no more than I." Then, after a meditative pause, "How many, think ye, we muster of our company of the Rose to-day?"

Wilkes looked doubtfully at Gascoyne. " There be only seventeen of us here now," said he at last. " Brinton and Lambourne are away to Roby Castle in Lord George's train, and will not be back till Saturday next. And Watt Newton is in the infirmary."

" Seventeen be'st enou," said Myles, grimly. "Let us get together this afternoon, such as may, in the Brutus Tower, for I, as I did say will no longer suffer these vile bachelors."

Gascoyne and Wilkes exchanged looks, and then the former blew a long whistle.

So that afternoon a gloomy set of young faces were gathered together in the Eyry—fifteen of the Knights of the Rose—and all knew why they were assembled. The talk which followed was conducted mostly by Myles. He addressed the others with a straightforward vim and earnestness, but the response was only half-hearted, and when at last, having heated himself up with his own fire, he sat down, puffing out his red cheeks and glaring round, a space of silence followed, the lads looked doubtfully at one another. Myles felt the chill of their silence strike coldly on his enthusiasm, and it vexed him.

" What wouldst thou do, Falworth?" said one of the knights, at last. " Wouldst have us open a quarrel with they bachelors?"

"Nay," said Myles, gruffly. "I had thought that ye would all lend me a hand in a pitched battle, but now I see that ye ha' no stomach for that. Ne'theless, I tell ye plainly I will not submit longer to the bachelors. So now I will ask ye not to take any venture upon yourselves, but only this: that ye will stand by me when I do my fighting, and not let five or seven of them fall upon me at once."

"There is Walter Blunt; he is parlous strong," said one of the others, after a time of silence. "Methinks he could conquer any two of us."

"Nay," said Myles; "ye do fear him too greatly. I tell ye I fear not to stand up to try battle with him, and will do so, too, if the need arise. Only say ye that ye will stand by my back."

"Marry," said Gascoyne, quaintly, "an thou wilt dare take the heavy end upon thee, I for one am willing to stand by and see that thou have thy fill of fighting."

"I too will stand thee by, Myles," said Edmund Wilkes.

"And I, and I, and I," said others, chiming in.

Those who would still have held back were carried along by the stream, and so it was settled that if the need should arise for Myles to do a bit of fighting, the others should stand by to see that he had fair play.

"When thinkest thou that thou wilt take thy stand against them, Myles?" asked Wilkes.

Myles hesitated a moment. "To-morrow," said he, grimly.

Several of the lads whistled softly.

Gascoyne was prepared for an early opening of the war, but perhaps not for such an early opening as this. "By 'r Lady, Myles, thou art hungry for brawling," said he.

CHAPTER XIII.

AFTER the first excitement of meeting, discussing, and deciding had passed, Myles began to feel the weight of the load he had so boldly taken upon himself. He began to reckon what a serious thing it was for him to stand as a single champion against the tyranny that had grown so strong through years of custom. Had he let himself do so, he might almost have repented, but it was too late now for repentance. He had laid his hand to the plough, and he must drive the furrow.

Somehow the news of impending battle had leaked out among the rest of the body of squires, and a buzz of suppressed excitement hummed through the dormitory that evening. The bachelors, to whom, no doubt, vague rumors had been blown, looked lowering, and talked together in low voices, standing apart in a group. Some of them made a rather marked show of secreting knives in the straw of their beds, and no doubt it had its effect upon more than one young heart that secretly thrilled at the sight of the shining blades. However, all was undisturbed that evening. The lights were put out, and the lads retired with more than usual quietness, only for the murmur of whispering.

All night Myles's sleep was more or less disturbed by dreams in which he was now conquering, now being conquered, and before the day had fairly broken he was awake. He lay upon his cot, keying himself up for the encounter which he had set upon himself to face, and it would not be the truth to say that the sight of those knives hidden in the straw the night before had made no impression upon him. By-and-by he knew the others were beginning to awake, for he heard them softly stirring, and as the light grew broad and strong, saw them arise, one by one, and begin dressing in the gray morning. Then he himself arose and put on his doublet and hose, strapping his belt tightly about his waist; then he sat down on the side of his cot.

Presently that happened for which he was waiting; two of the younger squires started to bring the bachelors' morning supply of water. As they crossed the room Myles called to them in a loud voice—a little uneven, perhaps:

"Stop! We draw no more water for any one

in this house, saving only for ourselves. Set ye down those buckets, and go back to your places!"

The two lads stopped, half turned, and then stood still, holding the three buckets undecidedly.

In a moment all was uproar and confusion, for by this time every one of the lads had arisen, some sitting on the edge of their beds, some nearly, others quite dressed. A half-dozen of the Knights of the Rose came over to where Myles stood, gathering in a body behind him, and the others followed, one after another.

The bachelors were hardly prepared for such prompt and vigorous action.

"What is to do?" cried one of them, who stood near the two lads with the buckets. "Why fetch ye not the water?"

"Falworth says we shall not fetch it," answered one of the lads, a boy by the name of Gosse.

"What mean ye by that, Falworth?" the young man called to Myles.

Myles's heart was beating thickly and heavily within him, but nevertheless he spoke up boldly enough. "I mean," said he, "that from henceforth ye shall fetch and carry for yourselves."

"Look'ee, Blunt," called the bachelor; "here is Falworth says they squires will fetch no more water for us."

The head bachelor had heard all that had passed, and was even then hastily slipping on his doublet and hose. " Now, then, Falworth," said he at last, striding forward, " what is to do? Ye will fetch no more water, eh? By 'r Lady, I will know the reason why."

He was still advancing towards Myles, with two or three of the older bachelors at his heels, when Gascoyne spoke.

" Thou hadst best stand back, Blunt," said he, " else thou mayst be hurt. We will not have ye bang Falworth again as ye once did, so stand thou back !"

Blunt stopped short and looked upon the lads standing behind Myles, some of them with faces a trifle pale perhaps, but all grim and determined looking enough. Then he turned upon his heel suddenly, and walked back to the far end of the dormitory, where the bachelors were presently clustered together. A few words passed between them, and then the thirteen began at once arming themselves, some with wooden clogs, and some with the knives which they had so openly concealed the night before. At the sign of imminent battle, all those not actively interested scuttled away to right and left, climbing up on the benches and cots, and leaving a free field to the combatants. The next moment would have brought bloodshed.

107

Now Myles, thanks to the training of the Crosbey-Dale smith, felt tolerably sure that in a wrestling bout he was a match—perhaps more than a match—for any one of the body of squires, and he had determined, if possible, to bring the battle to a single-handed encounter upon that footing. Accordingly he suddenly stepped forward before the others.

"Look'ee, fellow," he called to Blunt, "thou art he who struck me whilst I was down some while since. Wilt thou let this quarrel stand between thee and me, and meet me man to man without weapon? See, I throw me down mine own, and will meet thee with bare hands." And as he spoke, he tossed the clog he held in his hand back upon the cot.

"So be it," said Blunt, with great readiness, tossing down a similar weapon which he himself held.

"Do not go, Myles," cried Gascoyne, "he is a villain and a traitor, and would betray thee to thy death. I saw him when he first gat from bed hide a knife in his doublet."

"Thou liest!" said Blunt. "I swear, by my faith, I be barehanded as ye see me! Thy friend accuses me, Myles Falworth, because he knoweth thou art afraid of me."

"There thou liest most vilely!" exclaimed Myles.

"Swear that thou hast no knife, and I will meet thee."

"Hast thou not heard me say that I have no knife?" said Blunt. "What more wouldst thou have?"

"Then I will meet thee half-way," said Myles.

Gascoyne caught him by the sleeve, and would have withheld him, assuring him that he had seen the bachelor conceal a knife. But Myles, hot for the fight, broke away from his friend without listening to him.

As the two advanced steadily towards one another a breathless silence fell upon the dormitory in sharp contrast to the uproar and confusion that had filled it a moment before. The lads, standing some upon benches, some upon beds, all watched with breathless interest the meeting of the two champions.

As they approached one another they stopped and stood for a moment a little apart, glaring the one upon the other. They seemed ill enough matched; Blunt was fully half a head taller than Myles, and was thick-set and close-knit in young manhood. Nothing but Myles's undaunted pluck could have led him to dare to face an enemy so much older and stouter than himself.

The pause was only for a moment. They who looked saw Blunt slide his hand furtively towards his bosom. Myles saw too, and in the flash of an instant knew what the gesture meant, and sprang upon the other before the hand could grasp what it sought. As he clutched his enemy he felt what he had in that instant expected to feel—the handle of a dagger. The next moment he cried, in a loud voice:

"Oh, thou villain! Help, Gascoyne! He hath a knife under his doublet!"

In answer to his cry for help, Myles's friends started to his aid. But the bachelors shouted, "Stand back and let them fight it out alone, else we will knife ye too." And as they spoke, some of them leaped from the benches whereon they stood, drawing their knives and flourishing them.

For just a few seconds Myles's friends stood cowed, and in those few seconds the fight came to an end with a suddenness unexpected to all.

A struggle fierce and silent followed between the two; Blunt striving to draw his knife, and Myles, with the energy of despair, holding him tightly by the wrist. It was in vain the elder lad writhed and twisted; he was strong enough to overbear Myles, but still was not able to clutch the haft of his knife.

"Thou shalt not draw it!" gasped Myles at last. "Thou shalt not stab me!"

Then again some of his friends started forward

to his aid, but they were not needed, for before they came, the fight was over.

Blunt, finding that he was not able to draw the weapon, suddenly ceased his endeavors, and flung his arms around Myles, trying to bear him down upon the ground, and in that moment his battle was lost.

In an instant—so quick, so sudden, so unexpected that no one could see how it happened—his feet were whirled away from under him, he spun with flying arms across Myles's loins, and pitched with a thud upon the stone pavement, where he lay still, motionless, while Myles, his face white with passion and his eyes gleaming, stood glaring around like a young wild-boar beset·by the dogs.

The next moment the silence was broken, and the uproar broke forth with redoubled violence. The bachelors, leaping from the benches, came hurrying forward on one side, and Myles's friends from the other.

"Thou shalt smart for this, Falworth," said one of the older lads. "Belike thou hast slain him!"

Myles turned upon the speaker like a flash, and with such a passion of fury in his face that the other, a fellow nearly a head taller than he, shrank back, cowed in spite of himself. Then Gascoyne came and laid his hand on his friend's shoulder.

"Who touches me?" cried Myles, hoarsely, turning sharply upon him; and then, seeing who it was, "Oh, Francis, they would ha' killed me!"

"Come away, Myles," said Gascoyne; "thou knowest not what thou doest; thou art mad; come away. What if thou hadst killed him?"

The words called Myles somewhat to himself. 'I care not!" said he, but sullenly and not passionately, and then he suffered Gascoyne and Wilkes to lead him away.

Meantime Blunt's friends had turned him over, and, after feeling his temples, his wrist, and his heart, bore him away to a bench at the far end of the room. There they fell to chafing his hands and sprinkling water in his face, a crowd of the others gathering about. Blunt was hidden from Myles by those who stood around, and the lad listened to the broken talk that filled the room with its confusion, his anxiety growing keener as he became cooler. But at last, with a heartfelt joy, he gathered from the confused buzz of words that the other lad had opened his eyes and, after a while, he saw him sit up, leaning his head upon the shoulder of one of his fellow-bachelors, white and faint and sick as death.

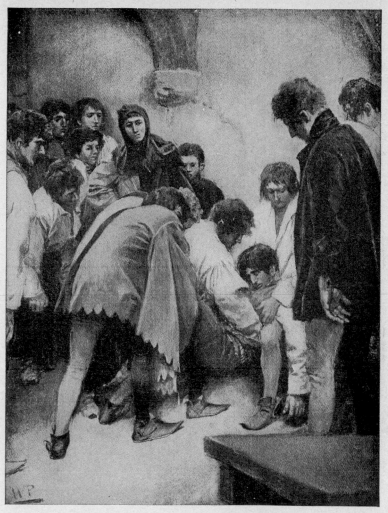

"They bore him away to a bench at the far end of the room"

"Thank Heaven that thou didst not kill him!" said Edmond Wilkes, who had been standing with the crowd looking on at the efforts of Blunt's friends to revive him, and who had now come and sat down upon the bed not far from Myles.

"Aye," said Myles, gruffly, "I do thank Heaven for that."

CHAPTER XIV.

IF Myles fancied that one single victory over his enemy would cure the evil against which he fought, he was grievously mistaken; wrongs are not righted so easily as that. It was only the beginning. Other and far more bitter battles lay before him ere he could look around him and say, "I have won the victory."

For a day—for two days—the bachelors were demoralized at the fall of their leader, and the Knights of the Rose were proportionately uplifted.

The day that Blunt met his fall, the wooden tank in which the water had been poured every morning was found to have been taken away. The bachelors made a great show of indignation and inquiry. Who was it stole their tank? If they did but know, he should smart for it.

"Ho! ho!" roared Edmond Wilkes, so that the whole dormitory heard him, "smoke ye not their tricks, lads? See ye not that they have stolen their own water-tank, so that they might have no need for another fight over the carrying of the water?"

The bachelors made an obvious show of not having heard what he said, and a general laugh went around. No one doubted that Wilkes had spoken the truth in his taunt, and that the bachelors had indeed stolen their own tank. So no more water was ever carried for the head squires, but it was plain to see that the war for the upperhand was not yet over.

Even if Myles had entertained comforting thoughts to the contrary, he was speedily undeceived. One morning, about a week after the fight, as he and Gascoyne were crossing the armory court, they were hailed by a group of the bachelors standing at the stone steps of the great building.

"Holloa, Falworth!" they cried. "Knowest thou that Blunt is nigh well again?"

"Nay," said Myles; "I knew it not. But I am right glad to hear it."

"Thou wilt sing a different song anon," said one of the bachelors. "I tell thee he is hot against thee, and swears when he cometh again he will carve thee soothly."

"Aye, marry!" said another. "I would not be in thy skin a week hence for a ducat! Only this morning he told Philip Mowbray that he would have thy blood for the fall thou gavest him. Look to thyself, Falworth; he cometh again Wednesday or Thursday next; thou standest in a parlous state."

"Myles," said Gascoyne, as they entered the great quadrangle, "I do indeed fear me that he meaneth to do thee evil."

"I know not," said Myles, boldly; "but I fear him not." Nevertheless his heart was heavy with the weight of impending ill.

One evening the bachelors were more than usually noisy in their end of the dormitory, laughing and talking and shouting to one another.

"Holloa, you sirrah, Falworth!" called one of them along the length of the room. "Blunt cometh again to-morrow day."

Myles saw Gascoyne direct a sharp glance at him; but he answered nothing either to his enemy's words or his friend's look.

As the bachelor had said, Blunt came the next morning. It was just after chapel, and the whole body of squires was gathered in the armory waiting for the orders of the day and the calling of the roll of those chosen for household duty. Myles was sitting on a bench along the wall, talking and jesting with some who stood by, when of a sudden his heart gave a great leap within him.

It was Walter Blunt. He came walking in at the door as if nothing had passed, and at his unexpected coming the hubbub of talk and laughter was suddenly checked. Even Myles stopped in his speech for a moment, and then continued with a beating heart and a carelessness of manner that was altogether assumed. In his hand Blunt carried the house orders for the day, and without seeming to notice Myles, he opened it and read the list of those called upon for household service.

Myles had risen, and was now standing listening with the others. When Blunt had ended reading the list of names, he rolled up the parchment, and thrust it into his belt; then swinging suddenly on his heel, he strode straight up to Myles, facing him front to front. A moment or two of deep silence followed; not a sound broke the stillness. When Blunt spoke every one in the armory heard his words.

"Sirrah!" said he, "thou didst put foul shame upon me some time sin. Never will I forget or forgive that offence, and will have a reckoning with thee right soon that thou wilt not forget to the last day of thy life."

When Myles had seen his enemy turn upon him, he did not know at first what to expect; he would not have been surprised had they come to

blows there and then, and he held himself pre
pared for any event. He faced the other pluckily
enough and without flinching, and spoke up bold
ly in answer. "So be it, Walter Blunt; I fear thee
not in whatever way thou mayst encounter me."

"Dost thou not?" said Blunt. "By 'r Lady,
thou'lt have cause to fear me ere I am through
with thee." He smiled a baleful, lingering smile,
and then turned slowly and walked away.

"What thinkest thou, Myles?" said Gascoyne,
as the two left the armory together.

"I think naught," said Myles, gruffly. "He
will not dare to touch me to harm me. I fear
him not." Nevertheless, he did not speak the
full feelings of his heart.

"I know not, Myles," said Gascoyne, shaking
his head doubtfully. "Walter Blunt is a parlous
evil-minded knave, and methinks will do whatever evil he promiseth."

"I fear him not," said Myles again; but his
heart foreboded trouble.

The coming of the head squire made a very
great change in the condition of affairs. Even
before that coming the bachelors had somewhat
recovered from their demoralization, and now
again they began to pluck up their confidence
and to order the younger squires and pages
upon this personal service or upon that.

"See ye not," said Myles one day, when the Knights of the Rose were gathered in the Brutus Tower—"see ye not that they grow as bad as ever? An we put not a stop to this overmastery now, it will never stop."

"Best let it be, Myles," said Wilkes. "They will kill thee an thou cease not troubling them. Thou hast bred mischief enow for thyself already.'

"No matter for that," said Myles; "it is not to be borne that they order others of us about as they do. I mean to speak to them to-night, and tell them it shall not be."

He was as good as his word. That night, as the youngsters were shouting and romping and skylarking, as they always did before turning in, he stood upon his cot and shouted: "Silence! List to me a little!" And then, in the hush that followed—"I want those bachelors to hear this: that we squires serve them no longer, and if they would ha' some to wait upon them, they must get them otherwheres than here. There be twenty of us to stand against them and haply more, and we mean that they shall ha' service of us no more."

Then he jumped down again from his elevated stand, and an uproar of confusion instantly filled the place. What was the effect of his words upon the bachelors he could not see. What was the result he was not slow in discovering.

The next day Myles and Gascoyne were throwing their daggers for a wager at a wooden target against the wall back of the armorer's smithy. Wilkes, Gosse, and one or two others of the squires were sitting on a bench looking on, and now and then applauding a more than usually well-aimed cast of the knife. Suddenly that impish little page spoken of before, Robin Ingoldsby, thrust his shock head around the corner of the smithy, and said:

"Ho, Falworth! Blunt is going to serve thee out to-day, and I myself heard him say so. He says he is going to slit thine ears." And then he was gone as suddenly as he had appeared.

Myles darted after him, caught him midway in the quadrangle, and brought him back by the scuff of the neck, squalling and struggling.

"There!" said he, still panting from the chase, and seating the boy by no means gently upon the bench beside Wilkes. "Sit thou there, thou imp of evil! And now tell me what thou didst mean by thy words anon—an thou stop not thine outcry, I will cut thy throat for thee;" and he made a ferocious gesture with his dagger.

It was by no means easy to worm the story from the mischievous little monkey; he knew

"*But tell me, Robin Ingoldsby, dost know aught more of this matter?*"

Myles too well to be in the least afraid of his threats. But at last, by dint of bribing and coaxing, Myles and his friends managed to get at the facts. The youngster had been sent to clean the riding-boots of one of the bachelors, instead of which he had lolled idly on a cot in the dormitory, until he had at last fallen asleep. He had been awakened by the opening of the dormitory door, and by the sound of voices—among them was that of his taskmaster. Fearing punishment for his neglected duty, he had slipped out of the cot, and hidden himself beneath it.

Those who had entered were Walter Blunt and three of the older bachelors. Blunt's companions were trying to persuade him against something, but without avail. It was—Myles's heart thrilled and his blood boiled — to lie in wait for him, to overpower him by numbers, and to mutilate him by slitting his ears—a disgraceful punishment administered, as a rule, only for thieving and poaching.

" He would not dare to do such a thing !" cried Myles, with heaving breast and flashing eyes.

" Aye, but he would," said Gascoyne. " His father, Lord Reginald Blunt, is a great man over Nottingham way, and my Lord would not dare to punish him even for such a matter as that. But tell me, Robin Ingoldsby, dost know aught more of this matter? Prithee tell it me, Robin. Where do they propose to lie in wait for Falworth?"

" In the gate-way of the Buttery Court, so as to catch him when he passes by to the armory,' answered the boy.

"Are they there now?" said Wilkes.

"Aye, nine of them," said Robin. " I heard Blunt tell Mowbray to go and gather the others. He heard thee tell Gosse, Falworth, that thou wert going thither for thy arbalist this morn to shoot at the rooks withal."

" That will do, Robin," said Myles. " Thou mayst go."

And therewith the little imp scurried off, pulling the lobes of his ears suggestively as he darted around the corner.

The others looked at one another for a while in silence.

" So, comrades," said Myles at last, "what shall we do now?"

"Go, and tell Sir James," said Gascoyne, promptly.

" Nay," said Myles; "I take no such coward's part as that. I say an they hunger to fight, give them their stomachful."

The others were very reluctant for such extreme measures, but Myles, as usual, carried his way, and so a pitched battle was decided upon. It was Gascoyne who suggested the plan which they afterwards followed.

Then Wilkes started away to gather together those of the Knights of the Rose not upon household duty, and Myles, with the others, went to the armor smith to have him make for them a set of knives with which to meet their enemies —knives with blades a foot long, pointed and double-edged.

The smith, leaning with his hammer upon the anvil, listened to them as they described the weapons.

" Nay, nay, Master Myles," said he, when Myles had ended by telling the use to which he intended putting them. " Thou art going all wrong in this matter. With such blades, ere this battle is ended, some one would be slain, and so murder done. Then the family of him who was killed would haply have ye cited, and mayhap it might e'en come to the hanging, for some of they boys ha' great folkeys behind them. Go ye to Tom Fletcher, Master Myles, and buy of him good yew staves, such as one might break a head withal, and with them, gin ye keep your wits, ye may hold your own against knives or short swords. I tell thee, e'en though my trade be making of blades, rather would I ha' a good stout cudgel in my hand than the best dagger that ever was forged.

Myles stood thoughtfully for a moment or two; then, looking up, "Methinks thou speaketh truly, Robin," said he; "and it were ill done to have blood upon our hands."

CHAPTER XV.

FROM the long, narrow stone-paved Armory Court, and connecting it with the inner Buttery Court, ran a narrow arched passage-way, in which was a picket-gate, closed at night and locked from within. It was in this arched passage-way that, according to little Robert Ingoldsby's report, the bachelors were lying in wait for Myles. Gascoyne's plan was that Myles should enter the court alone, the Knights of the Rose lying ambushed behind the angle of the armory building until the bachelors should show themselves.

It was not without trepidation that Myles walked alone into the court, which happened then to be silent and empty. His heart beat more quickly than it was wont, and he gripped his cudgel behind his back, looking sharply this way and that, so as not to be taken unawares by a flank movement of his enemies. Midway in the court he stopped and hesitated for a moment; then he turned as though to enter the armory.

The next moment he saw the bachelors come pouring out from the archway.

Instantly he turned and rushed back towards where his friends lay hidden, shouting: "To the rescue! To the rescue!"

"Stone him!" roared Blunt. "The villain escapes!"

He stooped and picked up a cobble-stone as he spoke, flinging it after his escaping prey. It narrowly missed Myles's head; had it struck him, there might have been no more of this story to tell.

"To the rescue! To the rescue!" shouted Myles's friends in answer, and the next moment he was surrounded by them. Then he turned, and swinging his cudgel, rushed back upon his foes.

The bachelors stopped short at the unexpected sight of the lads with their cudgels. For a moment they rallied and drew their knives; then they turned and fled towards their former place of hiding.

One of them turned for a moment, and flung his knife at Myles with a deadly aim; but Myles, quick as a cat, ducked his body, and the weapon flew clattering across the stony court. Then he who had flung it turned again to fly, but in his attempt he had delayed one instant too long.

Myles reached him with a long-arm stroke of his cudgel just as he entered the passage-way, knocking him over like a bottle, stunned and senseless.

The next moment the picket-gate was banged in their faces and the bolt shot in the staples, and the Knights of the Rose were left shouting and battering with their cudgels against the palings.

By this time the uproar of fight had aroused those in the rooms and offices fronting upon the Armory Court; heads were thrust from many of the windows with the eager interest that a fight always evokes.

" Beware!" shouted Myles. " Here they come again!" He bore back towards the entrance of the alley-way as he spoke, those behind him scattering to right and left, for the bachelors had rallied, and were coming again to the attack, shouting.

They were not a moment too soon in this retreat, either, for the next instant the pickets flew open, and a volley of stones flew after the retreating Knights of the Rose. One smote Wilkes upon the head, knocking him down headlong. Another struck Myles upon his left shoulder, benumbing his arm from the finger-tips to the armpit, so that he thought at first the limb was broken.

"Get ye behind the buttresses!" shouted those who looked down upon the fight from the windows—"get ye behind the buttresses!" And in answer the lads, scattering like a newly-flushed covey of partridges, fled to and crouched in the sheltering angles of masonry to escape from the flying stones.

And now followed a lull in the battle, the bachelors fearing to leave the protection of the arched passage-way lest their retreat should be cut off, and the Knights of the Rose not daring to quit the shelter of the buttresses and angles of the wall lest they should be knocked down by the stones.

The bachelor whom Myles had struck down with his cudgel was sitting up rubbing the back of his head, and Wilkes had gathered his wits enough to crawl to the shelter of the nearest buttress. Myles, peeping around the corner behind which he stood, could see that the bachelors were gathered into a little group consulting together. Suddenly it broke asunder, and Blunt turned around.

"Ho, Falworth!" he cried. "Wilt thou hold truce whiles we parley with ye?"

"Aye," answered Myles.

"Wilt thou give me thine honor that ye will hold your hands from harming us whiles we talk together?"

"Yea," said Myles, "I will pledge thee mine honor."

"I accept thy pledge. See! here we throw aside our stones and lay down our knives. Lay ye by your clubs, and meet us in parley at the horse-block yonder."

"So be it," said Myles, and thereupon, standing his cudgel in the angle of the wall, he stepped boldly out into the open court-yard. Those of his party came scatteringly from right and left, gathering about him; and the bachelors advanced in a body, led by the head squire.

"Now what is it thou wouldst have, Walter Blunt?" said Myles, when both parties had met at the horse-block.

"It is to say this to thee, Myles Falworth," said the other. "One time, not long sin, thou didst challenge me to meet thee hand to hand in the dormitory. Then thou didst put a vile af front upon me, for the which I ha' brought on this battle to-day, for I knew not then that thou wert going to try thy peasant tricks of wrestling, and so, without guarding myself, I met thee as thou didst desire."

"But thou hadst thy knife, and would have stabbed him couldst thou ha' done so," said Gascoyne.

"Thou liest!" said Blunt. "I had no knife."

And then, without giving time to answer, " Thou canst not deny that I met thee then at thy bidding, canst thou, Falworth ?"

" Nay," said Myles, "nor haply canst thou deny it either." And at this covert reminder of his defeat Myles's followers laughed scoffingly and Blunt bit his lip.

" Thou hast said it," said he. "Then sin I met thee at thy bidding, I dare thee to meet me now at mine, and to fight this battle out between our two selves, with sword and buckler and bascinet as gentles should, and not in a wrestling match like two country hodges."

" Thou art a coward caitiff, Walter Blunt !" burst out Wilkes, who stood by with a swelling lump upon his head, already as big as a walnut. "Well thou knowest that Falworth is no match for thee at broadsword play. Is he not four years younger than thou, and hast thou not had three times the practice in arms that he hath had ? I say thou art a coward to seek to fight with cutting weapons."

Blunt made no answer to Wilkes's speech, but gazed steadfastly at Myles, with a scornful smile curling the corners of his lips. Myles stood looking upon the ground without once lifting his eyes, not knowing what to answer, for he was well aware that he was no match for Blunt with the broadsword.

"Thou art afraid to fight me, Myles Falworth," said Blunt, tauntingly, and the bachelors gave a jeering laugh in echo.

Then Myles looked up, and I cannot say that his face was not a trifle whiter than usual. "Nay," said he, "I am not afraid, and I will fight thee, Blunt."

"So be it," said Blunt. "Then let us go at it straightway in the armory yonder, for they be at dinner in the Great Hall, and just now there be'st no one by to stay us."

"Thou shalt not fight him, Myles!" burst out Gascoyne. "He will murther thee! Thou shalt not fight him, I say!"

Myles turned away without answering him.

"What is to do?" called one of those who were still looking out of the windows as the crowd of boys passed beneath.

"Blunt and Falworth are going to fight it out hand to hand in the armory," answered one of the bachelors, looking up.

The brawling of the squires was a jest to all the adjoining part of the house. So the heads were withdrawn again, some laughing at the "sparring of the cockerels."

But it was no jesting matter to poor Myles.

CHAPTER XVI.

I HAVE no intention to describe the fight between Myles Falworth and Walter Blunt. Fisticuffs of nowadays are brutal and debasing enough, but a fight with a sharp - edged broadsword was not only brutal and debasing, but cruel and bloody as well.

From the very first of the fight Myles Falworth was palpably and obviously overmatched. After fifteen minutes had passed, Blunt stood hale and sound as at first; but poor Myles had more than one red stain of warm blood upon doublet and hose, and more than one bandage had been wrapped by Gascoyne and Wilkes about sore wounds.

He had received no serious injury as yet, for not only was his body protected by a buckler, or small oblong shield, which he carried upon his left arm, and his head by a bascinet, or light helmet of steel, but perhaps, after all, Blunt was not over-anxious to do him any dangerous harm.

132

Nevertheless, there could be but one opinion as to how the fight tended, and Myles's friends were gloomy and downcast; the bachelors proportionately exultant, shouting with laughter, and taunting Myles at every unsuccessful stroke.

Once, as he drew back panting, leaning upon Gascoyne's shoulder, the faithful friend whispered, with trembling lips: " Oh, dear Myles, carry it no further. Thou hurtest him not, and he will slay thee ere he have done with thee."

Thereupon Blunt, who caught the drift of the speech, put in a word. " Thou art sore hurt, Myles Falworth," said he, " and I would do thee no grievous harm. Yield thee and own thyself beaten, and I will forgive thee. Thou hast fought a good fight, and there is no shame in yielding now."

" Never !" cried Myles, hoarsely—" never will I yield me ! Thou mayst slay me, Walter Blunt, and I reck not if thou dost do so, but never else wilt thou conquer me."

There was a tone of desperation in his voice that made all look serious.

" Nay," said Blunt; " I will fight thee no more, Myles Falworth; thou hast had enough."

" By heavens !" cried Myles, grinding his teeth, " thou shalt fight me, thou coward ! Thou hast brought this fight upon us, and either thou or I get our quittance here. Let go, Gascoyne!" he cried, shaking loose his friend's hold; " I tell thee he shall fight me!"

From that moment Blunt began to lose his head. No doubt he had not thought of such a serious fight as this when he had given his challenge, and there was a savage bull-dog tenacity about Myles that could not but have had a somewhat demoralizing effect upon him.

A few blows were given and taken, and then Myles's friends gave a shout. Blunt drew back, and placed his hand to his shoulder. When he drew it away again it was stained with red, and another red stain grew and spread rapidly down the sleeve of his jacket. He stared at his hand for a moment with a half-dazed look, and then glanced quickly to right and left.

" I will fight no more," said he, sullenly.

" Then yield thee!" cried Myles, exultantly.

The triumphant shouts of the Knights of the Rose stung Blunt like a lash, and the battle began again. Perhaps some of the older lads were of a mind to interfere at this point, certainly some looked very serious, but before they interposed, the fight was ended.

Blunt, grinding his teeth, struck one undercut at his opponent—the same undercut that Myles had that time struck at Sir James Lee at the knight's bidding when he first practised at the Devlen pels. Myles met the blow as Sir James had met the blow that he had given, and then struck in return as Sir James had struck—full and true. The bascinet that Blunt wore glanced the blow partly, but not entirely. Myles felt his sword bite through the light steel cap, and Blunt dropped his own blade clattering upon the floor. It was all over in an instant, but in that instant what he saw was stamped upon Myles's mind with an indelible imprint. He saw the young man stagger backward; he saw the eyes roll upward; and a red streak shoot out from under the cap and run down across the cheek.

Blunt reeled half around, and then fell prostrate upon his face; and Myles stood staring at him with the delirious turmoil of his battle dissolving rapidly into a dumb fear at that which he had done.

Once again he had won the victory—but what a victory! "Is he dead?" he whispered to Gascoyne.

"I know not," said Gascoyne, with a very pale face. "But come away, Myles." And he led his friend out of the room.

Some little while later one of the bachelors came to the dormitory where Myles, his wounds smarting and aching and throbbing, lay stretched upon his cot, and with a very serious face bade him to go presently to Sir James, who had just come from dinner, and was then in his office.

By this time Myles knew that he had not slain his enemy, and his heart was light in spite of the coming interview. There was no one in the office but Sir James and himself, and Myles, without concealing anything, told, point by point, the whole trouble. Sir James sat looking steadily at him for a while after he had ended.

"Never," said he, presently, "did I know any one of ye squires, in all the time that I have been here, get himself into so many broils as thou, Myles Falworth. Belike thou sought to take this lad's life."

"Nay," said Myles, earnestly, "God forbid!"

"Ne'theless," said Sir James, "thou fetched him a main shrewd blow, and it is by good hap, and no fault of thine, that he will live to do more mischief yet. This is thy second venture at him, the third time, haply, thou wilt end him for good." Then suddenly assuming his grimmest and sternest manner· "Now, sirrah, do I put a stop to this, and no more shall ye fight with edged tools. Get thee to the dormitory, and abide there a full week without coming forth. Michael shall bring thee bread and water twice a day for that time. That is all the food thou shalt have, and we

" 'Belike thou sought to take this lad's life,' said Sir James"

will see if that fare will not cool thy hot humors withal."

Myles had expected a punishment so much more severe than that which was thus meted to him, that in the sudden relief he broke into a convulsive laugh, and then, with a hasty sweep, wiped a brimming moisture from his eyes.

Sir James looked keenly at him for a moment. "Thou art white i' the face," said he. "Art thou wounded very sorely?"

"Nay," said Myles, "it is not much; but I be sick in my stomach."

"Aye, aye," said Sir James; "I know that feeling well. It is thus that one always feeleth in coming out from a sore battle when one hath suffered wounds and lost blood. An thou wouldst keep thyself hale, keep thyself from needless fighting. Now go thou to the dormitory, and, as I said, come thou not forth again for a week. Stay, sirrah!" he added, "I will send George-barber to thee to look to thy sores. Green wounds are best drawn and salved ere they grow cold."

I wonder what Myles would have thought had he known that so soon as he had left the office, Sir James had gone straight to the Earl and recounted the whole matter to him, with a deal of dry gusto, and that the Earl listened laughing.

"Aye," said he, when Sir James had done, "the boy hath mettle, sure. Nevertheless, we must transplant this fellow Blunt to the office of gentleman-in-waiting. He must be old enough now; and gin he stayeth in his present place, either he will do the boy a harm, or the boy will do him a harm."

So Blunt never came again to trouble the squires' quarters; and thereafter the youngsters rendered no more service to the elders.

Myles's first great fight in life was won.

CHAPTER XVII

THE summer passed away, and the bleak fall came. Myles had long since accepted his position as one set apart from the others of his kind, and had resigned himself to the evident fact that he was never to serve in the household in waiting upon the Earl. I cannot say that it never troubled him, but in time there came a compensation of which I shall have presently to speak.

And then he had so much the more time to himself. The other lads were sometimes occupied by their household duties when sports were afoot in which they would liked to have taken part. Myles was always free to enter into any matter of the kind after his daily exercise had been performed at the pels, the butts, or the tilting-court.

But even though he was never called to do service in " my Lord's house," he was not long in gaining a sort of second-hand knowledge of all the family. My Lady, a thin, sallow, faded dame, not yet past middle age, but looking ten years older. The Lady Anne, the daughter of the house; a tall, thin, dark-eyed, dark-haired, handsome young dame of twenty or twenty-one years of age, hawk-nosed like her father, and silent, proud, and haughty, Myles heard the squires say. Lady Alice, the Earl of Mackworth's niece and ward, a great heiress in her own right, a strikingly pretty black-eyed girl of fourteen or fifteen.

These composed the Earl's personal family; but besides them was Lord George Beaumont, his Earl's brother, and him Myles soon came to know better than any of the chief people of the castle excepting Sir James Lee.

For since Myles's great battle in the armory, Lord George had taken a laughing sort of liking to the lad, encouraging him at times to talk of his adventures, and of his hopes and aspirations.

Perhaps the Earl's younger brother—who was himself somewhat a soldier of fortune, having fought in Spain, France, and Germany—felt a certain kinship in spirit with the adventurous youngster who had his unfriended way to make in the world. However that might have been, Lord George was very kind and friendly to the lad, and the willing service that Myles rendered him reconciled him not a little to the Earl's obvious neglect.

Besides these of the more immediate family of the Earl were a number of knights, ladies, and gentlemen, some of them cadets, some of them retainers, of the house of Beaumont, for the princely nobles of those days lived in state little less royal than royalty itself.

Most of the knights and gentlemen Myles soon came to know by sight, meeting them in Lord George's apartments in the south wing of the great house, and some of them, following the lead of Lord George, singled him out for friendly notice, giving him a nod or a word in passing.

Every season has its pleasures for boys, and the constant change that they bring is one of the greatest delights of boyhood's days.

All of us, as we grow older, have in our memory pictures of by-gone times that are somehow more than usually vivid, the colors of some not blurring by time as others do. One of which, in remembering, always filled Myles's heart in after-years with an indefinable pleasure, was the recollection of standing with others of his fellow-squires in the crisp brown autumn grass of the paddock, and shooting with the long-bow at wild-fowl, which, when the east wind was straining, flew low overhead to pitch to the lake in the forbidden precincts of the deer park beyond the brow of the hill. More than once a brace or two of these wild-fowl, shot in their southward flight by the lads and cooked by fat, good-natured Mother Joan, graced the rude mess-table of the squires in the long hall, and even the toughest and fishiest drake, so the fruit of their skill, had a savor that, somehow or other, the daintiest fare lacked in after-years.

Then fall passed and winter came, bleak, cold, and dreary—not winter as we know it nowadays, with warm fires and bright lights to make the long nights sweet and cheerful with comfort, but winter with all its grimness and sternness. In the great cold stone-walled castles of those days the only fire and almost the only light were those from the huge blazing logs that roared and crackled in the great open stone fireplace, around which the folks gathered, sheltering their faces as best they could from the scorching heat, and cloaking their shoulders from the biting cold, for at the farther end of the room, where giant shadows swayed and bowed and danced huge and black against the high walls, the white frost glistened in the moonlight on the stone pavements, and the breath went up like smoke.

In those days were no books to read, but at the best only rude stories and jests, recited by some strolling mummer or minstrel to the listening circle, gathered around the blaze and welcoming the coarse, gross jests, and coarser, grosser songs with roars of boisterous laughter.

Yet bleak and dreary as was the winter in those days, and cold and biting as was the frost in the cheerless, windy halls and corridors of the castle, it was not without its joys to the young lads, for then, as now, boys could find pleasure even in slushy weather, when the sodden snow is fit for nothing but to make snowballs of.

Thrice that bitter winter the moat was frozen over, and the lads, making themselves skates of marrow-bones, which they bought from the hall cook at a groat a pair, went skimming over the smooth surface, red-cheeked and shouting, while the crows and the jackdaws looked down at them from the top of the bleak gray walls.

Then at Yule-tide, which was somewhat of a rude semblance to the Merry Christmas season of our day, a great feast was held in the hall, and all the castle folk were fed in the presence of the Earl and the Countess. Oxen and sheep were roasted whole; huge suet puddings, made of barley meal sweetened with honey and stuffed with plums, were boiled in great caldrons in the open court-yard; whole barrels of ale and malmsey were broached, and all the folk, gentle and simple, were bidden to the feast. Afterwards the minstrels danced and played a rude play, and in the evening a miracle show was performed on a raised platform in the north hall.

For a week afterwards the castle was fed upon the remains of the good things left from that great feast, until every one grew to loathe fine victuals, and longed for honest beef and mustard again.

Then at last in that constant change the winter was gone, and even the lads who had enjoyed its passing were glad when the winds blew warm once more, and the grass showed green in sunny places, and the leader of the wild-fowl blew his horn, as they who in the fall had flown to the south flew, arrow-like, northward again; when the buds swelled and the leaves burst forth once more, and crocuses and then daffodils gleamed in the green grass, like sparks and flames of gold.

With the spring came the out-door sports of the season; among others that of ball—for boys were boys, and played at ball even in those far-away days—a game called trap-ball. Even yet in some parts of England it is played just as it was in Myles Falworth's day, and enjoyed just as Myles and his friends enjoyed it.

So now that the sun was warm and the weather pleasant the game of trap-ball was in full swing every afternoon, the play-ground being an open space between the wall that surrounded the

144

castle grounds and that of the privy garden—
the pleasance in which the ladies of the Earl's
family took the air every day, and upon which
their apartments opened.

Now one fine breezy afternoon, when the lads
were shouting and playing at this, then their favorite game, Myles himself was at the trap barehanded and barearmed. The wind was blowing
from behind him, and, aided perhaps by it, he
had already struck three or four balls nearly the
whole length of the court—an unusual distance
—and several of the lads had gone back almost
as far as the wall of the privy garden to catch
any ball that might chance to fly as far as that.
Then once more Myles struck, throwing all his
strength into the blow. The ball shot up into
the air, and when it fell, it was to drop within the
privy garden.

The shouts of the young players were instantly stilled, and Gascoyne, who stood nearest Myles,
thrust his hands into his belt, giving a long shrill
whistle.

" This time thou hast struck us all out, Myles,'
said he. " There be no more play for us until
we get another ball."

The outfielders came slowly trooping in until
they had gathered in a little circle around Myles.

" I could not help it," said Myles, in answer to

their grumbling. " How knew I the ball would fly so far ? But if I ha' lost the ball, I can get it again. I will climb the wall for it."

" Thou shalt do naught of the kind, Myles," said Gascoyne, hastily. " Thou art as mad as a March hare to think of such a venture! Wouldst get thyself shot with a bolt betwixt the ribs, like poor Diccon Cook ?"

Of all places about the castle the privy garden was perhaps the most sacred. It was a small plot of ground, only a few rods long and wide, and was kept absolutely private for the use of the Count-ess and her family. Only a little while before Myles had first come to Devlen, one of the cook's men had been found climbing the wall, where-upon the soldier who saw him shot him with his cross bow. The poor fellow dropped from the wall into the garden, and when they found him, he still held a bunch of flowers in his hand, which he had perhaps been gathering for his sweet-heart.

Had Myles seen him carried on a litter to the infirmary as Gascoyne and some of the others had done, he might have thought twice before venturing to enter the ladies' private garden. As it was, he only shook his stubborn head, and said again, " I will climb the wall and fetch it."

Now at the lower extremity of the court, and

about twelve or fifteen feet distant from the garden wall, there grew a pear-tree, some of the branches of which overhung into the garden beyond. So, first making sure that no one was looking that way, and bidding the others keep a sharp lookout, Myles shinned up this tree, and choosing one of the thicker limbs, climbed out upon it for some little distance. Then lowering his body, he hung at arm's-length, the branch bending with his weight, and slowly let himself down hand under hand, until at last he hung directly over the top of the wall, and perhaps a foot above it. Below him he could see the leafy top of an arbor covered with a thick growth of clematis, and even as he hung there he noticed the broad smooth walks, the grassy terrace in front of the Countess's apartments in the distance, the quaint flower-beds, the yew-trees trimmed into odd shapes, and even the deaf old gardener working bare-armed in the sunlight at a flower-bed in the far corner by the tool-house.

The top of the wall was pointed like a house roof, and immediately below him was covered by a thick growth of green moss, and it flashed through his mind as he hung there that maybe it would offer a very slippery foothold for one dropping upon the steep slopes of the top. But it was too late to draw back now.

Bracing himself for a moment, he loosed his hold upon the limb above. The branch flew back with a rush, and he dropped, striving to grasp the sloping angle with his feet. Instantly the treacherous slippery moss slid away from beneath him; he made a vain clutch at the wall, his fingers sliding over the cold stones, then, with a sharp exclamation, down he pitched bodily into the garden beneath! A thousand thoughts flew through his brain like a cloud of flies, and then a leafy greenness seemed to strike up against him. A splintering crash sounded in his ears as the lattice top of the arbor broke under him, and with one final clutch at the empty air he fell heavily upon the ground beneath.

He heard a shrill scream that seemed to find an instant echo; even as he fell he had a vision of faces and bright colors, and when he sat up, dazed and bewildered, he found himself face to face with the Lady Anne, the daughter of the house, and her cousin, the Lady Alice, who clutching one another tightly, stood staring at him with wide scared eyes.

CHAPTER XVIII.

For a little time there was a pause of deep silence, during which the fluttering leaves came drifting down from the broken arbor above.

It was the Lady Anne who first spoke. "Who art thou, and whence comest thou?" said she, tremulously.

Then Myles gathered himself up sheepishly. "My name is Myles Falworth," said he, "and I am one of the squires of the body."

"Oh! aye!" said the Lady Alice, suddenly. "Methought I knew thy face. Art thou not the young man that I have seen in Lord George's train?"

"Yes, lady," said Myles, wrapping and twining a piece of the broken vine in and out among his fingers. "Lord George hath often had me of late about his person."

"And what dost thou do here, sirrah?" said Lady Anne, angrily. "How darest thou come so into our garden?"

"I meant not to come as I did," said Myles, clumsily, and with a face hot and red, "but I slipped over the top of the wall and fell hastily into the garden. Truly, lady, I meant ye no harm or fright thereby."

He looked so drolly abashed as he stood before them, with his clothes torn and soiled from the fall, his face red, and his eyes downcast, all the while industriously twisting the piece of clematis in and around his fingers, that Lady Anne's half-frightened anger could not last. She and her cousin exchanged glances, and smiled at one another.

"But," said she at last, trying to draw her pretty brows together into a frown, "tell me; why didst thou seek to climb the wall?"

"I came to seek a ball," said Myles, "which I struck over hither from the court beyond."

"And wouldst thou come into our privy garden for no better reason than to find a ball?" said the young lady.

"Nay," said Myles; "it was not so much to find the ball, but, in good sooth, I did truly strike it harder than need be, and so, gin I lost the ball, I could do no less than come and find it again, else our sport is done for the day. So it was I came hither."

The two young ladies had by now recovered

from their fright. The Lady Anne slyly nudged her cousin with her elbow, and the younger could not suppress a half-nervous laugh. Myles heard it, and felt his face grow hotter and redder than ever.

"Nay," said Lady Anne, "I do believe Master Giles—"

"My name be'st Myles," corrected Myles.

"Very well, then, Master Myles; I say I do believe that thou meanest no harm in coming hither; ne'theless it was ill of thee so to do. An my father should find thee here, he would have thee shrewdly punished for such trespassing. Dost thou not know that no one is permitted to enter this place—no, not even my uncle George? One fellow who came hither to steal apples once had his ears shaven close to his head, and not more than a year ago one of the cook's men who climbed the wall early one morning was shot by the watchman."

"Aye," said Myles, "I knew of him who was shot, and it did go somewhat against my stomach to venture, knowing what had happed to him. Ne'theless, an I gat not the ball, how were we to play more to-day at the trap?"

"Marry, thou art a bold fellow, I do believe me," said the young lady, "and sin thou hast come in the face of such peril to get thy ball, thou shalt not go away empty. Whither didst thou strike it?"

"Over yonder by the cherry-tree," said Myles, jerking his head in that direction. "An I may go get it, I will trouble ye no more." As he spoke he made a motion to leave them.

"Stay!" said the Lady Anne, hastily; "remain where thou art. An thou cross the open, some one may haply see thee from the house, and will give the alarm, and thou wilt be lost. I will go get thy ball."

And so she left Myles and her cousin, crossing the little plots of grass and skirting the rose-bushes to the cherry-tree.

When Myles found himself alone with Lady Alice, he knew not where to look or what to do, but twisted the piece of clematis which he still held in and out more industriously than ever.

Lady Alice watched him with dancing eyes for a little while. "Haply thou wilt spoil that poor vine," said she by·and·by, breaking the silence and laughing, then turning suddenly serious again. "Didst thou hurt thyself by thy fall?"

"Nay," said Myles, looking up; "such a fall as that was no great matter. Many and many a time I have had worse."

"Hast thou so?" said the Lady Alice. "Thou didst fright me parlously, and my coz likewise."

Myles entertains the Lady Anne and the Lady Alice with his adventures

Myles hesitated for a moment, and then blurted out, "Thereat I grieve, for thee I would not fright for all the world."

The young lady laughed and blushed. "All the world is a great matter," said she.

"Yea," said he, "it is a great matter; but it is a greater matter to fright thee, and so I would not do it for that, and more."

The young lady laughed again, but she did not say anything further, and a space of silence fell so long that by-and-by she forced herself to say, "My cousin findeth not the ball presently."

"Nay," said Myles, briefly, and then again neither spoke, until by-and-by the Lady Anne came, bringing the ball. Myles felt a great sense of relief at that coming, and yet was somehow sorry. Then he took the ball, and knew enough to bow his acknowledgment in a manner neither ill nor awkward.

"Didst thou hurt thyself?" said Lady Anne.

"Nay," said Myles, giving himself a shake; "seest thou not I be whole, limb and bone? Nay, I have had shrewdly worse falls than that. Once I fell out of an oak-tree down by the river and upon a root, and bethought me I did break a rib or more. And then one time when I was a boy in Crosbey-Dale—that was where I lived before I came hither—I did catch me hold of the blade of the windmill, thinking it was moving slowly, and that I would have a ride i' th' air, and so was like to have had a fall ten thousand times worse than this."

"Oh, tell us more of that!" said the Lady Anne, eagerly. "I did never hear of such an adventure as that. Come, coz, and sit down here upon the bench, and let us have him tell us all of that happening."

Now the lads upon the other side of the wall had been whistling furtively for some time, not knowing whether Myles had broken his neck or had come off scot-free from his fall. "I would like right well to stay with ye," said he, irresolutely, "and would gladly tell ye that and more an ye would have me to do so; but hear ye not my friends call me from beyond? Mayhap they think I break my back, and are calling to see whether I be alive or no. An I might whistle them answer and toss me this ball to them, all would then be well, and they would know that I was not hurt, and so, haply, would go away."

"Then answer them," said the Lady Anne, "and tell us of that thing thou spokest of anon— how thou tookest a ride upon the windmill. We young ladies do hear little of such matters, not being allowed to talk with lads. All that we hear of perils are of knights and ladies and jousting, and such like.   It would pleasure us right well to have thee tell of thy adventures."

So Myles tossed back the ball, and whistled in answer to his friends.

Then he told the two young ladies not only of his adventure upon the windmill, but also of other boyish escapades, and told them well, with a straightforward smack and vigor, for he enjoyed adventure and loved to talk of it.   In a little while he had regained his ease; his shyness and awkwardness left him, and nothing remained but the delightful fact that he was really and actually talking to two young ladies, and that with just as much ease and infinitely more pleasure than could be had in discourse with his fellow-squires.   But at last it was time for him to go.   " Marry," said he, with a half-sigh, " methinks I did never ha' so sweet and pleasant a time in all my life before. Never did I know a real lady to talk with, saving only my mother, and I do tell ye plain methinks I would rather talk with ye than with any he in Christendom — saving, perhaps, only my friend Gascoyne.   I would I might come hither again."

The honest frankness of his speech was irresistible; the two girls exchanged glances and then began laughing.   " Truly," said Lady Anne, who, as was said before, was some three or four years older than Myles, "thou art a bold lad to ask such a thing. How wouldst thou come hither? Wouldst tumble through our clematis arbor again, as thou didst this day?"

"Nay," said Myles, "I would not do that again, but if ye will bid me do so, I will find the means to come hither."

"Nay," said Lady Anne, "I dare not bid thee do such a foolhardy thing. Nevertheless, if thou hast the courage to come—"

"Yea," said Myles, eagerly, "I have the courage."

"Then, if thou hast so, we will be here in the garden on Saturday next at this hour. I would like right well to hear more of thy adventures. But what didst thou say was thy name? I have forgot it again."

"It is Myles Falworth."

"Then we shall yclep thee Sir Myles, for thou art a soothly errant-knight. And stay! Every knight must have a lady to serve. How wouldst thou like my Cousin Alice here for thy true lady?"

"Aye," said Myles, eagerly, "I would like it right well." And then he blushed fiery red at his boldness.

"I want no errant-knight to serve me," said the Lady Alice, blushing, in answer. "Thou dost ill tease me, coz! An thou art so free in choosing him a lady to serve, thou mayst choose him thyself for thy pains."

"Nay," said the Lady Anne, laughing; "I say thou shalt be his true lady, and he shall be thy true knight. Who knows? Perchance he may serven thee in some wondrous adventure, like as Chaucer telleth of. But now, Sir Errant-Knight, thou must take thy leave of us, and I must e'en let thee privily out by the postern-wicket. And if thou wilt take the risk upon thee and come hither again, prithee be wary in that coming, lest in venturing thou have thine ears clipped in most unknightly fashion."

That evening, as he and Gascoyne sat together on a bench under the trees in the great quadrangle, Myles told of his adventure of the afternoon, and his friend listened with breathless interest.

"But, Myles," cried Gascoyne, "did the Lady Anne never once seem proud and unkind?"

"Nay," said Myles; "only at first, when she chid me for falling through the roof of their arbor. And to think, Francis! Lady Anne herself bade me hold the Lady Alice as my true lady, and to serve her in all knightliness!" Then he told his friend that he was going to the privy garden again on the next Saturday, and that the Lady Anne had given him permission so to do.

Gascoyne gave a long, wondering whistle, and then sat quite still, staring into the sky. By-and-by he turned to his friend and said, " I give thee my pledge, Myles Falworth, that never in all my life did I hear of any one that had such marvellous strange happenings befall him as thou."

Whenever the opportunity occurred for sending a letter to Crosbey-Holt, Myles wrote one to his mother; and one can guess how they were treasured by the good lady, and read over and over again to the blind old Lord as he sat staring into darkness with his sightless eyes. About the time of this escapade he wrote a letter telling of those doings, wherein, after speaking of his misadventure of falling from the wall, and of his acquaintance with the young ladies, he went on to speak of the manner in which he repeated his visits. The letter was worded in the English of that day—the quaint and crabbed language in which Chaucer wrote. Perhaps few boys could read it nowadays, so, modernizing it somewhat, it ran thus:

"And now to let ye weet that thing that followed that happening that made me acquaint with they two young Damoiselles. I take me to the south wall of that garden one day four and twenty great spikes, which Peter Smith did forge for me, and for which I pay him fivepence, and that all the money that I had left of my half-year's wage, and wot not where I may get more at these present, withouten I do betake me to Sir James, who, as I did tell ye, hath consented to hold those moneys that Prior Edward gave me till I need them.

"Now these same spikes, I say, I take me them down behind the corner of the wall, and there drave them betwixt the stones, my very dear comrade and true friend Gascoyne helping me thereto to do. And so come Saturday, I climb me over the wall and to the roof of the tool-house below, seeking a fitting opportunity when I might so do without being in too great jeopardy.

"Yea; and who should be there but they two ladies, biding my coming, who, seeing me, made as though they had expected me not, and gave me greatest rebuke for aventuring so moughtily. Yet, methinks, were they right well pleasured that I should so aventure, which indeed I might not otherwise do, seeing as I have telled to thee, that one of them is mine own true lady for to serven, and so was the only way that I might come to speech with her."

Such was Myles's own quaint way of telling how he accomplished his aim of visiting the forbidder garden, and no doubt the smack of adventure and the savor of danger in the undertaking recommended him not a little to the favor of the young ladies.

After this first acquaintance perhaps a month passed, during which Myles had climbed the wall some half a dozen times (for the Lady Anne would not permit of too frequent visits), and during which the first acquaintance of the three ripened rapidly to an honest, pleasant friendship. More than once Myles, when in Lord George's train, caught a covert smile or half nod from one or both of the girls, not a little delightful in its very secret friendliness.

CHAPTER XIX.

As was said, perhaps a month passed; then Myles's visits came to an abrupt termination, and with it ended, in a certain sense, a chapter of his life.

One Saturday afternoon he climbed the garden wall, and skirting behind a long row of rosebushes that screened him from the Countess's terrace, came to a little summer-house where the two young ladies had appointed to meet him that day.

A pleasant half-hour or so was passed, and then it was time for Myles to go. He lingered for a while before he took his final leave, leaning against the door-post, and laughingly telling how he and some of his brother squires had made a figure of straw dressed in men's clothes, and had played a trick with it one night upon a watchman against whom they bore a grudge.

The young ladies were listening with laughing faces, when suddenly, as Myles looked, he saw the smile vanish from Lady Alice's eyes and a wide terror take its place. She gave a half-articulate cry, and rose abruptly from the bench upon which she was sitting.

Myles turned sharply, and then his very heart seemed to stand still within him; for there, standing in the broad sunlight without, and glaring in upon the party with baleful eyes, was the Earl of Mackworth himself.

How long was the breathless silence that followed, Myles could never tell. He knew that the Lady Anne had also risen, and that she and her cousin were standing as still as statues. Presently the Earl pointed to the house with his staff, and Myles noted stupidly how it trembled in his hand.

"Ye wenches," said he at last, in a hard, harsh voice—"ye wenches, what meaneth this? Would ye deceive me so, and hold parlance thus secretly with this fellow? I will settle with him anon. Meantime get ye straightway to the house and to your rooms, and there abide until I give ye leave to come forth again. Go, I say!"

"Father," said Lady Anne, in a breathless voice —she was as white as death, and moistened her lips with her tongue before she spoke—"father, thou wilt not do harm to this young man. Spare him, I do beseech thee, for truly it was I who bade him come hither. I know that he would not have come but at our bidding."

The Earl stamped his foot upon the gravel. "Did ye not hear me?" said he, still pointing towards the house with his trembling staff. "I bade ye go to your rooms. I will settle with this fellow, I say, as I deem fitting."

"Father," began Lady Anne again; but the Earl made such a savage gesture that poor Lady Alice uttered a faint shriek, and Lady Anne stopped abruptly, trembling. Then she turned and passed out the farther door of the summer-house, poor little Lady Alice following, holding her tight by the skirts, and trembling and shuddering as though with a fit of the ague.

The Earl stood looking grimly after them from under his shaggy eyebrows, until they passed away behind the yew-trees, appeared again upon the terrace behind, entered the open doors of the women's house, and were gone. Myles heard their footsteps growing fainter and fainter, but he never raised his eyes. Upon the ground at his feet were four pebbles, and he noticed how they almost made a square, and would do so if he pushed one of them with his toe, and then it seemed strange to him that he should think of such a little foolish thing at that dreadful time.

He knew that the Earl was looking gloomily at

him, and that his face must be very pale. Suddenly Lord Mackworth spoke. "What hast thou to say?" said he, harshly.

Then Myles raised his eyes, and the Earl smiled grimly as he looked his victim over. "I have naught to say," said the lad, huskily.

"Didst thou not hear what my daughter spake but now?" said the Earl. "She said that thou came not of thy own free-will; what sayst thou to that, sirrah — is it true?"

Myles hesitated for a moment or two; his throat was tight and dry. "Nay," said he at last, "she belieth herself. It was I who first came into the garden. I fell by chance from the tree yonder — I was seeking a ball — then I asked those two if I might not come hither again, and so have done some several times in all. But as for her — nay; it was not at her bidding that I came, but through mine own asking."

The Earl gave a little grunt in his throat. "And how often hast thou been here?" said he, presently.

Myles thought a moment or two. "This maketh the seventh time," said he.

Another pause of silence followed, and Myles began to pluck up some heart that maybe all would yet be well. The Earl's next speech dashed that hope into a thousand fragments. "Well thou knowest," said he, "that it is forbid for any to come here. Well thou knowest that twice have men been punished for this thing that thou hast done, and yet thou camest in spite of all. Now dost thou know what thou wilt suffer?"

Myles picked with nervous fingers at a crack in the oaken post against which he leaned. "Mayhap thou wilt kill me," said he at last, in a dull, choking voice.

Again the Earl smiled a grim smile. "Nay," said he, " I would not slay thee, for thou hast gentle blood. But what sayest thou should I shear thine ears from thine head, or perchance have thee scourged in the great court?"

The sting of the words sent the blood flying back to Myles's face again, and he looked quickly up. "Nay," said he, with a boldness that surprised himself; "thou shalt do no such unlordly thing upon me as that. I be thy peer, sir, in blood; and though thou mayst kill me, thou hast no right to shame me!"

Lord Mackworth bowed with a mocking courtesy. "Marry!" said he. "Methought it was one of mine own saucy popinjay squires that I caught sneaking here and talking to those two foolish young lasses, and, lo! it is a young Lord—or mayhap thou art a young Prince—and commandeth me that I shall not do this and I shall not do that.

I crave your Lordship's honorable pardon, if I have said aught that may have galled you."

The fear Myles had felt was now beginning to dissolve in rising wrath. "Nay," said he, stoutly, "I be no Lord and I be no Prince, but I be as good as thou. For am I not the son of thy one-time very true comrade and thy kinsman—to wit, the Lord Falworth, whom, as thou knowest, is poor and broken, and blind, and helpless, and outlawed, and banned? Yet," cried he, grinding his teeth, as the thought of it all rushed in upon him, "I would rather be in his place than in yours; for though he be ruined, you—"

He had just sense enough to stop there.

The Earl, gripping his staff behind his back, and with his head a little bent, was looking keenly at the lad from under his shaggy gray brows. "Well," said he, as Myles stopped, "thou hast gone too far now to draw back. Say thy say to the end. Why wouldst thou rather be in thy father's stead than in mine?"

Myles did not answer.

"Thou shalt finish thy speech, or else show thyself a coward. Though thy father is ruined, thou didst say I am—what?"

Myles keyed himself up to the effort, and then blurted out, "Thou art attainted with shame."

A long breathless silence followed.

"Myles Falworth," said the Earl at last (and even in the whirling of his wits Myles wondered that he had the name so pat)—"Myles Falworth, of all the bold, mad, hare-brained fools, thou art the most foolish. How dost thou dare say such words to me? Dost thou not know that thou makest thy coming punishment ten times more bitter by such a speech?"

"Aye!" cried Myles, desperately; "but what else could I do? An I did not say the words, thou callest me coward, and coward I am not."

"By 'r Lady!" said the Earl, "I do believe thee. Thou art a bold, impudent varlet as ever lived— to beard me so, forsooth! Hark'ee; thou sayst I think naught of mine old comrade. I will show thee that thou dost belie me. I will suffer what thou hast said to me for his sake, and for his sake will forgive thee thy coming hither — which I would not do in another case to any other man. Now get thee gone straightway, and come hither no more. Yonder is the postern-gate; mayhap thou knowest the way. But stay! How camest thou hither?"

Myles told him of the spikes he had driven in the wall, and the Earl listened, stroking his beard. When the lad had ended, he fixed a sharp look upon him. "But thou drove not those spikes alone," said he; "who helped thee do it?"

"That I may not tell," said Myles, firmly.

"So be it," said the Earl. "I will not ask thee to tell his name. Now get thee gone! And as for those spikes, thou mayst e'en knock them out of the wall, sin thou drave them in. Play no more pranks an thou wouldst keep thy skin whole. And now go, I say!"

Myles needed no further bidding, but turned and left the Earl without another word. As he went out the postern-gate he looked over his shoulder, and saw the tall figure, in its long fur-trimmed gown, still standing in the middle of the path, looking after him from under the shaggy eyebrows.

As he ran across the quadrangle, his heart still fluttering in his breast, he muttered to himself, "The old grizzle-beard; an I had not faced him a bold front, mayhap he would have put such shame upon me as he said. I wonder why he stood so staring after me as I left the garden."

Then for the time the matter slipped from his mind, saving only that part that smacked of adventure.

CHAPTER XX.

So for a little while Myles was disposed to congratulate himself upon having come off so well from his adventure with the Earl. But after a day or two had passed, and he had time for second thought, he began to misdoubt whether, after all, he might not have carried it with a better air if he had shown more chivalrous boldness in the presence of his true lady; whether it would not have redounded more to his credit if he had in some way asserted his rights as the young dame's knight-errant and defender. Was it not ignominious to resign his rights and privileges so easily and tamely at a signal from the Earl?

" For, in sooth," said he to Gascoyne, as the two talked the matter over, " she hath, in a certain way, accepted me for her knight, and yet I stood me there without saying so much as one single word in her behalf."

" Nay," said Gascoyne, " I would not trouble me on that score. Methinks that thou didst come off wondrous well out of the business. I would not have thought it possible that my Lord could ha' been so patient with thee as he showed himself. Methinks, forsooth, he must hold thee privily in right high esteem."

" Truly," said Myles, after a little pause of meditative silence, " I know not of any esteem, yet I do think he was passing patient with me in this matter. But ne'theless, Francis, that changeth not my stand in the case. Yea, I did shamefully, so to resign my lady without speaking one word ; nor will I so resign her even yet. I have bethought me much of this matter of late, Francis, and now I come to thee to help me from my evil case. I would have thee act the part of a true friend to me—like that one I have told thee of in the story of the Emperor Justinian. I would have thee, when next thou servest in the house, to so contrive that my Lady Alice shall get a letter which I shall presently write, and wherein I may set all that is crooked straight again."

" Heaven forbid," said Gascoyne, hastily, " that I should be such a fool as to burn my fingers in drawing thy nuts from the fire ! Deliver thy letter thyself, good fellow !"

So spoke Gascoyne, yet after all he ended, as he usually did, by yielding to Myles's superior will and persistence. So the letter was written, and one day the good-natured Gascoyne carried it with him to the house, and the opportunity offering, gave it to one of the young ladies attendant upon the Countess's family—a lass with whom he had friendly intimacy—to be delivered to Lady Alice.

But if Myles congratulated himself upon the success of this new adventure, it was not for long. That night, as the crowd of pages and squires were making themselves ready for bed, the call came through the uproar for " Myles Falworth! Myles Falworth !"

" Here I be," cried Myles, standing up on his cot. " Who calleth me?"

It was the groom of the Earl's bedchamber, and seeing Myles standing thus raised above the others, he came walking down the length of the room towards him, the wonted hubbub gradually silencing as he advanced and the youngsters turning, staring, and wondering.

" My Lord would speak with thee, Myles Falworth," said the groom, when he had come close enough to where Myles stood. " Busk thee and make ready; he is at livery even now."

The groom's words fell upon Myles like a blow. He stood for a while staring wide-eyed. " My Lord speak with me, sayst thou!" he ejaculated at last.

"Aye," said the other, impatiently; "get thee ready quickly. I must return anon."

Myles's head was in a whirl as he hastily changed his clothes for a better suit, Gascoyne helping him. What could the Earl want with him at this hour? He knew in his heart what it was; the interview could concern nothing but the letter that he had sent to Lady Alice that day. As he followed the groom through the now dark and silent courts, and across the corner of the great quadrangle, and so to the Earl's house, he tried to brace his failing courage to meet the coming interview. Nevertheless, his heart beat tumultuously as he followed the other down the long corridor, lit only by a flaring link set in a wrought-iron bracket. Then his conductor lifted the arras at the door of the bedchamber, whence came the murmuring sound of many voices, and holding it aside, beckoned him to enter, and Myles passed within. At the first, he was conscious of nothing but a crowd of people, and of the brightness of many lighted candles; then he saw that he stood in a great airy room spread with a woven mat of rushes. On three sides the walls were hung with tapestry representing hunting and battle scenes; at the farther end, where the bed stood, the stone wall of the fourth side was covered with cloth of blue, embroidered with silver goshawks. Even now, in the ripe spring-time of May, the room was still chilly, and a great fire roared and crackled in the huge gaping mouth of the stone fireplace. Not far from the blaze were clustered the greater part of those present, buzzing in talk, now and then swelled by murmuring laughter. Some of those who knew Myles nodded to him, and two or three spoke to him as he stood waiting, whilst the groom went forward to speak to the Earl; though what they said and what he answered, Myles, in his bewilderment and trepidation, hardly knew.

As was said before, the livery was the last meal of the day, and was taken in bed. It was a simple repast—a manchette, or small loaf of bread of pure white flour, a loaf of household bread, sometimes a lump of cheese, and either a great flagon of ale or of sweet wine, warm and spiced. The Earl was sitting upright in bed, dressed in a furred dressing-gown, and propped up by two cylindrical bolsters of crimson satin. Upon the coverlet, and spread over his knees, was a large wide napkin of linen fringed with silver thread, and on it rested a silver tray containing the bread and some cheese. Two pages and three gentlemen were waiting upon him, and Mad Noll, the Jester, stood at the head of the bed, now and then jingling his bawble and passing some quaint jest upon the chance of making his master smile. Upon a table near by were some dozen or so waxen tapers stuck upon as many spiked candlesticks of silver-gilt, and illuminating that end of the room with their bright twinkling flames. One of the gentlemen was in the act of serving the Earl with a goblet of wine, poured from a silver ewer by one of the squires, as the groom of the chamber came forward and spoke. The Earl, taking the goblet, turned his head, and as Myles looked, their eyes met. Then the Earl turned away again and raised the cup to his lips, while Myles felt his heart beat more rapidly than ever.

But at last the meal was ended, and the Earl washed his hands and his mouth and his beard from a silver basin of scented water held by another one of the squires. Then, leaning back against the pillows, he beckoned to Myles.

In answer Myles walked forward the length of the room, conscious that all eyes were fixed upon him. The Earl said something, and those who stood near drew back as he came forward. Then Myles found himself standing beside the bed, looking down upon the quilted counterpane, feeling that the other was gazing fixedly at him.

"I sent for thee," said the Earl at last, still looking steadily at him, "because this afternoon came a letter to my hand which thou hadst writ-

"Myles found himself standing beside the bed"

ten to my niece, the Lady Alice. I have it here," said he, thrusting his hand under the bolster, "and have just now finished reading it." Then, after a moment's pause, whilst he opened the parchment and scanned it again, " I find no matter of harm in it, but hereafter write no more such." He spoke entirely without anger, and Myles looked up in wonder "Here, take it," said the Earl, folding the letter and tossing it to Myles, who instinctively caught it, "and henceforth trouble thou my niece no more either by letter or any other way. I thought haply thou wouldst be at some such saucy trick, and I made Alice promise to let me know when it happed. Now, I say, let this be an end of the matter. Dost thou not know thou mayst injure her by such witless folly as that of meeting her privily, and privily writing to her?"

"I meant no harm," said Myles.

"I believe thee," said the Earl. "That will do now; thou mayst go."

Myles hesitated.

"What wouldst thou say?" said Lord Mackworth.

"Only this," said Myles, "an I have thy leave so to do, that the Lady Alice hath chosen me to be her knight, and so, whether I may see her or speak with her or no, the laws of chivalry give me, who am gentle born, the right to serve her as a true knight may."

"As a true fool may," said the Earl, dryly. "Why, how now, thou art not a knight yet, nor anything but a raw lump of a boy. What rights do the laws of chivalry give thee, sirrah? Thou art a fool!"

Had the Earl been ever so angry, his words would have been less bitter to Myles than his cool, unmoved patience; it mortified his pride and galled it to the quick.

"I know that thou dost hold me in contempt," he mumbled.

"Out upon thee!" said the Earl, testily. "Thou dost tease me beyond patience. I hold thee in contempt, forsooth! Why, look thee, hadst thou been other than thou art, I would have had thee whipped out of my house long since. Thinkest thou I would have borne so patiently with another one of ye squires had such an one held secret meeting with my daughter and niece, and tampered, as thou hast done, with my household, sending through one of my people that letter? Go to; thou art a fool, Myles Falworth!"

Myles stood staring at the Earl without making an effort to speak. The words that he had heard suddenly flashed, as it were, a new light into his mind. In that flash he fully recognized, and for the first time, the strange and wonderful forbearance the great Earl had shown to him, a poor obscure boy. What did it mean? Was Lord Mackworth his secret friend, after all, as Gascoyne had more than once asserted? So Myles stood silent, thinking many things.

Meantime the other lay back upon the cylindrical bolsters, looking thoughtfully at him. " How old art thou?" said he at last.

" Seventeen last April," answered Myles.

" Then thou art old enough to have some of the thoughts of a man, and to lay aside those of a boy. Haply thou hast had foolish things in thy head this short time past; it is time that thou put them away. Harkee, sirrah! the Lady Alice is a great heiress in her own right, and mayst command the best alliance in England—an Earl —a Duke. She groweth apace to a woman, and then her kind lieth in Courts and great houses. As for thee, thou art but a poor lad, penniless and without friends to aid thee to open advancement. Thy father is attainted, and one whisper of where he lieth hid would bring him thence to the Tower, and haply to the block. Besides that, he hath an enemy, as Sir James Lee hath already told thee— an enemy perhaps more great and powerful than myself. That enemy watcheth for thy father and for thee; shouldst thou dare raise thy head or thy fortune ever so little, he would haply crop them both, and that parlously quick. Myles Falworth, how dost thou dare to lift thine eyes to the Lady Alice de Mowbray?"

Poor Myles stood silent and motionless. "Sir," said he at last, in a dry choking voice, "thou art right, and I have been a fool. Sir, I will never raise mine eyes to look upon the Lady Alice more."

"I say not that either, boy," said the Earl; "but ere thou dost so dare, thou must first place thyself and thy family whence ye fell. Till then, as thou art an honest man, trouble her not. Now get thee gone."

As Myles crossed the dark and silent courtyards, and looked up at the clear, still twinkle of the stars, he felt a kind of dull wonder that they and the night and the world should seem so much the same, and he be so different.

The first stroke had been given that was to break in pieces his boyhood life—the second was soon to follow.

CHAPTER XXI.

THERE are now and then times in the life of every one when new and strange things occur with such rapidity that one has hardly time to catch one's breath between the happenings. It is as though the old were crumbling away—breaking in pieces—to give place to the new that is soon to take its place.

So it was with Myles Falworth about this time. The very next day after this interview in the bed-chamber, word came to him that Sir James Lee wished to speak with him in the office. He found the lean, grizzled old knight alone, sitting at the heavy oaken table with a tankard of spiced ale at his elbow, and a dish of wafers and some fragments of cheese on a pewter platter before him. He pointed to his clerk's seat—a joint stool somewhat like a camp-chair, but made of heavy oaken braces and with a seat of hog-skin—and bade Myles be seated.

It was the first time that Myles had ever heard

of such courtesy being extended to one of the company of squires, and, much wondering, he obeyed the invitation, or rather command, and took the seat.

The old knight sat regarding him for a while in silence, his one eye, as bright and as steady as that of a hawk, looking keenly from under the penthouse of its bushy brows, the while he slowly twirled and twisted his bristling wiry mustaches, as was his wont when in meditation. At last he broke the silence. " How old art thou?" said he, abruptly.

" I be turned seventeen last April," Myles answered, as he had the evening before to Lord Mackworth.

" Humph!" said Sir James; " thou be'st big of bone and frame for thine age. I would that thy heart were more that of a man likewise, and less that of a giddy, hare-brained boy, thinking continually of naught but mischief."

Again he fell silent, and Myles sat quite still, wondering if it was on account of any special one of his latest escapades that he had been summoned to the office—the breaking of the window in the Long Hall by the stone he had flung at the rook, or the climbing of the South Tower for the jackdaw's nest.

" Thou hast a friend," said Sir James, suddenly

breaking into his speculations, " of such a kind that few in this world possess. Almost ever since thou hast been here he hath been watching over thee. Canst thou guess of whom I speak?"

" Haply it is Lord George Beaumont," said Myles; "he hath always been passing kind to me."

" Nay," said Sir James, " it is not of him that I speak, though methinks he liketh thee well enow. Canst thou keep a secret, boy?" he asked, suddenly.

" Yea," answered Myles.

" And wilt thou do so in this case if I tell thee who it is that is thy best friend here?"

" Yea."

" Then it is my Lord who is that friend — the Earl himself; but see that thou breathe not a word of it."

Myles sat staring at the old knight in utter and profound amazement, and presently Sir James continued:

" Yea, almost ever since thou hast come here my Lord hath kept oversight upon all thy doings, upon all thy mad pranks and thy quarrels and thy fights, thy goings out and comings in. What thinkest thou of that, Myles Falworth?"

Again the old knight stopped and regarded the lad, who sat silent, finding no words to answer.

He seemed to find a grim pleasure in the young-ster's bewilderment and wonder. Then a sudden thought came to Myles.

"Sir," said he, "did my Lord know that I went to the privy garden as I did?"

"Nay," said Sir James; "of that he knew naught at first until thy father bade thy mother write and tell him."

"My father!" ejaculated Myles.

"Aye," said Sir James, twisting his mustaches more vigorously than ever. "So soon as thy fa-ther heard of that prank, he wrote straightway to my Lord that he should put a stop to what might in time have bred mischief."

"Sir," said Myles, in an almost breathless voice, "I know not how to believe all these things, or whether I be awake or a-dreaming."

"Thou be'st surely enough awake," answered the old man; "but there are other matters yet to be told. My Lord thinketh, as others of us do —Lord George and myself—that it is now time for thee to put away thy boyish follies, and learn those things appertaining to manhood. Thou hast been here a year now, and hast had freedom to do as thou might list; but, boy"—and the old warrior spoke seriously, almost solemnly—"upon thee doth rest matters of such great import that did I tell them to thee thou couldst not grasp them. My Lord deems that thou hast, mayhap, promise beyond the common of men; ne'theless it remaineth yet to be seen an he be right; it is yet to test whether that promise may be fulfilled. Next Monday I and Sir Everard Willoughby take thee in hand to begin training thee in the knowledge and the use of the jousting lance, of arms, and of horsemanship. Thou art to go to Ralph Smith, and have him fit a suit of plain armor to thee which he hath been charged to make for thee against this time. So get thee gone, think well over all these matters, and prepare thyself by next Monday. But stay, sirrah," he added, as Myles, dazed and bewildered, turned to obey; " breathe to no living soul what I ha' told thee—that my Lord is thy friend—neither speak of anything concerning him. Such is his own heavy command laid upon thee."

Then Myles turned again without a word to leave the room. But as he reached the door Sir James stopped him a second time.

" Stay !" he called. " I had nigh missed telling thee somewhat else. My Lord hath made thee a present this morning that thou wottest not of. It is "—then he stopped for a few moments, perhaps to enjoy the full flavor of what he had to say—" it is a great Flemish horse of true breed and right mettle; a horse such as a knight of the noblest strain might be proud to call his own. Myles Falworth, thou wert born upon a lucky day!"

"Sir," cried Myles, and then stopped short. Then, "Sir," he cried again, "didst thou say it—the horse—was to be mine?"

"Aye, it is to be thine."

"My very own?"

"Thy very own."

How Myles Falworth left that place he never knew. He was like one in some strange, some wonderful dream. He walked upon air, and his heart was so full of joy and wonder and amazement that it thrilled almost to agony. Of course his first thought was of Gascoyne. How he ever found him he never could tell, but find him he did.

"Come, Francis!" he cried, "I have that to tell thee so marvellous that had it come upon me from paradise it could not be more strange."

Then he dragged him away to their Eyry—it had been many a long day since they had been there—and to all his friend's speeches, to all his wondering questions, he answered never a word until they had climbed the stairs, and so come to their old haunt. Then he spoke.

"Sit thee down, Francis," said he, "till I tell thee that which passeth wonder." As Gascoyne obeyed, he himself stood looking about him.

The Earl of Mackworth received King Henry IV.

" This is the last time I shall ever come hither,"
said he. And thereupon he poured out his heart
to his listening friend in the murmuring solitude
of the airy height. He did not speak of the Earl,
but of the wonderful new life that had thus suddenly opened before him, with its golden future
of limitless hopes, of dazzling possibilities, of he-
roic ambitions. He told everything, walking up
and down the while—for he could not remain
quiet—his cheeks glowing and his eyes sparkling.

Gascoyne sat quite still, staring straight before
him. He knew that his friend was ruffling eagle
pinions for a flight in which he could never hope
to follow, and somehow his heart ached, for he
knew that this must be the beginning of the end
of the dear, delightful friendship of the year past.

N

CHAPTER XXII.

And so ended Myles Falworth's boyhood. Three years followed, during which he passed through that state which immediately follows boyhood in all men's lives—a time when they are neither lads nor grown men, but youths passing from the one to the other period through what is often an uncouth and uncomfortable age.

He had fancied, when he talked with Gascoyne in the Eyry that time, that he was to become a man all at once; he felt just then that he had forever done with boyish things. But that is not the way it happens in men's lives. Changes do not come so suddenly and swiftly as that, but by little and little. For three or four days, maybe, he went his new way of life big with the great change that had come upon him, and then, now in this and now in that, he drifted back very much into his old ways of boyish doings. As was said, one's young days do not end all at once, even when they be so suddenly and sharply shaken, and Myles was not different from others. He had been stirred to the core by that first wonderful sight of the great and glorious life of manhood opening before him, but he had yet many a sport to enjoy, many a game to play, many a boisterous romp to riot in the dormitory, many an expedition to make to copse and spinney and river on days when he was off duty, and when permission had been granted.

Nevertheless, there was a great and vital change in his life; a change which he hardly felt or realized. Even in resuming his old life there was no longer the same vitality, the same zest, the same enjoyment in all these things. It seemed as though they were no longer a part of himself. The savor had gone from them, and by-and-by it was pleasanter to sit looking on at the sports and the games of the younger lads than to take active part in them.

These three years of his life that had thus passed had been very full; full mostly of work, grinding and monotonous; of training dull, dry, laborious. For Sir James Lee was a taskmaster as hard as iron and seemingly as cold as a stone. For two, perhaps for three, weeks Myles entered into his new exercises with all the enthusiasm that novelty brings; but these exercises hardly varied a tittle from day to day, and soon became

187

a duty, and finally a hard and grinding task. He used, in the earlier days of his castle life, to hate the dull monotony of the tri-weekly hacking at the pels with a heavy broadsword as he hated nothing else; but now, though he still had that exercise to perform, it was almost a relief from the heavy dulness of riding, riding, riding in the tilt-yard with shield and lance—couch—recover —*en passant*.

But though he had nowadays but little time for boyish plays and escapades, his life was not altogether without relaxation. Now and then he was permitted to drive in mock battle with other of the younger knights and bachelors in the paddock near the outer walls. It was a still more welcome change in the routine of his life when, occasionally, he would break a light lance in the tilting-court with Sir Everard Willoughby; Lord George, perhaps, and maybe one or two others of the Hall folk, looking on.

Then one gilded day, when Lord Dudleigh was visiting at Devlen, Myles ran a course with a heavier lance in the presence of the Earl, who came down to the tilt-yard with his guest to see the young novitiate ride against Sir Everard. He did his best, and did it well. Lord Dudleigh praised his poise and carriage, and Lord George, who was present, gave him an approving smile and nod. But the Earl of Mackworth only sat stroking his beard impassively, as was his custom. Myles would have given much to know his thoughts.

In all these years Sir James Lee almost never gave any expression either of approbation or disapproval—excepting when Myles exhibited some carelessness or oversight. Then his words were sharp and harsh enough. More than once Myles's heart failed him, and bitter discouragement took possession of him; then nothing but his bull-dog tenacity and stubbornness brought him out from the despondency of the dark hours.

"Sir," he burst out one day, when his heart was heavy with some failure, "tell me, I beseech thee, do I get me any of skill at all? Is it in me ever to make a worthy knight, fit to hold lance and sword with other men, or am I only soothly a dull heavy block, worth naught of any good?"

"Thou art a fool, sirrah!" answered Sir James, in his grimmest tones. "Thinkest thou to learn all of knightly prowess in a year and a half? Wait until thou art ripe, and then I will tell thee if thou art fit to couch a lance or ride a course with a right knight."

"Thou art an old bear!" muttered Myles to himself, as the old one-eyed knight turned on his heel and strode away. " Beshrew me! an I show thee not that I am as worthy to couch a lance as thou one of these fine days!"

However, during the last of the three years the grinding routine of his training had not been quite so severe as at first. His exercises took him more often out into the fields, and it was during this time of his knightly education that he sometimes rode against some of the castle knights in friendly battle with sword or lance or wooden mace. In these encounters he always held his own; and held it more than well, though, in his boyish simplicity, he was altogether unconscious of his own skill, address, and strength. Perhaps it was his very honest modesty that made him so popular and so heartily liked by all.

He had by this time risen to the place of head squire or chief bachelor, holding the same position that Walter Blunt had occupied when he himself had first come, a raw country boy, to Devlen. The lesser squires and pages fairly worshipped him as a hero, albeit imposing upon his good-nature. All took a pride in his practice in knightly exercises, and fabulous tales were current among the young fry concerning his strength and skill.

Yet, although Myles was now at the head of his class, he did not, as other chief bachelors had done, take a leading position among the squires in the Earl's household service. Lord Mackworth, for his own good reasons, relegated him to the position of Lord George's especial attendant. Nevertheless, the Earl always distinguished him from the other esquires, giving him a cool nod whenever they met; and Myles, upon his part—now that he had learned better to appreciate how much his Lord had done for him—would have shed the last drop of blood in his veins for the head of the house of Beaumont.

As for the two young ladies, he often saw them, and sometimes, even in the presence of the Earl, exchanged a few words with them, and Lord Mackworth neither forbade it nor seemed to notice it.

Towards the Lady Anne he felt the steady friendly regard of a lad for a girl older than himself; towards the Lady Alice, now budding into ripe young womanhood, there lay deep in his heart the resolve to be some day her true knight in earnest as he had been her knight in pretence in that time of boyhood when he had so perilously climbed into the privy garden.

In body and form he was now a man, and in thought and heart was quickly ripening to manhood, for, as was said before, men matured quickly in those days. He was a right comely youth, for the promise of his boyish body had been fulfilled in a tall, powerful, well-knit frame. His face was still round and boyish, but on cheek and chin and lip was the curl of adolescent beard—soft, yellow, and silky. His eyes were as blue as steel, and quick and sharp in glance as those of a hawk; and as he walked, his arms swung from his broad, square shoulders, and his body swayed with pent-up strength ready for action at any moment.

If little Lady Alice, hearing much talk of his doings and of his promise in these latter times, thought of him now and then it is a matter not altogether to be wondered at.

Such were the changes that three years had wrought. And from now the story of his manhood really begins.

Perhaps in all the history of Devlen Castle, even at this, the high tide of pride and greatness of the house of Beaumont, the most notable time was in the early autumn of the year 1411, when for five days King Henry IV. was entertained by the Earl of Mackworth. The King was at that time making a progress through certain of the midland counties, and with him travelled the Comte de Vermoise. The Count was the secret emissary of the Dauphin's faction in France, at that time in the very bitterest intensity of the struggle with the Duke of Burgundy, and had come to England seeking aid for his master in his quarrel.

It was not the first time that royalty had visited Devlen. Once, in Earl Robert's day, King Edward II. had spent a week at the castle during the period of the Scottish wars. But at that time it was little else than a military post, and was used by the King as such. Now the Beaumonts were in the very flower of their prosperity, and preparations were made for the coming visit of royalty upon a scale of such magnificence and splendor as Earl Robert, or perhaps even King Edward himself, had never dreamed.

For weeks the whole castle had been alive with folk hurrying hither and thither; and with the daily and almost hourly coming of pack-horses, laden with bales and boxes, from London. From morning to night one heard the ceaseless chip-chipping of the masons' hammers, and saw carriers of stones and mortar ascending and descending the ladders of the scaffolding that covered the face of the great North Hall. Within, that part of the building was alive with the scraping of the carpenters' saws, the clattering of lumber, and the rapping and banging of hammers.

The North Hall had been assigned as the lodging place for the King and his court, and

St. George's Hall (as the older building adjoining it was called) had been set apart as the lodging of the Comte de Vermoise and the knights and gentlemen attendant upon him.

The great North Hall had been very much altered and changed for the accommodation of the King and his people; a beautiful gallery of carved wood-work had been built within and across the south end of the room for the use of the ladies who were to look down upon the ceremonies below. Two additional windows had been cut through the wall and glazed, and passage-ways had been opened connecting with the royal apartments beyond. In the bedchamber a bed of carved wood and silver had been built into the wall, and had been draped with hangings of pale blue and silver, and a magnificent screen of wrought-iron and carved wood had been erected around the couch; rich and beautiful tapestries brought from Italy and Flanders were hung upon the walls; cushions of velvets and silks stuffed with down covered benches and chairs. The floor of the hall was spread with mats of rushes stained in various colors, woven into curious patterns; and in tne smaller rooms precious carpets of arras were laid on the cold stones.

All of the cadets of the House had been assembled; all of the gentlemen in waiting, retainers and clients. The castle seemed full to overflowing; even the dormitory of the squires was used as a lodging place for many of the lesser gentry.

So at last, in the midst of all this bustle of preparation, came the day of days when the King was to arrive. The day before a courier had come bringing the news that he was lodging at Donaster Abbey overnight, and would make progress the next day to Devlen.

That morning, as Myles was marshalling the pages and squires, and, with the list of names in his hand, was striving to evolve some order out of the confusion, assigning the various individuals their special duties—these to attend in the household, those to ride in the escort—one of the gentlemen of Lord George's household came with an order for him to come immediately to the young nobleman's apartments. Myles hastily turned over his duties to Gascoyne and Wilkes, and then hurried after the messenger. He found Lord George in the antechamber, three gentlemen squires arming him in a magnificent suit of ribbed Milan.

He greeted Myles with a nod and a smile as the lad entered. "Sirrah," said he, "I have had a talk with Mackworth this morn concerning thee, and have a mind to do thee an honor in my poor way. How wouldst thou like to ride to-day as my special squire of escort?"

Myles flushed to the roots of his hair. "Oh, sir!" he cried, eagerly, "an I be not too ungainly for thy purpose, no honor in all the world could be such joy to me as that!"

Lord George laughed. "A little matter pleases thee hugely," said he; "but as to being ungainly, who so sayeth that of thee belieth thee, Myles; thou art not ungainly, sirrah. But that is not to the point. I have chosen thee for my equerry to-day; so make thou haste and don thine armor, and then come hither again, and Hollingwood will fit thee with a wreathed bascinet I have within, and a juppon embroidered with my arms and colors."

When Myles had made his bow and left his patron, he flew across the quadrangle, and burst into the armory upon Gascoyne, whom he found still lingering there, chatting with one or two of the older bachelors.

"What thinkest thou, Francis?" he cried, wild with excitement. "An honor hath been done me this day I could never have hoped to enjoy. Out of all this household, Lord George hath chosen me his equerry for the day to ride to meet the King. Come, hasten to help me to arm! Art thou not glad of this thing for my sake, Francis?"

"Aye, glad am I indeed!" cried Gascoyne, that generous friend; "rather almost would I have this befall thee than myself!" And indeed he was hardly less jubilant than Myles over the honor.

Five minutes later he was busy arming him in the little room at the end of the dormitory which had been lately set apart for the use of the head bachelor. "And to think," he said, looking up as he kneeled, strapping the thigh-plates to his friend's legs, "that he should have chosen thee before all others of the fine knights and lords and gentlemen of quality that are here!"

"Yea," said Myles, "it passeth wonder. I know not why he should so single me out for such an honor. It is strangely marvellous."

"Nay," said Gascoyne, "there is no marvel in it, and I know right well why he chooseth thee. It is because he sees, as we all see, that thou art the stoutest and the best-skilled in arms, and most easy of carriage of any man in all this place."

Myles laughed. "An thou make sport of me," said he, "I'll rap thy head with this dagger hilt. Thou art a silly fellow, Francis, to talk so. But tell me, hast thou heard who rides with my Lord?"

"Yea; I heard Wilkes say anon that it was Sir James Lee."

"I am right glad of that," said Myles; "for then he will show me what to do and how to bear myself. It frights me to think what would hap should I make some mistake in my awkwardness. Methinks Lord George would never have me with him more should I do amiss this day."

"Never fear," said Gascoyne; "thou wilt not do amiss."

And now, at last, the Earl, Lord George, and all their escort were ready; then the orders were given to horse, the bugle sounded, and away they all rode, with clashing of iron hoofs and ringing and jingling of armor, out into the dewy freshness of the early morning, the slant yellow sun of autumn blazing and flaming upon polished helmets and shields, and twinkling like sparks of fire upon spear points. Myles's heart thrilled within him for pure joy, and he swelled out his sturdy young breast with great draughts of the sweet fresh air that came singing across the sunny hill-tops. Sir James Lee, who acted as the Earl's equerry for the day, rode at a little distance, and there was an almost pathetic contrast between the grim, steadfast impassiveness of the tough old warrior and Myles's passionate exuberance of youth.

At the head of the party rode the Earl and his brother side by side, each clad *cap-a-pie* in a suit of Milan armor, the cuirass of each covered with a velvet juppon embroidered in silver with the arms and quarterings of the Beaumonts. The Earl wore around his neck an "S S" collar, with a jewelled St. George hanging from it, and upon his head a vizored bascinet, ornamented with a wreath covered with black and yellow velvet and glistening with jewels.

Lord George, as was said before, was clad in a beautiful suit of ribbed Milan armor. It was rimmed with a thin thread of gold, and, like his brother, he wore a bascinet wreathed with black and yellow velvet.

Behind the two brothers and their equerries rode the rest in their proper order—knights, gentlemen, esquires, men-at-arms—to the number, perhaps, of two hundred and fifty; spears and lances aslant, and banners, pennons, and pencels of black and yellow fluttering in the warm September air.

From the castle to the town they rode, and then across the bridge, and thence clattering up through the stony streets, where the folk looked down upon them from the windows above, or crowded the fronts of the shops of the tradesmen. Lusty cheers were shouted for the Earl, but the great Lord rode staring ever straight before him, as unmoved as a stone. Then out of the town they clattered, and away in a sweeping cloud of dust across the country-side.

It was not until they had reached the windy top of Willoughby Croft, ten miles away, that they met the King and his company. As the two parties approached to within forty or fifty yards of one another they stopped.

As they came to a halt, Myles observed that a gentleman dressed in a plain blue-gray riding-habit, and sitting upon a beautiful white gelding, stood a little in advance of the rest of the party, and he knew that that must be the King. Then Sir James nodded to Myles, and leaping from his horse, flung the reins to one of the attendants. Myles did the like; and then, still following Sir James's lead as he served Lord Mackworth, went forward and held Lord George's stirrup while he dismounted. The two noblemen quickly removed each his bascinet, and Myles, holding the bridle-rein of Lord George's horse with his left hand, took the helmet in his right, resting it upon his hip.

Then the two brothers walked forward bare-headed, the Earl a little in advance. Reaching the King he stopped, and then bent his knee—stiffly in the armored plates—until it touched the ground. Thereupon the King reached him his hand, and he, rising again, took it, and set it to his lips.

Then Lord George, advancing, kneeled as his brother had kneeled, and to him also the King gave his hand.

Myles could hear nothing, but he could see that a few words of greeting passed between the three, and then the King, turning, beckoned to a knight who stood just behind him and a little in advance of the others of the troop. In answer, the knight rode forward; the King spoke a few words of introduction, and the stranger, ceremoniously drawing off his right gauntlet, clasped the hand, first of the Earl, and then of Lord George. Myles knew that he must be the great Comte de Vermoise, of whom he had heard so much of late.

A few moments of conversation followed, and then the King bowed slightly. The French nobleman instantly reined back his horse, an order was given, and then the whole company moved forward, the two brothers walking upon either side of the King, the Earl lightly touching the bridle-rein with his bare hand.

Whilst all this was passing, the Earl of Mackworth's company had been drawn up in a double line along the road-side, leaving the way open to the other party. As the King reached the head of the troop, another halt followed while he spoke a few courteous words of greeting to some of the lesser nobles attendant upon the Earl whom he knew.

In that little time he was within a few paces of Myles, who stood motionless as a statue, holding the bascinet and the bridle-rein of Lord George's horse.

What Myles saw was a plain, rather stout man, with a face fat, smooth, and waxy, with pale-blue eyes, and baggy in the lids; clean shaven, except for a mustache and tuft covering lips and chin. Somehow he felt a deep disappointment. He had expected to see something lion-like, something regal, and, after all, the great King Henry was commonplace, fat, unwholesome-looking. It came to him with a sort of a shock that, after all, a King was in nowise different from other men.

Meanwhile the Earl and his brother replaced their bascinets, and presently the whole party moved forward upon the way to Mackworth.

CHAPTER XXIII.

THAT same afternoon the squires' quarters were thrown into such a ferment of excitement as had, perhaps, never before stirred them. About one o'clock in the afternoon the Earl himself and Lord George came walking slowly across the Armory Court wrapped in deep conversation, and entered Sir James Lee's office.

All the usual hubbub of noise that surrounded the neighborhood of the dormitory and the armory was stilled at their coming, and when the two noblemen had entered Sir James's office, the lads and young men gathered in knots discussing with an almost awesome interest what that visit might portend.

After some time Sir James Lee came to the door at the head of the long flight of stone steps, and whistling, beckoned one of the smaller pages to him. He gave a short order that sent the little fellow flying on some mission. In the course of a few minutes he returned, hurrying across

the stony court with Myles Falworth, who presently entered Sir James's office. It was then
and at this sight that the intense half-suppressed
excitement reached its height of fever-heat.
What did it all mean? The air was filled with
a thousand vague, wild rumors—but the very
wildest surmises fell short of the real truth.

Perhaps Myles was somewhat pale when he
entered the office; certainly his nerves were in a
tremor, for his heart told him that something
very portentous was about to befall him. The
Earl sat at the table, and in the seat that Sir
James Lee usually occupied, Lord George half
sat, half leaned in the window-place. Sir James
stood with his back to the empty fireplace, and
his hands clasped behind him. All three were
very serious.

"Give thee good den, Myles Falworth," said
the Earl, as Myles bowed first to him and then
to the others; "and I would have thee prepare
thyself for a great happening." Then, continu-
ing directly to the point: "Thou knowest, sirrah,
why we have been training thee so closely these
three years gone; it is that thou shouldst be
able to hold thine own in the world. Nay, not
only hold thine own, but to show thyself to be a
knight of prowess shouldst it come to a battle
between thee and thy father's enemy; for there

lieth no half-way place for thee, and thou must be either great or else nothing. Well, sir, the time hath now come for thee to show thy mettle. I would rather have chosen that thou hadst labored a twelvemonth longer; but now, as I said, hath come a chance to prove thyself that may never come again. Sir James tells me that thou art passably ripe in skill. Thou must now show whether that be so or no. Hast thou ever heard of the Sieur de la Montaigne?"

"Yea, my Lord. I have heard of him often," answered Myles. It was he who won the prize at the great tourney at Rochelle last year."

"I see that thou hast his fame pat to thy tongue's end," said the Earl; "he is the chevalier of whom I speak, and he is reckoned the best knight of Dauphiny. That one of which thou spokest was the third great tourney in which he was adjudged the victor. I am glad that thou holdest his prowess highly. Knowest thou that he is in the train of the Comte de Vermoise?"

"Nay," said Myles, flushing; "I did hear news he was in England, but knew not that he was in this place."

"Yea," said Lord Mackworth; "he is here." He paused for a moment; then said, suddenly, "Tell me, Myles Falworth, an thou wert a knight and of rank fit to run a joust with the Sieur de la Montaigne, wouldst thou dare encounter him in the lists?"

The Earl's question fell upon Myles so suddenly and unexpectedly that for a moment or so he stood staring at the speaker with mouth agape. Meanwhile the Earl sat looking calmly back at him, slowly stroking his beard the while.

It was Sir James Lee's voice that broke the silence. "Thou heardst thy Lord speak," said he, harshly. "Hast thou no tongue to answer, sirrah?"

"Be silent, Lee," said Lord Mackworth, quietly. "Let the lad have time to think before he speaketh."

The sound of the words aroused Myles. He advanced to the table, and rested his hand upon it. "My Lord—my Lord," said he, "I know not what to say, I—I am amazed and afeard."

"How! how!" cried Sir James Lee, harshly. "Afeard, sayst thou? An thou art afeard, thou knave, thou needst never look upon my face or speak to me more! I have done with thee forever an thou art afeard even were the champion a Sir Alisander."

"Peace, peace, Lee," said the Earl, holding up his hand. "Thou art too hasty. The lad shall have his will in this matter, and thou and no one shall constrain him. Methinks, also, thou dost not understand him. Speak from thy heart, Myles; why art thou afraid?"

"Because," said Myles, "I am so young, sir; I am but a raw boy. How should I dare be so hardy as to venture to set lance against such an one as the Sieur de la Montaigne? What would I be but a laughing-stock for all the world who would see me so foolish as to venture me against one of such prowess and skill?

"Nay, Myles," said Lord George, "thou think-est not well enough of thine own skill and prow-ess. Thinkest thou we would undertake to set thee against him, an we did not think that thou couldst hold thine own fairly well?"

"Hold mine own?" cried Myles, turning to Lord George. "Sir; thou dost not mean—thou canst not mean, that I may hope or dream to hold mine own against the Sieur de la Mon-taigne."

"Aye," said Lord George, "that was what I did mean."

"Come, Myles," said the Earl; "now tell me: wilt thou fight the Sieur de la Montaigne?"

"Yea," said Myles, drawing himself to his full height and throwing out his chest. "Yea," and his cheeks and forehead flushed red; "an thou bid me do so, I will fight him."

207

"There spake my brave lad!" cried Lord George, heartily.

"I give thee joy, Myles," said the Earl, reaching him his hand, which Myles took and kissed. "And I give thee double joy. I have talked with the King concerning thee this morning, and he hath consented to knight thee—yea, to knight thee with all honors of the Bath—provided thou wilt match thee against the Sieur de la Montaigne for the honor of England and Mackworth. Just now the King lieth to sleep for a little while after his dinner; have thyself in readiness when he cometh forth, and I will have thee presented."

Then the Earl turned to Sir James Lee, and questioned him as to how the bachelors were fitted with clothes. Myles listened, only half hearing the words through the tumbling of his thoughts. He had dreamed in his day-dreams that some time he might be knighted, but that time always seemed very, very distant. To be knighted now, in his boyhood, by the King, with the honors of the Bath, and under the patronage of the Earl of Mackworth; to joust—to actually joust—with the Sieur de la Montaigne, one of the most famous chevaliers of France! No wonder he only half heard the words; half heard the Earl's questions concerning his clothes and the discussion which followed; half heard Lord George volunteer to array him in fitting garments from his own wardrobe.

"Thou mayst go now," said the Earl, at last turning to him. "But be thou at George's apartments by two of the clock to be dressed fittingly for the occasion."

Then Myles went out stupefied, dazed, bewildered. He looked around, but he did not see Gascoyne. He said not a word to any of the others in answer to the eager questions poured upon him by his fellow-squires, but walked straight away. He hardly knew where he went, but by-and-by he found himself in a grassy angle below the end of the south stable; a spot overlooking the outer wall and the river beyond. He looked around; no one was near, and he flung himself at length, burying his face in his arms. How long he lay there he did not know, but suddenly some one touched him upon the shoulder, and he sprang up quickly. It was Gascoyne.

"What is to do, Myles?" said his friend, anxiously. "What is all this talk I hear concerning thee up yonder at the armory?"

"Oh, Francis!" cried Myles, with a husky choking voice; "I am to be knighted—by the King —by the King himself; and I—I am to fight the Sieur de la Montaigne."

He reached out his hand, and Gascoyne took it. They stood for a while quite silent, and when at last the stillness was broken, it was Gascoyne who spoke, in a choking voice.

"Thou art going to be great, Myles," said he. "I always knew that it must be so with thee, and now the time hath come. Yea, thou wilt be great, and live at court amongst noble folk, and Kings haply. Presently thou wilt not be with me any more, and wilt forget me by-and-by."

"Nay, Francis, never will I forget thee!" answered Myles, pressing his friend's hand. "I will always love thee better than any one in the world, saving only my father and my mother."

Gascoyne shook his head and looked away, swallowing at the dry lump in his throat. Suddenly he turned to Myles. "Wilt thou grant me a boon?"

"Yea," answered Myles. "What is it?"

"That thou wilt choose me for thy squire."

"Nay," said Myles; "how canst thou think to serve me as squire? Thou wilt be a knight thyself some day, Francis, and why dost thou wish now to be my squire?"

"Because," said Gascoyne, with a short laugh, "I would rather be in thy company as a squire than in mine own as a knight, even if I might be banneret"

Myles flung his arm around his friend's neck, and kissed him upon the cheek. "Thou shalt have thy will," said he; "but whether knight or squire, thou art ever mine own true friend."

Then they went slowly back together, hand in hand, to the castle world again.

At two o'clock Myles went to Lord George's apartments, and there his friend and patron dressed him out in a costume better fitted for the ceremony of presentation — a fur-trimmed jacket of green brocaded velvet embroidered with golden thread, a black velvet hood-cap rolled like a turban and with a jewel in the front, a pair of crimson hose, and a pair of black velvet shoes trimmed and stitched with gold-thread. Myles had never worn such splendid clothes in his life before, and he could not but feel that they became him well.

"Sir," said he, as he looked down at himself, "sure it is not lawful for me to wear such clothes as these."

In those days there was a law, known as a sumptuary law, which regulated by statute the clothes that each class of people were privileged to wear. It was, as Myles said, against the law for him to wear such garments as those in which he was clad — either velvet, crimson stuff, fur or silver or gold embroidery — nevertheless such a solemn ceremony as presentation to the King excused the temporary overstepping of the law, and so Lord George told him. As he laid his hand upon the lad's shoulder and held him off at arm's-length, he added, "And I pledge thee my word, Myles, that thou art as lusty and handsome a lad as ever mine eyes beheld."

"Thou art very kind to me, sir," said Myles, in answer.

Lord George laughed; and then giving him a shake, let go his shoulder.

It was about three o'clock when little Edmond de Montefort, Lord Mackworth's favorite page, came with word that the King was then walking in the Earl's pleasance.

"Come, Myles," said Lord George, and then Myles arose from the seat where he had been sitting, his heart palpitating and throbbing tumultuously.

At the wicket-gate of the pleasance two gentlemen-at-arms stood guard in half-armor; they saluted Lord George, and permitted him to pass with his protégé. As he laid his hand upon the latch of the wicket he paused for a moment and turned.

"Myles," said he, in a low voice, "thou art a thoughtful and cautious lad; for thy father's sake be thoughtful and cautious now. Do not speak his name or betray that thou art his son." Then he opened the wicket-gate and entered.

Any lad of Myles's age, even one far more used to the world than he, would perhaps have felt all the oppression that he experienced under the weight of such a presentation. He hardly knew what he was doing as Lord George led him to where the King stood, a little apart from the attendants, with the Earl and the Comte de Vermoise. Even in his confusion he knew enough to kneel, and somehow his honest, modest diffidence became the young fellow very well. He was not awkward, for one so healthful in mind and body as he could not bear himself very ill, and he felt the assurance that in Lord George he had a kind friend at his side, and one well used to court ceremonies to lend him countenance. Then there is something always pleasing in frank, modest manliness such as was stamped on Myles's handsome, sturdy face. No doubt the King's heart warmed towards the fledgling warrior kneeling in the path-way before him. He smiled very kindly as he gave the lad his hand to kiss, and that ceremony done, held fast to the hard, brown, sinewy fist of the young man with his soft white hand, and raised him to his feet.

" By the mass!" said he, looking Myles over with smiling eyes, "thou art a right champion in good sooth. Such as thou art haply was Sir Galahad when he came to Arthur's court. And so, they tell me, thou hast stomach to brook the Sieur de la Montaigne, that tough old boar of Dauphiny. Hast thou in good sooth the courage to face him? Knowest thou what a great thing it is that thou hast set upon thyself—to do battle, even in sport, with him?"

"Yea, your Majesty," answered Myles, "well I wot it is a task haply beyond me. But gladly would I take upon me even a greater venture, and one more dangerous, to do your Majesty's pleasure!"

The King looked pleased. "Now that was right well said, young man," said he, "and I like it better that it came from such young and honest lips. Dost thou speak French?"

"Yea, your Majesty," answered Myles. "In some small measure do I so."

"I am glad of that," said the King; "for so I may make thee acquainted with Sieur de la Montaigne."

He turned as he ended speaking, and beckoned to a heavy, thick-set, black-browed chevalier who stood with the other gentlemen attendants at a little distance. He came instantly forward in answer to the summons, and the King introduced the two to one another. As each took the other formally by the hand, he measured his opponent hastily, body and limb, and perhaps each thought that he had never seen a stronger, stouter, better-knit man than the one upon whom he looked. But nevertheless the contrast betwixt the two was very great — Myles, young, boyish, fresh-faced; the other, bronzed, weather beaten, and seamed with a great white scar that ran across his forehead and cheek; the one a novice, the other a warrior seasoned in twoscore battles.

A few polite phrases passed between the two, the King listening smiling, but with an absent and far-away look gradually stealing upon his face. As they ended speaking, a little pause of silence followed, and then the King suddenly aroused himself.

"So," said he, "I am glad that ye two are acquainted. And now we will leave our youthful champion in thy charge, Beaumont — and in thine, Mon Sieur, as well—and so soon as the proper ceremonies are ended, we will dub him knight with our own hands." And now, Mackworth, and thou my Lord Count, let us walk a little; I have bethought me further concerning these threescore extra men for Dauphiny.

Then Myles withdrew, under the charge of Lord George and the Sieur de la Montaigne.

and while the King and the two nobles walked slowly up and down the gravel path between the tall rose-bushes, Myles stood talking with the gentlemen attendants, finding himself, with a certain triumphant exultation, the peer of any and the hero of the hour.

That night was the last that Myles and Gascoyne spent lodging in the dormitory in their squirehood service. The next day they were assigned apartments in Lord George's part of the house, and thither they transported themselves and their belongings, amid the awestruck wonder and admiration of their fellow-squires.

"Lord George led him to where the King stood"

CHAPTER XXIV.

In Myles Falworth's day one of the greatest ceremonies of courtly life was that of the bestowal of knighthood by the King, with the honors of the Bath. By far the greater number of knights were at that time created by other knights, or by nobles, or by officers of the crown. To be knighted by the King in person distinguished the recipient for life. It was this signal honor that the Earl, for his own purposes, wished Myles to enjoy, and for this end he had laid not a few plans.

The accolade was the term used for the creation of a knight upon the field of battle. It was a reward of valor or of meritorious service, and was generally bestowed in a more or less off-hand way; but the ceremony of the Bath was an occasion of the greatest courtly moment, and it was thus that Myles Falworth was to be knighted in addition to the honor of a royal belting.

A quaint old book treating of knighthood and

217

chivalry gives a full and detailed account of all the circumstances of the ceremony of a creation of a Knight of the Bath. It tells us that the candidate was first placed under the care of two squires of honor, "grave and well seen in courtship and nurture, and also in feats of chivalry," which same were likewise to be governors in all things relating to the coming honors.

First of all, the barber shaved him, and cut his hair in a certain peculiar fashion ordained for the occasion, the squires of honor supervising the operation. This being concluded, the candidate was solemnly conducted to the chamber where the bath of tepid water was prepared, "hung within and without with linen, and likewise covered with rich cloths and embroidered linen." While in the bath two "ancient, grave, and reverend knights" attended the bachelor, giving him "meet instructions in the order and feats of chivalry." The candidate was then examined as to his knowledge and acquirements, and then, all questions being answered to the satisfaction of his examiners, the elder of the two dipped a handful of water out from the bath, and poured it upon his head, at the same time signing his left shoulder with the sign of the cross.

As soon as this ceremony was concluded, the two squires of honor helped their charge from the bath, and conducted him to a plain bed without hangings, where they let him rest until his body was warm and dry. Then they clad him in a white linen shirt, and over it a plain robe of russet, "girdled about the loins with a rope, and having a hood like unto a hermit."

As soon as the candidate had arisen, the two "ancient knights" returned, and all being in readiness he was escorted to the chapel, the two walking, one upon either side of him, his squires of honor marching before, and the whole party preceded by "sundry minstrels making a loud noise of music."

When they came to the chapel, the two knights who escorted him took leave of the candidate, each saluting him with a kiss upon the cheek. No one remained with him but his squires of honor, the priest, and the chandler.

In the mean time the novitiate's armor, sword, lance, and helmet had been laid in readiness before the altar. These he watched and guarded while the others slept, keeping vigil until sunrise, during which time "he shall," says the ancient authority, "pass the night in orisons, prayers, and meditation." At daylight he confessed to the priest, heard matins, and communicated in mass, and then presented a lighted candle at the altar, with a piece of money stuck in it as close to the flame as could be done, the candle being offered to the honor of God, and the money to the honor of that person who was to make him a knight.

So concluded the sacred ceremony, which being ended his squires conducted the candidate to his chamber, and there made him comfortable, and left him to repose for a while before the second and final part of the ordinance.

Such is a shortened account of the preparatory stages of the ceremonies through which Myles Falworth passed.

Matters had come upon him so suddenly one after the other, and had come with such bewilder-ing rapidity that all that week was to him like some strange, wonderful, mysterious vision. He went through it all like one in a dream. Lord George Beaumont was one of his squires of honor; the other, by way of a fitting complement to the courage of the chivalrous lad, was the Sieur de la Montaigne, his opponent soon to be. They were well versed in everything relating to knight-craft, and Myles followed all their directions with passive obedience. Then Sir James Lee and the Comte de Vermoise administered the ceremony of the Bath, the old knight examining him in the laws of chivalry.

It occurs perhaps once or twice in one's life-time that one passes through great happenings—

sometimes of joy, sometimes of dreadful bitterness—in just such a dazed state as Myles passed
through this. It is only afterwards that all comes
back to one so sharply and keenly that the heart
thrills almost in agony in living it over again.
But perhaps of all the memory of that time, when
it afterwards came back piece by piece, none was
so clear to Myles's back-turned vision as the long
night spent in the chapel, watching his armor,
thinking such wonderful thoughts, and dreaming
sucn wonderful wide-eyed dreams. At such times
Myles saw again the dark mystery of the castle
chapel; he saw again the half-moon gleaming
white and silvery through the tall, narrow window, and throwing a broad form of still whiteness
across stone floor, empty seats, and still, motionless figures of stone effigies. At such times he
stood again in front of the twinkling tapers that
lit the altar where his armor lay piled in a heap,
heard again the deep breathing of his companions
of the watch sleeping in some empty stall, wrapped
each in his cloak, and saw the old chandler bestir
himself, and rise and come forward to snuff the
candles. At such times he saw again the day
growing clearer and clearer through the tall, glazed
windows, saw it change to a rosy pink, and then
to a broad, ruddy glow that threw a halo of light
around Father Thomas's bald head bowed in

221

sleep, and lit up the banners and trophies hanging motionless against the stony face of the west wall; heard again the stirring of life without and the sound of his companions arousing themselves; saw them come forward, and heard them wish him joy that his long watch was ended.

It was nearly noon when Myles was awakened from a fitful sleep by Gascoyne bringing in his dinner, but, as might be supposed, he had but little hunger, and ate sparingly. He had hardly ended his frugal meal before his two squires of honor came in, followed by a servant carrying the garments for the coming ceremony. He saluted them gravely, and then arising, washed his face and hands in a basin which Gascoyne held; then kneeled in prayer, the others standing silent at a little distance. As he arose, Lord George came forward.

"The King and the company come presently to the Great Hall, Myles," said he; "it is needful for thee to make all the haste that thou art able."

Perhaps never had Devlen Castle seen a more brilliant and goodly company gathered in the great hall than that which came to witness King Henry create Myles Falworth a knight bachelor.

At the upper end of the hall was a raised dais, upon which stood a throne covered with crimson satin and embroidered with lions and flower-de-luces; it was the King's seat. He and his personal attendants had not yet come, but the rest of the company were gathered. The day being warm and sultry, the balcony was all aflutter with the feather fans of the ladies of the family and their attendants, who from this high place looked down upon the hall below. Up the centre of the hall was laid a carpet of arras, and the passage was protected by wooden railings. Upon the one side were tiers of seats for the castle gentle-folks and the guests. Upon the other stood the burghers from the town, clad in sober dun and russet, and yeomanry in green and brown. The whole of the great vaulted hall was full of the dull hum of many people waiting, and a ceaseless restlessness stirred the crowded throng. But at last a whisper went around that the King was coming. A momentary hush fell, and through it was heard the noisy clatter of horses' feet coming nearer and nearer, and then stopping before the door. The sudden blare of trumpets broke through the hush; another pause, and then in through the great door-way of the hall came the royal procession.

First of all marched, in the order of their rank, and to the number of a score or more, certain gentlemen, esquires and knights, chosen mostly from the King's attendants. Behind these came two pursuivants-at-arms in tabards, and following them a party of a dozen more bannerets and barons. Behind these again, a little space intervening, came two heralds, also in tabards, a group of the greater nobles attendant upon the King following in the order of their rank. Next came the King-at-arms and, at a little distance and walking with sober slowness, the King himself, with the Earl and the Count directly attendant upon him—the one marching upon the right hand and the other upon the left. A breathless silence filled the whole space as the royal procession advanced slowly up the hall. Through the stillness could be heard the muffled sound of the footsteps on the carpet, the dry rustling of silk and satin garments, and the clear clink and jingle of chains and jewelled ornaments, but not the sound of a single voice.

After the moment or two of bustle and confusion of the King taking his place had passed, another little space of expectant silence fell. At last there suddenly came the noise of acclamation of those who stood without the door—cheering and the clapping of hands—sounds heralding the immediate advent of Myles and his attendants. The next moment the little party entered the hall.

First of all, Gascoyne, bearing Myles's sword in both hands, the hilt resting against his breast, the point elevated at an angle of forty-five degrees. It was sheathed in a crimson scabbard, and the belt of Spanish leather studded with silver bosses was wound crosswise around it. From the hilt of the sword dangled the gilt spurs of his coming knighthood. At a little distance behind his squire followed Myles, the centre of all observation. He was clad in a novitiate dress, arranged under Lord George's personal supervision. It had been made somewhat differently from the fashion usual at such times, and was intended to indicate in a manner the candidate's extreme youthfulness and virginity in arms. The outer garment was a tabard robe of white wool, embroidered at the hem with fine lines of silver, and gathered loosely at the waist with a belt of lavender leather stitched with thread of silver. Beneath he was clad in armor (a present from the Earl), new and polished till it shone with dazzling brightness, the breastplate covered with a juppon of white satin, embroidered with silver. Behind Myles, and upon either hand, came his squires of honor, sponsors, and friends—a little company of some half-dozen in all. As they advanced slowly up the great, dim, high-vaulted room, the whole multitude broke forth into a humming buzz of applause. Then a sudden clapping of hands began near the door-way, ran down through the length of the room, and was taken up by all with noisy clatter.

"Saw I never youth so comely," whispered one of the Lady Anne's attendant gentlewomen. "Sure he looketh as Sir Galahad looked when he came first to King Arthur's court."

Myles knew that he was very pale; he felt rather than saw the restless crowd of faces upon either side, for his eyes were fixed directly before him, upon the dais whereon sat the King, with the Earl of Mackworth standing at his right hand, the Comte de Vermoise upon the left, and the others ranged around and behind the throne. It was with the same tense feeling of dreamy un-reality that Myles walked slowly up the length of the hall, measuring his steps by those of Gascoyne. Suddenly he felt Lord George Beaumont touch him lightly upon the arm, and almost in-stinctively he stopped short — he was standing just before the covered steps of the throne.

He saw Gascoyne mount to the third step, stop short, kneel, and offer the sword and the spurs he carried to the King, who took the weapon and laid it across his knees. Then the squire bowed low, and walking backward withdrew to one side, leaving Myles standing alone facing the throne.

The King unlocked the spur chains from the sword-hilt, and then, holding the gilt spurs in his hand for a moment, he looked Myles straight in the eyes and smiled. Then he turned, and gave one of the spurs to the Earl of Mackworth.

The Earl took it with a low bow, turned, and came slowly down the steps to where Myles stood. Kneeling upon one knee, and placing Myles's foot upon the other, Lord Mackworth set the spur in its place and latched the chain over the instep He drew the sign of the cross upon Myles's bended knee, set the foot back upon the ground, rose with slow dignity, and bowing to the King, drew a little to one side.

As soon as the Earl had fulfilled his office the King gave the second spur to the Comte de Vermoise, who set it to Myles's other foot with the same ceremony that the Earl had observed, withdrawing as he had done to one side.

An instant pause of motionless silence followed, and then the King slowly arose, and began deliberately to unwind the belt from around the scabbard of the sword he held. As soon as he stood, the Earl and the Count advanced, and taking Myles by either hand, led him forward and up the steps of the dais to the platform above. As they drew a little to one side, the King stooped and buckled the sword-belt around Myles's waist then, rising again, lifted his hand and struck him upon the shoulder, crying, in a loud voice,

"Be thou a good knight!"

Instantly a loud sound of applause and the clapping of hands filled the whole hall, in the midst of which the King laid both hands upon Myles's shoulders and kissed him upon the right cheek. So the ceremony ended; Myles was no longer Myles Falworth, but Sir Myles Falworth, Knight by Order of the Bath and by grace of the King!

CHAPTER XXV.

IT was the custom to conclude the ceremonies
of the bestowal of knighthood by a grand feast
given in honor of the newly-created knight. But
in Myles's instance the feast was dispensed with.
The Earl of Mackworth had planned that Myles
might be created a Knight of the Bath with all
possible pomp and ceremony; that his personal-
ity might be most favorably impressed upon the
King; that he might be so honorably knighted
as to make him the peer of any who wore spurs
in all England; and, finally, that he might cele-
brate his new honors by jousting with some
knight of high fame and approved valor. All
these *desiderata* chance had fulfilled in the visit
of the King to Devlen.

As the Earl had said to Myles, he would
rather have waited a little while longer until the
lad was riper in years and experience, but the opportunity was not to be lost. Young as he was,
Myles must take his chances against the years

and grim experience of the Sieur de la Montaigne. But it was also a part of the Earl's purpose that the King and Myles should not be brought too intimately together just at that time. Though every particular of circumstance should be fulfilled in the ceremony, it would have been ruination to the Earl's plans to have the knowledge come prematurely to the King that Myles was the son of the attainted Lord Falworth. The Earl knew that Myles was a shrewd, cool-headed lad; but the King had already hinted that the name was familiar to his ears, and a single hasty answer or unguarded speech upon the young knight's part might awaken him to a full knowledge. Such a mishap was, of all things, to be avoided just then, for, thanks to the machinations of that enemy of his father, of whom Myles had heard so much, and was soon to hear more, the King had always retained and still held a bitter and rancorous enmity against the unfortunate nobleman.

It was no very difficult matter for the Earl to divert the King's attention from the matter of the feast. His Majesty was very intent just then upon supplying a quota of troops to the Dauphin, and the chief object of his visit to Devlen was to open negotiations with the Earl looking to that end. He was interested—much

interested in Myles and in the coming jousting in which the young warrior was to prove
himself, but he was interested in it by way of
a relaxation from the other and more engross-
ing matter. So, though he made some passing
and half preoccupied inquiry about the feast,
he was easily satisfied with the Earl's reasons
for not holding it: which were that he had arranged a consultation for that morning in regard to the troops for the Dauphin, to which
meeting he had summoned a number of his own
more important dependent nobles; that the King
himself needed repose and the hour or so of rest
that his barber-surgeon had ordered him to take
after his mid-day meal; that Father Thomas had
laid upon Myles a petty penance—that for the
first three days of his knighthood he should eat
his meals without meat and in his own apartment
—and various other reasons equally good and
sufficient. So the King was satisfied, and the
feast was dispensed with.

The next morning had been set for the jousting, and all that day the workmen were busy
erecting the lists in the great quadrangle upon
which, as was said before, looked the main buildings of the castle. The windows of Myles's
apartment opened directly upon the bustling
scene--the carpenters hammering and sawing,

the upholsterers snipping, cutting, and tacking. Myles and Gascoyne stood gazing out from the open casement, with their arms lying across one another's shoulders in the old boyhood fashion, and Myles felt his heart shrink with a sudden tight pang as the realization came sharply and vividly upon him that all these preparations were being made for him, and that the next day he should, with almost the certainty of death, meet either glory or failure under the eyes not only of all the greater and lesser castle folk, but of the King himself and noble strangers critically used to deeds of chivalry and prowess. Perhaps he had never fully realized the magnitude of the reality before. In that tight pang at his heart he drew a deep breath, almost a sigh. Gascoyne turned his head abruptly, and looked at his friend, but he did not ask the cause of the sigh. No doubt the same thoughts that were in Myles's mind were in his also.

It was towards the latter part of the afternoon that a message came from the Earl, bidding Myles attend him in his private closet. After Myles had bowed and kissed his lordship's hand, the Earl motioned him to take a seat, telling him that he had some final words to say that might occupy a considerable time. He talked to the young man for about half an hour in his quiet, measured voice, only now and then showing a little agitation by rising and walking up and down the room for a turn or two. Very many things were disclosed in that talk that had caused Myles long hours of brooding thought, for the Earl spoke freely, and without conceal- ment to him concerning his father and the fort- unes of the house of Falworth.

Myles had surmised many things, but it was not until then that he knew for a certainty who was his father's malignant and powerful enemy— that it was the great Earl of Alban, the rival and bitter enemy of the Earl of Mackworth. It was not until then that he knew that the present Earl of Alban was the Lord Brookhurst, who had killed Sir John Dale in the anteroom at Fal- worth Castle that morning so long ago in his early childhood. It was not until then that he knew all the circumstances of his father's blind- ness; that he had been overthrown in the mêlée at the great tournament at York, and that that same Lord Brookhurst had ridden his iron-shod war-horse twice over his enemy's prostrate body before his squire could draw him from the press, and had then and there given him the wound from which he afterwards went blind. The Earl swore to Myles that Lord Brookhurst had done what he did wilfully, and had afterwards boasted of it. Then, with some hesitation, he told Myles the reason of Lord Brookhurst's enmity, and that it had arisen on account of Lady Falworth, whom he had one time sought in marriage, and that he had sworn vengeance against the man who had won her.

Piece by piece the Earl of Mackworth recounted every circumstance and detail of the revenge that the blind man's enemy had afterwards wreaked upon him. He told Myles how, when his father was attainted of high-treason, and his estates forfeited to the crown, the King had granted the barony of Easterbridge to the then newly-created Earl of Alban in spite of all the efforts of Lord Falworth's friends to the contrary; that when he himself had come out from an audience with the King, with others of his father's friends, the Earl of Alban had boasted in the anteroom, in a loud voice, evidently intended for them all to hear, that now that he had Falworth's fat lands, he would never rest till he had hunted the blind man out from his hiding, and brought his head to the block.

"Ever since then," said the Earl of Mackworth, "he hath been striving by every means to discover thy father's place of concealment. Some time, haply, he may find it, and then—"

Myles had felt for a long time that he was being moulded and shaped, and that the Earl of
Mackworth's was the hand that was making him
what he was growing to be; but he had never
realized how great were the things expected of
him should he pass the first great test, and show
himself what his friends hoped to see him. Now
he knew that all were looking upon him to act,
sometime, as his father's champion, and when
that time should come, to challenge the Earl of
Alban to the ordeal of single combat, to purge
his father's name of treason, to restore him to
his rank, and to set the house of Falworth where
it stood before misfortune fell upon it.

But it was not alone concerning his and his
father's affairs that the Earl of Mackworth talked
to Myles. He told him that the Earl of Alban
was the Earl of Mackworth's enemy also; that in
his younger days he had helped Lord Falworth,
who was his kinsman, to win his wife, and that
then Lord Brookhurst had sworn to compass his
·ruin as he had sworn to compass the ruin of his
friend. He told Myles how, now that Lord Brookhurst was grown to be Earl of Alban, and great
and powerful, he was forever plotting against him,
and showed Myles how, if Lord Falworth were
discovered and arrested for treason, he also would
be likely to suffer for aiding and abetting him.

Then it dawned upon Myles that the Earl looked to him to champion the house of Beaumont as well as that of Falworth.

"Mayhap," said the Earl, "thou didst think that it was all for the pleasant sport of the matter that I have taken upon me this toil and endeavor to have thee knighted with honor that thou mightst fight the Dauphiny knight. Nay, nay, Myles Falworth, I have not labored so hard for such a small matter as that. I have had the King, unknown to himself, so knight thee that thou mayst be the peer of Alban himself, and now I would have thee to hold thine own with the Sieur de la Montaigne, to try whether thou be'st Alban's match, and to approve thyself worthy of the honor of thy knighthood. I am sorry, ne'theless," he added, after a moment's pause, "that this could not have been put off for a while longer, for my plans for bringing thee to battle with that vile Alban are not yet ripe. But such a chance of the King coming hither haps not often. And then I am glad of this much—that a good occasion offers to get thee presently away from England. I would have thee out of the King's sight so soon as may be after this jousting. He taketh a liking to thee, and I fear me lest he should inquire more nearly concerning thee and so all be discovered and spoiled. My brother George goeth upon the first of next month to France to take service with the Dauphin, having under his command a company of tenscore men—knights and archers; thou shalt go with him, and there stay till I send for thee to return."

With this, the protracted interview concluded, the Earl charging Myles to say nothing further about the French expedition for the present—even to his friend—for it was as yet a matter of secrecy, known only to the King and a few nobles closely concerned in the venture.

Then Myles arose to take his leave. He asked and obtained permission for Gascoyne to accompany him to France. Then he paused for a moment or two, for it was strongly upon him to speak of a matter that had been lying in his mind all day—a matter that he had dreamed of much with open eyes during the long vigil of the night before.

The Earl looked up inquiringly. " What is it thou wouldst ask?" said he.

Myles's heart was beating quickly within him at the thought of his own boldness, and as he spoke his cheeks burned like fire. "Sir," said he, mustering his courage at last, " haply thou hast forgot it, but I have not; ne'theless, a long time since when I spoke of serving the—the Lady

Alice as her true knight, thou didst wisely laugh at my words, and bade me wait first till I had earned my spurs. But now, sir, I have gotten my spurs, and—and do now crave thy gracious leave that I may serve that lady as her true knight."

A space of dead silence fell, in which Myles's heart beat tumultuously within him.

"I know not what thou meanest," said the Earl at last, in a somewhat constrained voice. " How wouldst thou serve her? What wouldst thou have?"

" I would have only a little matter just now," answered Myles. " I would but crave of her a favor for to wear in the morrow's battle, so that she may know that I hold her for my own true lady, and that I may have the courage to fight more boldly, having that favor to defend."

The Earl sat looking at him for a while in brooding silence, stroking his beard the while. Suddenly his brow cleared. "So be it," said he. " I grant thee my leave to ask the Lady Alice for a favor, and if she is pleased to give it to thee, I shall not say thee nay. But I set this upon thee as a provision: that thou shalt not see her without the Lady Anne be present. Thus it was, as I remember, thou saw her first, and with it thou must now be satisfied. Go thou to the

Long Gallery, and thither they will come anon if naught hinder them."

Myles waited in the Long Gallery perhaps some fifteen or twenty minutes. No one was there but himself. It was a part of the castle connecting the Earl's and the Countess's apartments, and was used but little. During that time he stood looking absently out of the open casement into the stony court-yard beyond, trying to put into words that which he had to say; wondering, with anxiety, how soon the young ladies would come; wondering whether they would come at all. At last the door at the farther end of the gallery opened, and turning sharply at the sound, he saw the two young ladies enter, Lady Alice leaning upon Lady Anne's arm. It was the first time that he had seen them since the ceremony of the morning, and as he advanced to meet them, the Lady Anne came frankly forward, and gave him her hand, which Myles raised to his lips.

" I give thee joy of thy knighthood, Sir Myles," said she, " and do believe, in good sooth, that if any one deserveth such an honor, thou art he."

At first little Lady Alice hung back behind her cousin, saying nothing until the Lady Anne, turning suddenly, said: "Come, coz, hast thou naught to say to our new-made knight? Canst thou not also wish him joy of his knighthood?"

Lady Alice hesitated a minute, then gave Myles a timid hand, which he, with a strange mixture of joy and confusion, took as timidly as it was offered. He raised the hand, and set it lightly and for an instant to his lips, as he had done with the Lady Anne's hand, but with very different emotions.

"I give you joy of your knighthood, sir," said Lady Alice, in a voice so low that Myles could hardly hear it.

Both flushed red, and as he raised his head again, Myles saw that the Lady Anne had withdrawn to one side. Then he knew that it was to give him the opportunity to proffer his request.

A little space of silence followed, the while he strove to key his courage to the saying of that which lay at his mind. "Lady," said he at last, and then again—"Lady, I—have a favor for to ask thee."

"What is it thou wouldst have, Sir Myles?" she murmured, in reply.

"Lady," said he, "ever sin I first saw thee I have thought that if I might choose of all the world, thou only wouldst I choose for—for my true lady, to serve as a right knight should." Here he stopped, frightened at his own boldness.

Lady Alice stood quite still, with her face turned away. " Thou—thou art not angered at what I say ?" he said.

She shook her head.

"I have longed and longed for the time," said he, "to ask a boon of thee, and now hath that time come. Lady, to-morrow I go to meet a right good knight, and one skilled in arms and in jousting, as thou dost know. Yea, he is famous in arms, and I be nobody. Ne'theless, I fight for the honor of England and Mackworth —and—and for thy sake. I— Thou art not angered at what I say ?"

Again the Lady Alice shook her head.

" I would that thou — I would that thou would give me some favor for to wear — thy veil or thy necklace."

He waited anxiously for a little while, but Lady Alice did not answer immediately.

"I fear me," said Myles, presently, " that I have in sooth offended thee in asking this thing. I know that it is a parlous bold matter for one so raw in chivalry and in courtliness as I am, and one so poor in rank, to ask thee for thy favor. An I ha' offended, I prithee let it be as though I had not asked it."

Perhaps it was the young man's timidity that brought a sudden courage to Lady Alice; per-

haps it was the graciousness of her gentle breeding that urged her to relieve Myles's somewhat
awkward humility, perhaps it was something
more than either that lent her bravery to speak,
even knowing that the Lady Anne heard all.
She turned quickly to him: "Nay, Sir Myles,"
she said, "I am foolish, and do wrong thee by my
foolishness and silence, for, truly, I am proud to
have thee wear my favor." She unclasped, as
she spoke, the thin gold chain from about her
neck. "I give thee this chain," said she, "and it
will bring me joy to have it honored by thy true
knightliness, and, giving it, I do wish thee all success." Then she bowed her head, and, turning,
left him holding the necklace in his hand.

Her cousin left the window to meet her, bowing her head with a smile to Myles as she took
her cousin's arm again and led her away. He
stood looking after them as they left the room,
and when they were gone, he raised the necklace
to his lips with a heart beating tumultuously with
a triumphant joy it had never felt before.

CHAPTER XXVI

AND now, at last, had come the day of days for Myles Falworth, the day when he was to put to the test all that he had acquired in the three years of his training; the day that was to disclose what promise of future greatness there was in his strong young body. And it was a noble day, one of those of late September, when the air seems sweeter and fresher than at other times; the sun bright and as yellow as gold; the wind lusty and strong, before which the great white clouds go sailing majestically across the bright blueness of the sky above, while their dusky shadows skim across the brown face of the rusty earth beneath.

As was said before, the lists had been set up in the great quadrangle of the castle, than which, level and smooth as a floor, no more fitting place could be chosen. The course was of the usual size — sixty paces long — and separated along its whole length by a barrier about five

feet high.   Upon the west side of the course,
and about twenty paces distant from it, a scaffolding had been built facing towards the east
so as to avoid the glare of the afternoon sun.
In the centre was a raised dais, hung round with
cloth of blue embroidered with lions rampant.
Upon the dais stood a cushioned throne for the
King, and upon the steps below, ranged in the
order of their dignity, were seats for the Earl,
his guests, the family, the ladies, knights, and gentlemen of the castle.   In front, the scaffolding
was covered with the gayest tapestries and bright-
est-colored hangings that the castle could afford.
And above, parti-colored pennants and stream-
ers, surmounted by the royal ensign of England,
waved and fluttered in the brisk wind.

At either end of the lists stood the pavilions
of the knights.   That of Myles was at the south-
ern extremity, and was hung, by the Earl's desire, with cloth of the Beaumont colors (black and
yellow), while a wooden shield bearing three goshawks spread (the crest of the house) was nailed
to the roof, and a long streamer of black and yellow trailed out in the wind from the staff above.
Myles, partly armed, stood at the door-way of the
pavilion, watching the folk gathering at the scaffolding.   The ladies of the house were already
seated, and the ushers were bustling hither and

thither, assigning the others their places   A considerable crowd of common folk and burghers from the town had already gathered at the barriers opposite, and as he looked at the restless and growing multitude he felt his heart beat quickly and his flesh grow cold with a nervous trepidation—just such as the lad of to-day feels when he sees the auditorium filling with friends and strangers who are to listen by-and-by to the reading of his prize poem.

Suddenly there came a loud blast of trumpets. A great gate at the farther extremity of the lists was thrown open, and the King appeared, riding upon a white horse, preceded by the King-at-arms and the heralds, attended by the Earl and the Comte de Vermoise, and followed by a crowd of attendants. Just then Gascoyne, who, with Wilkes, was busied lacing some of the armor plates with new thongs, called Myles, and he turned and entered the pavilion

As the two squires were adjusting these last pieces, strapping them in place and tying the thongs, Lord George and Sir James Lee entered the pavilion. Lord George took the young man by the hand, and with a pleasant smile wished him success in the coming encounter.

Sir James seemed anxious and disturbed. He said nothing, and after Gascoyne had placed the open bascinet that supports the tilting helm in its place, he came forward and examined the armor piece by piece, carefully and critically, testing the various straps and leather points and thongs to make sure of their strength.

" Sir," said Gascoyne, who stood by watching him anxiously, " I do trust that I have done all meetly and well."

" I see nothing amiss, sirrah," said the old knight, half grudgingly. "So far as I may know, he is ready to mount."

Just then a messenger entered, saying that the King was seated, and Lord George bade Myles make haste to meet the challenger.

" Francis," said Myles, " prithee give me my pouch yonder."

Gascoyne handed him the velvet bag, and he opened it, and took out the necklace that the Lady Alice had given him the day before.

" Tie me this around my arm," said he. He looked down, keeping his eyes studiously fixed on Gascoyne's fingers, as they twined the thin golden chain around the iron plates of his right arm, knowing that Lord George's eyes were upon him, and blushing fiery red at the knowledge.

Sir James was at that moment examining the great tilting helm, and Lord George watched him, smiling amusedly. "And hast thou then already chosen thee a lady?" he said, presently.

"Aye, my Lord," answered Myles, simply.

"Marry, I trust we be so honored that she is one of our castle folk," said the Earl's brother.

For a moment Myles did not reply; then he looked up. "My Lord," said he, "the favor was given to me by the Lady Alice."

Lord George looked grave for the moment; then he laughed. "Marry, thou art a bold archer to shoot for such high game."

Myles did not answer, and at that moment two grooms led his horse up to the door of the pavilion. Gascoyne and Wilkes helped him to his saddle, and then, Gascoyne holding his horse by the bridle-rein, he rode slowly across the lists to the little open space in front of the scaffolding and the King's seat just as the Sieur de la Montaigne approached from the opposite direction.

As soon as the two knights champion had reached each his appointed station in front of the scaffolding, the Marshal bade the speaker read the challenge, which, unrolling the parchment, he began to do in a loud, clear voice, so that all might hear. It was a quaint document, wrapped up in the tangled heraldic verbiage of the time. The pith of the matter was that the Sieur Brian Philip Francis de la Montaigne pro claimed before all men the greater chivalry and skill at arms of the knights of France and of Dauphiny, and likewise the greater fairness of the ladies of France and Dauphiny, and would there defend those sayings with his body without fear or attaint as to the truth of the same. As soon as the speaker had ended, the Marshal bade him call the defendant of the other side.

Then Myles spoke his part, with a voice trembling somewhat with the excitement of the moment, but loudly and clearly enough: " I, Myles Edward Falworth, knight, so created by the hand and by the grace of his Majesty King Henry IV. of England, do take upon me the gage of this battle, and will defend with my body the chivalry of the knights of England and the fairness of the ladies thereof!"

Then, after the speaker ended his proclamation and had retired to his place, the ceremony of claiming and redeeming the helmet, to which all young knights were subjected upon first entering the lists, was performed.

One of the heralds cried in a loud voice, " I, Gilles Hamerton, herald to the most noble Clarencieux King-at-arms, do claim the helm of Sir Myles Edward Falworth by this reason, that he hath never yet entered joust or tourney."

To which Myles answered, " I do acknowledge

"'My Lord,' said he, 'the favor was given to me by the Lady Alice'"

the right of that claim, and herewith proffer thee in ransom for the same this purse of one hundred marks in gold."

As he spoke, Gascoyne stepped forward and delivered the purse, with the money, to the Herald. It was a more than usually considerable ransom, and had been made up by the Earl and Lord George that morning.

" Right nobly hast thou redeemed thy helm," said the Herald, " and hereafter be thou free to enter any jousting whatsoever, and in whatever place."

So, all being ended, both knights bowed to the King, and then, escorted each by his squire, returned to his pavilion, saluted by the spectators with a loud clapping of hands.

Sir James Lee met Myles in front of his tent. Coming up to the side of the horse, the old man laid his hand upon the saddle, looking up into the young man's face.

" Thou wilt not fail in this venture and bring shame upon me ?" said he.

" Nay, my dear master," said Myles; " I will do my best."

" I doubt it not," said the old man; " and I believe me thou wilt come off right well. From what he did say this morning, methinks the Sieur de la Montaigne meaneth only to break

R

249

three lances with thee, and will content himself therewith, without seeking to unhorse thee. Ne'theless, be thou bold and watchful, and if thou find that he endeavor to cast thee, do thy best to unhorse him. Remember also those things which I have told thee ten thousand times before: hold thy toes well down and grip the stirrup hard, more especially at the moment of meeting; bend thy body forward, and keep thine elbow close to thy side. Bear thy lance point one foot above thine adversary's helm until within two lengths of meeting, and strike thou in the very middle of his shield. So, Myles, thou mayst hold thine own, and come off with glory."

As he ended speaking he drew back, and Gascoyne, mounting upon a stool, covered his friend's head and bascinet with the great jousting helm, making fast the leathern points that held it to the iron collar.

As he was tying the last thong a messenger came from the Herald, saying that the challenger was ready, and then Myles knew the time had come, and reaching down and giving Sir James a grip of the hand, he drew on his gauntlet, took the jousting lance that Wilkes handed him, and turned his horse's head towards his end of the lists.

CHAPTER XXVII.

As Myles took his place at the south end of the lists, he found the Sieur de la Montaigne already at his station. Through the peep-hole in the face of the huge helmet, a transverse slit known as the occularium, he could see, like a strange narrow picture, the farther end of the lists, the spectators upon either side moving and shifting with ceaseless restlessness, and in the centre of all, his opponent, sitting with spear point directed upward, erect, motionless as a statue of iron, the sunlight gleaming and flashing upon his polished plates of steel, and the trappings of his horse swaying and fluttering in the rushing of the fresh breeze.

Upon that motionless figure his sight gradually centred with every faculty of mind and soul. He knew the next moment the signal would be given that was to bring him either glory or shame from that iron statue. He ground his teeth together with stern resolve to do his best in the coming encounter, and murmured a brief prayer in the hollow darkness of his huge helm. Then with a shake he settled himself more firmly in his saddle, slowly raised his spear point until the shaft reached the exact angle, and there suffered it to rest motionless. There was a moment of dead, tense, breathless pause, then he rather felt than saw the Marshal raise his baton. He gathered himself together, and the next moment a bugle sounded loud and clear. In one blinding rush he drove his spurs into the sides of his horse, and in instant answer felt the noble steed spring forward with a bound.

Through all the clashing of his armor reverberating in the hollow depths of his helmet, he saw the mail-clad figure from the other end of the lists rushing towards him, looming larger and larger as they came together. He gripped his saddle with his knees, clutched the stirrup with the soles of his feet, and bent his body still more forward. In the instant of meeting, with almost the blindness of instinct, he dropped the point of his spear against the single red flower-de-luce in the middle of the on-coming shield. There was a thunderous crash that seemed to rack every joint, he heard the crackle of splintered wood, he felt the momentary trembling recoil of the horse beneath him, and in the next instant had passed by. As he checked the onward rush of his horse at the far end of the course, he heard faintly in the dim hollow recess of the helm the loud shout and the clapping of hands of those who looked on, and found himself gripping with nervous intensity the butt of a broken spear, his mouth clammy with excitement, and his heart thumping in his throat.

Then he realized that he had met his opponent, and had borne the meeting well. As he turned his horse's head towards his own end of the lists, he saw the other trotting slowly back towards his station, also holding a broken spear shaft in his hand.

As he passed the iron figure a voice issued from the helmet, "Well done, Sir Myles, nobly done!" and his heart bounded in answer to the words of praise. When he had reached his own end of the lists, he flung away his broken spear, and Gascoyne came forward with another.

"Oh, Myles!" he said, with a sob in his voice, "it was nobly done. Never did I see a better ridden course in all my life. I did not believe that thou couldst do half so well. Oh, Myles, prithee knock him out of his saddle an thou lovest me!"

Myles, in his high-keyed nervousness, could not forbear a short hysterical laugh at his friend's warmth of enthusiasm. He took the fresh lance in his hand, and then, seeing that his opponent was walking his horse slowly up and down at his end of the lists, did the same during the little time of rest before the next encounter.

When, in answer to the command of the Marshal, he took his place a second time, he found himself calmer and more collected than before, but every faculty no less intensely fixed than it had been at first. Once more the Marshal raised his baton, once more the horn sounded, and once more the two rushed together with the same thunderous crash, the same splinter of broken spears, the same momentary trembling recoil of the horse, and the same onward rush past one another. Once more the spectators applauded and shouted as the two knights turned their horses and rode back towards their station.

This time as they met midway the Sieur de la Montaigne reined in his horse. "Sir Myles," said his muffled voice, "I swear to thee, by my faith, I had not thought to meet in thee such an opponent as thou dost prove thyself to be. I had thought to find in thee a raw boy, but find instead a Paladin. Hitherto I have given thee grace as I would give grace to any mere lad, and thought of nothing but to give thee opportunity to break thy lance. Now I shall do my endeavor

254

to unhorse thee as I would an acknowledged peer in arms. Nevertheless, on account of thy youth, I give thee this warning, so that thou mayst hold thyself in readiness."

"I give thee gramercy for thy courtesy, my Lord," answered Myles, speaking in French, "and I will strive to encounter thee as best I may, and pardon me if I seem forward in so saying, but were I in thy place, my Lord, I would change me yon breast-piece and over-girth of my saddle; they are sprung in the stitches."

"Nay," said the Sieur de la Montaigne, laughing, "breast-piece and over-girth have carried me through more tilts than one, and shall through this. An thou give me a blow so true as to burst breast-piece and over-girth, I will own myself fairly conquered by thee." So saying, he saluted Myles with the butt of the spear he still held, and passed by to his end of the lists.

Myles, with Gascoyne running beside him, rode across to his pavilion, and called to Edmund Wilkes to bring him a cup of spiced wine. After Gascoyne had taken off his helmet, and as he sat wiping the perspiration from his face Sir James came up and took him by the hand.

"My dear boy," said he, gripping the hand he held, "never could I hope to be so overjoyed in mine old age as I am this day. Thou dost bring honor to me, for I tell thee truly thou dost ride like a knight seasoned in twenty tourneys."

"It doth give me tenfold courage to hear thee so say, dear master," answered Myles. "And truly," he added, "I shall need all my courage this bout, for the Sieur de la Montaigne telleth me that he will ride to unhorse me this time."

"Did he indeed so say?" said Sir James. "Then belike he meaneth to strike at thy helm. Thy best chance is to strike also at his. Doth thy hand tremble?"

"Not now," answered Myles.

"Then keep thy head cool and thine eye true. Set thy trust in God, and haply thou wilt come out of this bout honorably in spite of the rawness of thy youth."

Just then Edmund Wilkes presented the cup of wine to Myles, who drank it off at a draught, and thereupon Gascoyne replaced the helm and tied the thongs.

The charge that Sir James Lee had given to Myles to strike at his adversary's helm was a piece of advice he probably would not have given to so young a knight, excepting as a last resort. A blow perfectly delivered upon the helm was of all others the most difficult for the recipient to recover from, but then a blow upon the helm was not one time in fifty perfectly given. The huge cylindrical tilting helm was so constructed in front as to slope at an angle in all directions to one point. That point was the centre of a cross formed by two iron bands welded to the steel-face plates of the helm where it was weakened by the opening slit of the occularium, or peep-hole. In the very centre of this cross was a little flattened surface where the bands were riveted together, and it was upon that minute point that the blow must be given to be perfect, and that stroke Myles determined to attempt.

As he took his station Edmund Wilkes came running across from the pavilion with a lance that Sir James had chosen, and Myles, returning the one that Gascoyne had just given him, took it in his hand. It was of seasoned oak, some-what thicker than the other, a tough weapon, not easily to be broken even in such an encounter as he was like to have. He balanced the weapon, and found that it fitted perfectly to his grasp. As he raised the point to rest, his opponent took his station at the farther extremity of the lists, and again there was a little space of breathless pause. Myles was surprised at his own coolness; every nervous tremor was gone. Before, he had been conscious of the critical multitude looking down upon him; now it was a conflict of man to

man, and such a conflict had no terrors for his
young heart of iron.

The spectators had somehow come to the
knowledge that this was to be a more serious encounter than the two which had preceded it, and
a breathless silence fell for the moment or two
that the knights stood in place.

Once more he breathed a short prayer, " Holy
Mary, guard me !"

Then again, for the third time, the Marsha'
raised his baton, and the horn sounded, and foi
the third time Myles drove his spurs into his
horse's flanks. Again he saw the iron figure of
his opponent rushing nearer, nearer, nearer. He
centred, with a straining intensity, every faculty
of soul, mind, and body upon one point — the
cross of the occularium, the mark he was to
strike. He braced himself for the tremendous
shock which he knew must meet him, and then
in a flash dropped the lance point straight and
true. The next instant there was a deafening,
stunning crash — a crash like the stroke of a
thunder-bolt. There was a dazzling blaze of
blinding light, and a myriad sparks danced and
flickered and sparkled before his eyes. He felt
his horse stagger under him with the recoil, and
hardly knowing what he did, he drove his spurs
deep into its sides with a shout. At the same

moment there resounded in his ears a crashing rattle and clatter, he knew not of what, and then, as his horse recovered and sprang forward, and as the stunning bewilderment passed, he found that his helmet had been struck off. He heard a great shout arise from all, and thought, with a sickening, bitter disappointment, that it was because he had lost. At the farther end of the course he turned his horse, and then his heart gave a leap and a bound as though it would burst, the blood leaped to his cheeks tingling, and his bosom thrilled with an almost agonizing pang of triumph, of wonder, of amazement.

There, in a tangle of his horse's harness and of embroidered trappings, the Sieur de la Montaigne lay stretched upon the ground, with his saddle near by, and his riderless horse was trotting aimlessly about at the farther end of the lists.

Myles saw the two squires of the fallen knight run across to where their master lay, he saw the ladies waving their kerchiefs and veils, and the castle people swinging their hats and shouting in an ecstasy of delight. Then he rode slowly back to where the squires were now aiding the fallen knight to arise. The senior squire drew his dagger, cut the leather points, and drew off the helm, disclosing the knight's face—a face white as death, and convulsed with rage, mortification, and bitter humiliation.

"I was not rightly unhorsed!" he cried, hoarsely and with livid lips, to the Marshal and his attendants, who had ridden up. "I unhelmed him fairly enough, but my over-girth and breast-strap burst, and my saddle slipped. I was not unhorsed, I say, and I lay claim that I unhelmed him."

"Sir," said the Marshal calmly, and speaking in French, "surely thou knowest that the loss of helmet does not decide an encounter. I need not remind thee, my Lord, that it was so awarded by John of Gaunt, Duke of Lancaster, when in the jousting match between Reynand de Roye and John de Holland, the Sieur Reynand left every point of his helm loosened, so that the helm was beaten off at each stroke. If he then was justified in doing so of his own choice, and wilfully suffering to be unhelmed, how then can this knight be accused of evil who suffered it by chance?"

"Nevertheless," said the Sieur de la Montaigne, in the same hoarse, breathless voice, "I do affirm, and will make my affirmation good with my body, that I fell only by the breaking of my girth. Who says otherwise lies!"

"It is the truth he speaketh," said Myles. "I

myself saw the stitches were some little what burst, and warned him thereof before we ran this course."

"Sir," said the Marshal to the Sieur de la Montaigne, "how can you now complain of that thing which your own enemy advised you of and warned you against? Was it not right knightly for him so to do?"

The Sieur de la Montaigne stood quite still for a little while, leaning on the shoulder of his chief squire, looking moodily upon the ground; then, without making answer, he turned, and walked slowly away to his pavilion, still leaning on his squire's shoulder, whilst the other attendant followed behind, bearing his shield and helmet.

Gascoyne had picked up Myles's fallen helmet as the Sieur de la Montaigne moved away, and Lord George and Sir James Lee came walking across the lists to where Myles still sat. Then, the one taking his horse by the bridle-rein, and the other walking beside the saddle, they led him before the raised dais where the King sat.

Even the Comte de Vermoise, mortified and amazed as he must have been at the overthrow of his best knight, joined in the praise and congratulation that poured upon the young conqueror. Myles, his heart swelling with a passion of triumphant delight, looked up and met the gaze of Lady Alice fixed intently upon him. A red spot of excitement still burned in either cheek, and it flamed to a rosier red as he bowed his head to her before turning away.

Gascoyne had just removed Myles's breastplate and gorget, when Sir James Lee burst into the pavilion. All his grim coldness was gone, and he flung his arms around the young man's neck, hugging him heartily, and kissing him upon either cheek.

Ere he let him go, " Mine own dear boy," he said, holding him off at arm's-length, and winking his one keen eye rapidly, as though to wink away a dampness of which he was ashamed— " mine own dear boy, I do tell thee truly this is as sweet to me as though thou wert mine own son ; sweeter to me than when I first break mine own lance in triumph, and felt myself to be a right knight."

" Sir," answered Myles, "what thou sayest doth rejoice my very heart. Ne'theless, it is but just to say that both his breast-piece and over-girth were burst in the stitches before he ran his course, for so I saw with mine own eyes."

" Burst in the stitches !" snorted Sir James. " Thinkest thou he did not know in what condition was his horse's gearing? I tell thee he went down because thou didst strike fair and true, and he did not so strike thee. Had he been Guy of Warwick he had gone down all the same under such a stroke and in such case.'

CHAPTER XXVIII.

IT was not until more than three weeks after
the King had left Devlen Castle that Lord
George and his company of knights and archers
were ready for the expedition to France. Two
weeks of that time Myles spent at Crosby-Dale
with his father and mother It was the first time
that he had seen them since, four years ago, he
had quitted the low, narrow, white-walled farm-
house for the castle of the great Earl of Mackworth. He had never appreciated before how
low and narrow and poor the farm-house was.
Now with his eyes trained to the bigness of Devlen Castle, he looked around him with wonder
and pity at his father's humble surroundings.
He realized as he never else could have realized
how great was the fall in fortune that had cast
the house of Falworth down from its rightful station to such a level as that upon which it now
rested. And at the same time that he thus recognized how poor was their lot, how dependent

Prior Edward and Myles in the Priory Garden

upon the charity of others, he also recognized how generous was the friendship of Prior Edward, who perilled his own safety so greatly in affording the family of the attainted Lord an asylum in its bitter hour of need and peril.

Myles paid many visits to the gentle old priest during those two weeks' visit, and had many long and serious talks with him. One warm bright afternoon, as he and the old man walked together in the priory garden, after a game or two of draughts, the young knight talked more freely and openly of his plans, his hopes, his ambitions, than perhaps he had ever done. He told the old man all that the Earl had disclosed to him concerning the fallen fortunes of his father's house, and of how all who knew those circumstances looked to him to set the family in its old place once more. Prior Edward added many things to those which Myles already knew—things of which the Earl either did not know, or did not choose to speak. He told the young man, among other matters, the reason of the bitter and lasting enmity that the King felt for the blind nobleman: that Lord Falworth had been one of King Richard's council in times past; that it was not a little owing to him that King Henry, when Earl of Derby, had been banished from England, and that, though he was then living in the retirement

_s
265

of private life, he bitterly and steadfastly opposed King Richard's abdication. He told Myles that at the time when Sir John Dale found shelter at Falworth Castle, vengeance was ready to fall upon his father at any moment, and it needed only such a pretext as that of sheltering so prominent a conspirator as Sir John to complete his ruin.

Myles, as he listened intently, could not but confess in his own mind that the King had many rational, perhaps just, grounds for grievance against such an ardent opponent as the blind Lord had shown himself to be. "But, sir," said he, after a little space of silence, when Prior Edward had ended, "to hold enmity and to breed treason are very different matters. Haply my father was Bolingbroke's enemy, but, sure, thou dost not believe he is justly and rightfully tainted with treason?"

"Nay," answered the priest, "how canst thou ask me such a thing? Did I believe thy father a traitor, thinkest thou I would thus tell his son thereof? Nay, Myles, I do know thy father well, and have known him for many years, and this of him, that few men are so honorable in heart and soul as he. But I have told thee all these things to show that the King is not without some reason to be thy father's unfriend. Neither, haply, is the Earl of Alban without cause of enmity against him. So thou, upon thy part, shouldst not feel bitter rancor against the King for what hath happed to thy house, nor even against William Brookhurst—I mean the Earl of Alban—for, I tell thee, the worst of our enemies and the worst of men believe themselves always to have right and justice upon their side, even when they most wish evil to others."

So spoke the gentle old priest, who looked from his peaceful haven with dreamy eyes upon the sweat and tussle of the world's battle. Had he instead been in the thick of the fight, it might have been harder for him to believe that his enemies ever had right upon their side.

"But tell me this," said Myles, presently, "dost thou, then, think that I do evil in seeking to do a battle of life or death with this wicked Earl of Alban, who hath so ruined my father in body and fortune?"

"Nay," said Prior Edward, thoughtfully, "I say not that thou doest evil. War and bloodshed seem hard and cruel matters to me; but God hath given that they be in the world, and may He forbid that such a poor worm as I should say that they be all wrong and evil. Meseems even an evil thing is sometimes passing good when rightfully used."

Myles did not fully understand what the old man meant, but this much he gathered, that his spiritual father did not think ill of his fighting the Earl of Alban for his temporal father's sake.

So Myles went to France in Lord George's company, a soldier of fortune, as his Captain was. He was there for only six months, but those six months wrought a great change in his life. In the fierce factional battles that raged around the walls of Paris; in the evil life which he saw at the Burgundian court in Paris itself after the truce—a court brilliant and wicked, witty and cruel—the wonderful liquor of youth had evaporated rapidly, and his character had crystallized as rapidly into the hardness of manhood. The warfare, the blood, the evil pleasures which he had seen had been a fiery, crucible test to his soul, and I love my hero that he should have come forth from it so well. He was no longer the innocent Sir Galahad who had walked in pure white up the Long Hall to be knighted by the King, but his soul was of that grim, sterling, rugged sort that looked out calmly from his gray eyes upon the wickedness and debauchery around him, and loved it not.

Then one day a courier came, bringing a packet. It was a letter from the Earl, bidding Myles return straightway to England and to Mackworth House upon the Strand, nigh to London, without delay, and Myles knew that his time had come.

It was a bright day in April when he and Gascoyne rode clattering out through Temple Bar, leaving behind them quaint old London town, its blank stone wall, its crooked, dirty streets, its high-gabled wooden houses, over which rose the sharp spire of St. Paul's, towering high into the golden air. Before them stretched the straight, broad highway of the Strand, on one side the great houses and palaces of princely priests and powerful nobles; on the other the Covent Garden, (or the Convent Garden, as it was then called), and the rolling country, where great stone windmills swung their slow-moving arms in the damp, soft April breeze, and away in the distance the Scottish Palace, the White Hall, and Westminster.

It was the first time that Myles had seen famous London town. In that dim and distant time of his boyhood, six months before, he would have been wild with delight and enthusiasm. Now he jogged along with Gascoyne, gazing about him with calm interest at open shops and booths and tall, gabled houses; at the busy throng of merchants and craftsmen, jostling and elbowing one another; at townsfolk—men and dames—

picking their way along the muddy kennel of a sidewalk. He had seen so much of the world that he had lost somewhat of interest in new things. So he did not care to tarry, but rode, with a mind heavy with graver matters, through the streets and out through the Temple Bar direct for Mackworth House, near the Savoy Palace.

It was with a great deal of interest that Myles and his patron regarded one another when they met for the first time after that half-year which the young soldier had spent in France. To Myles it seemed somehow very strange that his Lordship's familiar face and figure should look so exactly the same. To Lord Mackworth, perhaps, it seemed even more strange that six short months should have wrought so great a change in the young man. The rugged exposure in camp and field during the hard winter that had passed had roughened the smooth bloom of his boyish complexion and bronzed his fair skin almost as much as a midsummer's sun could have done. His beard and mustache had grown again, (now heavier and more mannish from having been shaved), and the white seam of a scar over the right temple gave, if not a stern, at least a determined look to the strong, square-jawed young face. So the two stood for a while regarding one another. Myles was the first to break the silence.

"My Lord," said he, "thou didst send for me to come back to England; behold, here am I."

"When didst thou land, Sir Myles?" said the Earl.

"I and my squire landed at Dover upon Tuesday last," answered the young man.

The Earl of Mackworth stroked his beard softly. "Thou art marvellous changed," said he. "I would not have thought it possible."

Myles smiled somewhat grimly. "I have seen such things, my Lord, in France and in Paris," said he, quietly, "as, mayhap, may make a lad a man before his time."

"From which I gather," said the Earl, "that many adventures have befallen thee. Methought thou wouldst find troublesome times in the Dauphin's camp, else I would not have sent thee to France."

A little space of silence followed, during which the Earl sat musingly, half absently, regarding the tall, erect, powerful young figure standing before him, awaiting his pleasure in motionless, patient, almost dogged silence. The strong, sinewy hands were clasped and rested upon the long, heavy sword, around the scabbard of which the belt was loosely wrapped, and the plates of mail caught and reflected in flashing, broken pieces, the bright sunlight from the window behind.

"Sir Myles," said the Earl, suddenly, breaking the silence at last, "dost thou know why I sent for thee hither?"

"Aye," said Myles, calmly, "how can I else? Thou wouldst not have called me from Paris but for one thing. Methinks thou hast sent for me to fight the Earl of Alban, and lo! I am here."

"Thou speakest very boldly," said the Earl. "I do hope that thy deeds be as bold as thy words."

"That," said Myles, "thou must ask other men. Methinks no one may justly call me coward."

"By my troth!" said the Earl, smiling, "looking upon thee—limbs and girth, bone and sinew— I would not like to be the he that would dare accuse thee of such a thing. As for thy surmise, I may tell thee plain that thou art right, and that it was to fight the Earl of Alban I sent for thee hither. The time is now nearly ripe, and I will straightway send for thy father to come to London. Meantime it would not be safe either for thee or for me to keep thee in my service. I have spoken to his Highness the Prince of Wales, who, with other of the Princes,

is upon our side in this quarrel. He hath promised to take thee into his service until the fitting
time comes to bring thee and thine enemy together, and to-morrow I shall take thee to Scotland Yard, where his Highness is now lodging."

As the Earl ended his speech, Myles bowed,
but did not speak. The Earl waited for a little
while, as though to give him the opportunity to
answer.

"Well, sirrah," said he at last, with a shade of
impatience, "hast thou naught to say? Meseems
thou takest all this with marvellous coolness."

"Have I then my Lord's permission to speak
my mind?"

"Aye," said the Earl, "say thy say."

"Sir," said Myles, "I have thought and pon-
dered this matter much while abroad, and would
now ask thee a plain question in all honesty an
I ha' thy leave."

The Earl nodded his head.

"Sir, am I not right in believing that thou hast
certain weighty purposes and aims of thine own
to gain an I win this battle against the Earl of
Alban?"

"Has my brother George been telling thee
aught to such a purpose?" said the Earl, after a
moment or two of silence.

Myles did not answer.

"No matter," added Lord Mackworth. "I will not ask thee who told thee such a thing. As for thy question—well, sin thou ask it frankly, I will be frank with thee. Yea, I have certain ends to gain in having the Earl of Alban overthrown."

Myles bowed. "Sir," said he, "haply thine ends are as much beyond aught that I can comprehend as though I were a little child, only this I know, that they must be very great. Thou knowest well that in any case I would fight me this battle for my father's sake and for the honor of my house; nevertheless, in return for all that it will so greatly advantage thee, wilt thou not grant me a boon in return should I overcome mine enemy?"

"What is thy boon, Sir Myles?"

"That thou wilt grant me thy favor to seek the Lady Alice de Mowbray for my wife."

The Earl of Mackworth started up from his seat. "Sir Myles Falworth"—he began, violently, and then stopped short, drawing his bushy eyebrows together into a frown, stern, if not sinister.

Myles withstood his look calmly and impassively, and presently the Earl turned on his heel, and strode to the open window. A long time passed in silence while he stood there, gazing out of the window into the garden beyond with his back to the young man.

Suddenly he swung around again. "Sir Myles," said he, "the family of Falworth is as good as any in Derbyshire. Just now it is poor and fallen in estate, but if it is again placed in credit and honor, thou, who art the son of the house, shalt have thy suit weighed with as much respect and consideration as though thou wert my peer in all things. Such is my answer. Art thou satisfied?"

"I could ask no more," answered Myles.

CHAPTER XXIX.

THAT night Myles lodged at Mackworth House. The next morning, as soon as he had broken his fast, which he did in the privacy of his own apartments, the Earl bade him and Gascoyne to make ready for the barge, which was then waiting at the river stairs to take them to Scotland Yard.

The Earl himself accompanied them, and as the heavy snub-nosed boat, rowed by the six oarsmen in Mackworth livery, slid slowly and heavily up against the stream, the Earl, leaning back in his cushioned seat, pointed out the various inns of the great priests or nobles; palatial town residences standing mostly a little distance back from the water behind terraced high-walled gardens and lawns. Yon was the Bishop of Exeter's Close; yon was the Bishop of Bath's; that was York House; and that Chester Inn. So passing by gardens and lawns and palaces, they came at last to Scotland Yard stairs, a broad flight of marble steps that led upward to a stone platform above, upon which opened the gate-way of the garden beyond.

The Scotland Yard of Myles Falworth's day was one of the more pretentious and commodious of the palaces of the Strand. It took its name from having been from ancient times the London inn which the tributary Kings of Scotland occupied when on their periodical visits of homage to England. Now, during this time of Scotland's independence, the Prince of Wales had taken up his lodging in the old palace, and made it noisy with the mad, boisterous mirth of his court.

As the watermen drew the barge close to the landing-place of the stairs, the Earl stepped ashore, and followed by Myles and Gascoyne, ascended to the broad gate-way of the river wall of the garden. Three men-at-arms who lounged upon a bench under the shade of the little pent-roof of a guard-house beside the wall, arose and saluted as the well-known figure of the Earl mounted the steps. The Earl nodded a cool answer, and passing unchallenged through the gate, led the way up a pleached walk, beyond which, as Myles could see, there stretched a little grassy lawn and a stone-paved terrace. As the Earl and the two young men approached the end of the walk, they were met by the sound of voices and laughter, the clinking of glasses and the rattle of dishes. Turning a corner, they came suddenly upon a party of young gentlemen, who sat at a late breakfast under the shade of a wide-spreading lime-tree. They had evidently just left the tilt-yard, for two of the guests—sturdy, thick-set young knights—yet wore a part of their tilting armor.

Behind the merry scene stood the gray, hoary old palace, a steep flight of stone steps, and a long, open, stone-arched gallery, which evidently led to the kitchen beyond, for along it hurried serving-men, running up and down the tall flight of steps, and bearing trays and dishes and cups and flagons. It was a merry sight and a pleasant one. The day was warm and balmy, and the yellow sunlight fell in waving uncertain patches of light, dappling the table-cloth, and twinkling and sparkling upon the dishes, cups, and flagons.

At the head of the table sat a young man some three or four years older than Myles, dressed in a full suit of rich blue brocaded velvet, embroidered with gold-thread and trimmed with black fur. His face, which was turned towards them as they mounted from the lawn to the little stone-flagged terrace, was frank and open; the cheeks smooth and fair; the eyes dark and blue. He

was tall and rather slight, and wore his thick yellow hair hanging to his shoulders, where it was
cut square across, after the manner of the times.
Myles did not need to be told that it was the
Prince of Wales.

"Ho, Gaffer Fox!" he cried, as soon as he
caught sight of the Earl of Mackworth, "what
wind blows thee hither among us wild mallard
drakes? I warrant it is not for love of us, but
only to fill thine own larder after the manner of
Sir Fox among the drakes. Whom hast thou
with thee? Some gosling thou art about to
pluck?"

A sudden hush fell upon the company, and all
faces were turned towards the visitors.

The Earl bowed with a soft smile. "Your
Highness," said he, smoothly, "is pleased to be
pleasant. Sir, I bring you the young knight of
whom I spoke to you some time since—Sir Myles
Falworth. You may be pleased to bring to mind
that you so condescended as to promise to take
him into your train until the fitting time arrived
for that certain matter of which we spoke."

"Sir Myles," said the Prince of Wales, with a
frank, pleasant smile, "I have heard great reports
of thy skill and prowess in France, both from
Mackworth and from others. It will pleasure
me greatly to have thee in my household; more

especially," he added, "as it will get thee, callow as thou art, out of my Lord Fox's clutches. Our faction cannot do without the Earl of Mackworth's cunning wits, Sir Myles; ne'theless I would not like to put all my fate and fortune into his hands without bond. I hope that thou dost not rest thy fortunes entirely upon his aid and countenance."

All who were present felt the discomfort of the Prince's speech. It was evident that one of his mad, wild humors was upon him. In another case the hare-brained young courtiers around might have taken their cue from him, but the Earl of Mackworth was no subject for their gibes and witticisms. A constrained silence fell, in which the Earl alone maintained a perfect ease of manner.

Myles bowed to hide his own embarrassment. "Your Highness," said he, evasively, "I rest my fortune, first of all, upon God, His strength and justice."

"Thou wilt find safer dependence there than upon the Lord of Mackworth," said the Prince, dryly. "But come," he added, with a sudden chance of voice and manner, "these be jests that border too closely upon bitter earnest for a merry breakfast. It is ill to idle with edged tools. Wilt thou not stay and break thy fast with us, my Lord?"

"Pardon me, your Highness," said the Earl, bowing, and smiling the same smooth smile his lips had worn from the first—such a smile as Myles had never thought to have seen upon his haughty face; "I crave your good leave to decline. I must return home presently, for even now, haply, your uncle, his Grace of Winchester, is awaiting my coming upon the business you wot of. Haply your Highness will find more joyance in a lusty young knight like Sir Myles than in an old fox like myself. So I leave him with you, in your good care."

Such was Myles's introduction to the wild young madcap Prince of Wales, afterwards the famous Henry V., the conqueror of France.

For a month or more thereafter he was a member of the princely household, and, after a little while, a trusted and honored member. Perhaps it was the calm sturdy strength, the courage of the young knight, that first appealed to the Prince's royal heart; perhaps afterwards it was the more sterling qualities that underlaid that courage that drew him to the young man; certain it was that in two weeks Myles was the acknowledged favorite. He made no protestation of virtue; he always accompanied the Prince in those madcap ventures to London, where he beheld all manner of wild revelry; he never held himself aloof from his gay comrades, but he looked upon all their mad sports with the same calm gaze that had carried him without taint through the courts of Burgundy and the Dauphin. The gay, roistering young lords and gentlemen dubbed him Saint Myles, and jested with him about hair-cloth shirts and flagellations, but witticism and jest alike failed to move Myles's patient virtue ; he went his own gait in the habits of his life, and in so going knew as little as the others of the mad court that the Prince's growing liking for him was, perhaps, more than all else. on account of that very temperance.

Then, by-and-by, the Prince began to confide in him as he did in none of the others. There was no great love betwixt the King and his son ; it has happened very often that the Kings of England have felt bitter jealousy towards the heirs-apparent as they have grown in power, and such was the case with the great King Henry IV. The Prince often spoke to Myles of the clashing and jarring between himself and his father, and the thought began to come to Myles's mind by degrees that maybe the King's jealousy accounted not a little for the Prince's reckless intemperance.

Once, for instance, as the Prince leaned upon his shoulder waiting, whilst the attendants made ready the barge that was to carry them down the river to the city, he said, abruptly: "Myles, what thinkest thou of us all? Doth not thy honesty hold us in contempt?"

"Nay, Highness," said Myles. "How could I hold contempt?"

"Marry," said the Prince, "I myself hold contempt, and am not as honest a man as thou. But, prithee, have patience with me, Myles. Some day, perhaps, I too will live a clean life. Now, an I live seriously, the King will be more jealous of me than ever, and that is not a little. Maybe I live thus so that he may not know what I really am in soothly earnest."

The Prince also often talked to Myles concerning his own affairs; of the battle he was to fight for his father's honor, of how the Earl of Mackworth had plotted and planned to bring him face to face with the Earl of Alban. He spoke to Myles more than once of the many great changes of state and party that hung upon the downfall of the enemy of the house of Falworth, and showed him how no hand but his own could strike that enemy down; if he fell, it must be through the son of Falworth. Sometimes it seemed to Myles as though he and his blind father were the centre of a great web of plot and intrigue, stretching far and wide, that included not only the greatest houses of England, but royalty and the political balance of the country as well, and even before the greatness of it all he did not flinch.

Then, at last, came the beginning of the time for action. It was in the early part of May, and Myles had been a member of the Prince's household for a little over a month. One morning he was ordered to attend the Prince in his privy cabinet, and, obeying the summons, he found the Prince, his younger brother, the Duke of Bedford, and his uncle, the Bishop of Winchester, seated at a table, where they had just been refreshing themselves with a flagon of wine and a plate of wafers.

"My poor Myles," said the Prince, smiling, as the young knight bowed to the three, and then stood erect, as though on duty. "It shames my heart, brother—and thou, uncle—it shames my heart to be one privy to this thing which we are set upon to do. Here be we, the greatest Lords of England, making a cat's-paw of this lad —for he is only yet a boy—and of his blind father, for to achieve our ends against Alban's faction. It seemeth not over-honorable to my mind."

"Pardon me, your Highness," said Myles, blushing to the roots of his hair; "but, an I may be so bold as to speak, I reck nothing of what your aims may be; I only look to restoring my father's honor and the honor of our house."

"Truly," said the Prince, smiling, "that is the only matter that maketh me willing to lay my hands to this business. Dost thou know why I have sent for thee? It is because this day thou must challenge the Duke of Alban before the King. The Earl of Mackworth has laid all his plans and the time is now ripe. Knowest that thy father is at Mackworth House?"

"Nay," said Myles; "I knew it not."

"He hath been there for nearly two days," said the Prince. "Just now the Earl hath sent for us to come first to Mackworth House. Then to go to the palace, for he hath gained audience with the King, and hath so arranged it that the Earl of Alban is to be there as well. We all go straight-way; so get thyself ready as soon as may be."

Perhaps Myles's heart began beating more quickly within him at the nearness of that great happening which he had looked forward to for so long. If it did, he made no sign of his emotion, but only asked, "How must I clothe myself, your Highness?"

"Wear thy light armor," said the Prince, "but no helmet, a juppon bearing the arms and colors that the Earl gave thee when thou wert knighted, and carry thy right-hand gauntlet under thy belt for thy challenge. Now make haste, for time passes."

CHAPTER XXX.

ADJOINING the ancient palace of Westminster, where King Henry IV. was then holding his court, was a no less ancient stone building known as the Painted Room.   Upon the walls were depicted a series of battle scenes in long bands reaching around this room, one above another. Some of these pictures had been painted as far back as the days of Henry III., others had been added since his time.   They chronicled the various wars of the King of England, and it was from them that the little hall took its name of the Painted Room.

This ancient wing, or offshoot, of the main buildings was more retired from the hurly-burly of outer life than other parts of the palace, and thither the sick King was very fond of retiring from the business of State, which ever rested more and more heavily upon his shoulders, sometimes to squander in quietness a spare hour or two; sometimes to idle over a favorite book;

sometimes to play a game of chess with a favorite courtier. The cold painted walls had been hung with tapestry, and its floor had been spread with arras carpet. These and the cushioned couches and chairs that stood around gave its gloomy antiquity an air of comfort—an air even of luxury.

It was to this favorite retreat of the King's that Myles was brought that morning with his father to face the great Earl of Alban.

In the anteroom the little party of Princes and nobles who escorted the father and son had held a brief consultation. Then the others had entered, leaving Myles and his blind father in charge of Lord Lumley and two knights of the court, Sir Reginald Hallowell and Sir Piers Averell.

Myles, as he stood patiently waiting, with his father's arm resting in his, could hear the muffled sound of voices from beyond the arras. Among others, he recognized the well-remembered tones of the King. He fancied that he heard his own name mentioned more than once, and then the sound of talking ceased. The next moment the arras was drawn aside, and the Earl entered the antechamber again.

"All is ready, cousin," said he to Lord Falworth, in a suppressed voice. "Essex hath done

as he promised, and Alban is within there now."
Then, turning to Myles, speaking in the same
low voice, and betraying more agitation than
Myles had thought it possible for him to show.
"Sir Myles," said he, "remember all that hath
been told thee. Thou knowest what thou hast
to say and do." Then, without further word, he
took Lord Falworth by the hand, and led the
way into the room, Myles following close behind.

The King half sat, half reclined, upon a cushioned seat close to which stood the two Princes.
There were some dozen others present, mostly
priests and noblemen of high quality who clustered in a group at a little distance. Myles knew
most of them at a glance having seen them come
and go at Scotland Yard. But among them all,
he singled out only one—the Earl of Alban.
He had not seen that face since he was a little
child eight years old, but now that he beheld it
again, it fitted instantly and vividly into the re-
membrance of the time of that terrible scene at
Falworth Castle, when he had beheld the then
Lord Brookhurst standing above the dead body
of Sir John Dale, with the bloody mace clinched
in his hand. There were the same heavy black
brows, sinister and gloomy, the same hooked
nose, the same swarthy cheeks. He even remembered the deep dent in the forehead, where

the brows met in perpetual frown. So it was that upon that face his looks centred and rested.

The Earl of Alban had just been speaking to some Lord who stood beside him, and a half-smile still hung about the corners of his lips. At first, as he looked up at the entrance of the new-comers, there was no other expression; then suddenly came a flash of recognition, a look of wide-eyed amazement; then the blood left the cheeks and the lips, and the face grew very pale. No doubt he saw at a flash that some great danger overhung him in this sudden coming of his old enemy, for he was as keen and as astute a politician as he was a famous warrior. At least he knew that the eyes of most of those present were fixed keenly and searchingly upon him. After the first start of recognition, his left hand, hanging at his side, gradually closed around the scabbard of his sword, clutching it in a vice-like grip.

Meantime the Earl of Mackworth had led the blind Lord to the King, where both kneeled.

"Why, how now, my Lord?" said the King. "Methought it was our young Paladin whom we knighted at Devlen that was to be presented, and here thou bringest this old man. A blind man, ha! What is the meaning of this?"

"Majesty," said the Earl, "I have taken this chance to bring to thy merciful consideration one who hath most wofully and unjustly suffered from thine anger. Yonder stands the young knight of whom we spake; this is his father, Gilbert Reginald, whilom Lord Falworth, who craves mercy and justice at thy hands."

"Falworth," said the King, placing his hand to his head. "The name is not strange to mine ears, but I cannot place it. My head hath troubled me sorely to-day, and I cannot remember."

At this point the Earl of Alban came quietly and deliberately forward. "Sire," said he, "pardon my boldness in so venturing to address you, but haply I may bring the name more clearly to your mind. He is, as my Lord of Mackworth said, the whilom Baron Falworth, the outlawed, attainted traitor; so declared for the harboring of Sir John Dale, who was one of those who sought your Majesty's life at Windsor eleven years ago. Sire, he is mine enemy as well, and is brought hither by my proclaimed enemies. Should aught occur to my harm, I rest my case in your gracious hands."

The dusky red flamed into the King's pale, sickly face in answer, and he rose hastily from his seat.

"Aye," said he, "I remember me now—I remember me the man and the name! Who hath dared bring him here before us?" All the dull heaviness of sickness was gone for the moment, and King Henry was the King Henry of ten years ago as he rolled his eyes balefully from one to another of the courtiers who stood silently around.

The Earl of Mackworth shot a covert glance at the Bishop of Winchester, who came forward in answer.

"Your Majesty," said he, "here am I, your brother, who beseech you as your brother not to judge over-hastily in this matter. It is true that this man has been adjudged a traitor, but he has been so adjudged without a hearing. I beseech thee to listen patiently to whatsoever he may have to say."

The King fixed the Bishop with a look of the bitterest, deepest anger, holding his nether lip tightly under his teeth—a trick he had when strongly moved with anger—and the Bishop's eyes fell under the look. Meantime the Earl of Alban stood calm and silent. No doubt he saw that the King's anger was likely to befriend him more than any words that he himself could say, and he perilled his case with no more speech which could only prove superfluous.

At last the King turned a face red and swollen with anger to the blind Lord, who still kneeled before him.

"What hast thou to say?" he said, in a deep and sullen voice.

"Gracious and merciful Lord," said the blind nobleman, "I come to thee, the fountain-head of justice, craving justice. Sire, I do now and here deny my treason, which denial I could not before make, being blind and helpless, and mine enemies strong and malignant. But now, sire, Heaven hath sent me help, and therefore I do acclaim before thee that my accuser, William Bushy Brookhurst, Earl of Alban, is a foul and an attainted liar in all that he hath accused me of. To uphold which allegation, and to defend me, who am blinded by his unknightliness, I do offer a champion to prove all that I say with his body in combat."

The Earl of Mackworth darted a quick look at Myles, who came forward the moment his father had ended, and kneeled beside him. The King offered no interruption to his speech, but he bent a look heavy with anger upon the young man.

"My gracious Lord and King," said Myles, "I, the son of the accused, do offer myself as his champion in this cause, beseeching thee of thy grace leave to prove the truth of the same, being a belted knight by thy grace and of thy creation, and the peer of any who weareth spurs." Thereupon, rising, he drew his iron gauntlet from his girdle, and flung it clashing down upon the floor, and with his heart swelling within him with anger and indignation and pity of his blind father, he cried, in a loud voice, "I do accuse thee, William of Alban, that thou liest vilely as aforesaid, and here cast down my gage, daring thee to take it up."

The Earl of Alban made as though he would accept the challenge, but the King stopped him hastily.

"Stop!" he cried, harshly. "Touch not the gage! Let it lie—let it lie, I tell thee, my Lord! Now, then," said he, turning to the others, "tell me what meaneth all this coil? Who brought this man hither?"

He looked from one to another of those who stood silently around, but no one answered.

"I see," said he, "ye all have had to do with it. It is as my Lord of Alban sayeth; ye are his enemies, and ye are my enemies as well. In this I do smell a vile plot. I cannot undo what I have done, and since I have made this young man a knight with mine own hands, I cannot deny that he is fit to challenge my Lord of Alban. Ne'theless, the High Court of Chivalry shall adjudge this case. Meantime," said he, turning to the Earl Marshal, who was present,

"I give thee this attainted Lord in charge. Convey him presently to the Tower, and let him abide our pleasure there. Also, thou mayst take up yon gage, and keep it till it is redeemed according to our pleasure."

He stood thoughtfully for a moment, and then raising his eyes, looked fixedly at the Earl of Mackworth. "I know," he said, "that I be a right sick man, and there be some who are already plotting to overthrow those who have held up my hand with their own strength for all these years." Then speaking more directly: "My Lord Earl of Mackworth, I see your hand in this before all others. It was thou who so played upon me as to get me to knight this young man, and thus make him worthy to challenge my Lord of Alban. It was thy doings that brought him here to-day, backed by mine own sons and my brother and by these noblemen." Then turning suddenly to the Earl of Alban: "Come, my Lord," said he; "I am aweary with all this coil. Lend me thine arm to leave this place." So it was that he left the room, leaning upon the Earl of Alban's arm, and followed by the two or three of the Alban faction who were present.

"Your Royal Highness," said the Earl Marshal, "I must e'en do the King's bidding, and take this gentleman into arrest."

"Do thy duty," said the Prince. "We knew it must come to this. Meanwhile he is to be a prisoner of honor, and see that he be well lodged and cared for. Thou wilt find my barge at the stairs to convey him down the river, and I myself will come this afternoon to visit him."

CHAPTER XXXI.

It was not until the end of July that the High Court of Chivalry rendered its judgment. There were many unusual points in the case, some of which bore heavily against Lord Falworth, some of which were in his favor. He was very ably defended by the lawyers whom the Earl of Mackworth had engaged upon his side; nevertheless, under ordinary circumstances, the judgment, no doubt, would have been quickly rendered against him. As it was, however, the circumstances were not ordinary, and it was rendered in his favor. The Court besought the King to grant the ordeal by battle, to accept Lord Falworth's champion, and to appoint the time and place for the meeting.

The decision must have been a most bitter, galling one for the sick King. He was naturally of a generous, forgiving nature, but Lord Falworth in his time of power had been an unrelenting and fearless opponent, and his Majesty, who, like most generous men, could on occasions be very cruel and intolerant, had never forgiven him. He had steadily thrown the might of his influence with the Court against the Falworths' case, but that influence was no longer all-powerful for good or ill. He was failing in health, and it could only be a matter of a few years, probably of only a few months, before his successor sat upon the throne.

Upon the other hand, the Prince of Wales's faction had been steadily, and of late rapidly, increasing in power, and in the Earl of Mackworth, its virtual head, it possessed one of the most capable politicians and astute intriguers in Europe. So, as the outcome of all the plotting and counter-plotting, scheming and counter-scheming, the case was decided in Lord Falworth's favor. The knowledge of the ultimate result was known to the Prince of Wales's circle almost a week before it was finally decided. Indeed, the Earl of Mackworth had made pretty sure of that result before he had summoned Myles from France, but upon the King it fell like the shock of a sudden blow. All that day he kept himself in moody seclusion, nursing his silent, bitter anger, and making only one outbreak, in which he swore by the Holy Rood that should Myles be worsted in the encounter, he would not take the battle into his own

U

hands, but would suffer him to be slain, and furthermore, that should the Earl show signs of failing at any time, he would do all in his power to save him. One of the courtiers who had been present, and who was secretly inclined to the Prince of Wales's faction, had repeated this speech at Scotland Yard, and the Prince had said,

"That meaneth, Myles, that thou must either win or die."

"And so I would have it to be, my Lord," Myles had answered.

It was not until nearly a fortnight after the decision of the Court of Chivalry had been rendered that the King announced the time and place of battle—the time to be the 3d of September, the place to be Smithfield—a spot much used for such encounters.

During the three weeks or so that intervened between this announcement and the time of combat, Myles went nearly every day to visit the lists in course of erection. Often the Prince went with him; always two or three of his friends of the Scotland Yard court accompanied him.

The lists were laid out in the usual form. The true or principal list in which the combatants were to engage was sixty yards long and forty yards wide; this rectangular space being surrounded by a fence about six feet high, painted vermilion. Between the fence and the stand where the King and the spectators sat, and surrounding the central space, was the outer or false list, also surrounded by a fence. In the false list the Constable and the Marshal and their followers and attendants were to be stationed at the time of battle to preserve the general peace during the contest between the principals.

One day as Myles, his princely patron, and his friends entered the barriers, leaving their horses at the outer gate, they met the Earl of Alban and his followers, who were just quitting the lists, which they also were in the habit of visiting nearly every day. As the two parties passed one another, the Earl spoke to a gentleman walking beside him and in a voice loud enough to be clearly overheard by the others:

" Yonder is the young sprig of Falworth," said he. " His father, my Lords, is not content with forfeiting his own life for his treason, but must, forsooth, throw away his son's also. I have faced and overthrown many a better knight than that boy."

Myles heard the speech, and knew that it was intended for him to hear it; but he paid no attention to it, walking composedly at the Prince's side. The Prince had also overheard it, and after a little space of silence asked,

"Dost thou not feel anxiety for thy coming battle, Myles?"

"Yea, my Lord," said Myles; "sometimes I do feel anxiety, but not such as my Lord of Alban would have me feel in uttering the speech that he spake anon. It is anxiety for my father's sake and my mother's sake that I feel, for truly there are great matters for them pending upon this fight. Ne'theless, I do know that God will not desert me in my cause, for verily my father is no traitor."

"But the Earl of Alban," said the Prince, gravely, "is reputed one of the best-skilled knights in all England; moreover, he is merciless and without generosity, so that an he gain aught advantage over thee, he will surely slay thee."

"I am not afraid, my Lord," said Myles, still calmly and composedly.

"Nor am I afraid for thee, Myles," said the Prince, heartily, putting his arm, as he spoke, around the young man's shoulder; "for truly, wert thou a knight of forty years, instead of one of twenty, thou couldst not bear thyself with more courage."

As the time for the duel approached, the days seemed to drag themselves along upon leaden feet; nevertheless, the days came and went, as all days do, bringing with them, at last, the fateful 3d of September.

Early in the morning, while the sun was still level and red, the Prince himself, unattended, came to Myles's apartment, in the outer room of which Gascoyne was bustling busily about arranging the armor piece by piece; renewing straps and thongs, but not whistling over his work as he usually did. The Prince nodded to him, and then passed silently through to the inner chamber. Myles was upon his knees, and Father Ambrose, the Prince's chaplain, was beside him. The Prince stood silently at the door, until Myles, having told his last bead, rose and turned towards him.

"My dear Lord," said the young knight, "I give you gramercy for the great honor you do me in coming so early for to visit me."

"Nay, Myles, give me no thanks," said the Prince, frankly reaching him his hand, which Myles took and set to his lips. "I lay bethinking me of thee this morning, while yet in bed, and so, as I could not sleep any more, I was moved to come hither to see thee."

Quite a number of the Prince's faction were at the breakfast at Scotland Yard that morning; among others, the Earl of Mackworth. All were more or less oppressed with anxiety, for nearly all of them had staked much upon the coming battle. If Alban conquered, he would be more powerful to harm them and to revenge himself upon them than ever, and Myles was a very young champion upon whom to depend. Myles himself, perhaps, showed as little anxiety as any ; he certainly ate more heartily of his breakfast that morning than many of the others.

After the meal was ended, the Prince rose. "The boat is ready at the stairs," said he; "if thou wouldst go to the Tower to visit thy father, Myles, before hearing mass, I and Cholmondeley and Vere and Poins will go with thee, if ye, Lords and gentlemen, will grant me your pardon for leaving you. Are there any others that thou wouldst have accompany thee ?"

"I would have Sir James Lee and my squire, Master Gascoyne, if thou art so pleased to give them leave to go," answered Myles.

"So be it," said the Prince. "We will stop at Mackworth stairs for the knight."

The barge landed at the west stairs of the Tower wharf, and the whole party were received with more than usual civilities by the Governor, who conducted them at once to the Tower where Lord Falworth was lodged. Lady Falworth met them at the head of the stairs; her eyes were very red and her face pale, and as Myles raised her hand and set a long kiss upon it, her lips trembled, and she turned her face quickly away, pressing her handkerchief for one moment to her eyes. Poor lady! What agony of anxiety and dread did she not suffer for her boy's sake that day! Myles had not hidden both from her and his father that he must either win or die.

As Myles turned from his mother, Prior Edward came out from the inner chamber, and was greeted warmly by him. The old priest had arrived in London only the day before, having come down from Crosbey Priory to be with his friend's family during this their time of terrible anxiety.

After a little while of general talk, the Prince and his attendants retired, leaving the family together, only Sir James Lee and Gascoyne remaining behind.

Many matters that had been discussed before were now finally settled, the chief of which was the disposition of Lady Falworth in case the battle should go against them. Then Myles took his leave, kissing his mother, who began crying, and comforting her with brave assurances. Prior Edward accompanied him as far as the head of the Tower stairs, where Myles kneeled upon the stone steps, while the good priest blessed him and signed the cross upon his forehead. The Prince was waiting in the walled garden adjoining, and as they rowed back again up the river to Scotland Yard, all were thoughtful and serious, even Poins' and Vere's merry tongues being stilled from their usual quips and jesting.

It was about the quarter of the hour before eleven o'clock when Myles, with Gascoyne, set forth for the lists. The Prince of Wales, together with most of his court, had already gone on to Smithfield, leaving behind him six young knights of his household to act as escort to the young champion. Then at last the order to horse was given; the great gate swung open, and out they rode, clattering and jingling, the sunlight gleaming and flaming and flashing upon their polished armor. They drew rein to the right, and so rode in a little cloud of dust along the Strand Street towards London town, with the breeze blowing merrily, and the sunlight shining as sweetly and blithesomely as though they were riding to a wedding rather than to a grim and dreadful ordeal that meant either victory or death.

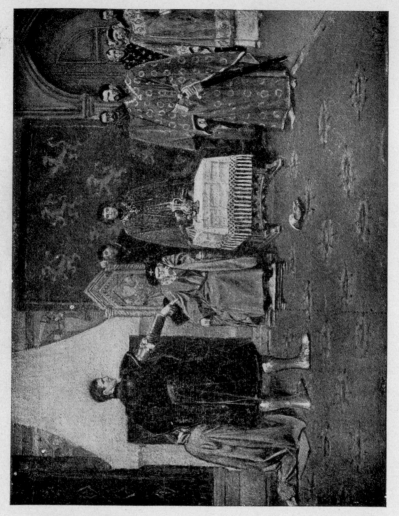

The Challenge

CHAPTER XXXII.

In the days of King Edward III. a code of laws relating to trial by battle had been compiled for one of his sons, Thomas of Woodstock. In this work each and every detail, to the most minute, had been arranged and fixed, and from that time judicial combats had been regulated in accordance with its mandates.

It was in obedience to this code that Myles Falworth appeared at the east gate of the lists (the east gate being assigned by law to the challenger), clad in full armor of proof, attended by Gascoyne, and accompanied by two of the young knights who had acted as his escort from Scotland Yard.

At the barriers he was met by the attorney Willingwood, the chief lawyer who had conducted the Falworth case before the High Court of Chivalry, and who was to attend him during the administration of the oaths before the King.

As Myles presented himself at the gate he was

met by the Constable, the Marshal, and their immediate attendants. The Constable, laying his hand upon the bridle-rein, said, in a loud voice: "Stand, Sir Knight, and tell me why thou art come thus armed to the gates of the lists. What is thy name? Wherefore art thou come?"

Myles answered, "I am Myles Falworth, a Knight of the Bath by grace of his Majesty King Henry IV. and by his creation, and do come hither to defend my challenge upon the body of William Bushy Brookhurst, Earl of Alban, proclaiming him an unknightly knight and a false and perjured liar, in that he hath accused Gilbert Reginald, Lord Falworth, of treason against our beloved Lord, his Majesty the King, and may God defend the right!"

As he ended speaking, the Constable advanced close to his side, and formally raising the umbril of the helmet, looked him in the face. Thereupon, having approved his identity, he ordered the gates to be opened, and bade Myles enter the lists with his squire and his friends.

At the south side of the lists a raised scaffolding had been built for the King and those who looked on. It was not unlike that which had been erected at Devlen Castle when Myles had first jousted as belted knight—here were the same raised seat for the King, the tapestries, the hangings, the fluttering pennons, and the royal standard floating above; only here were no fair-faced ladies looking down upon him, but instead, stern-browed Lords and knights in armor and squires, and here were no merry laughing and buzz of talk and flutter of fans and kerchiefs, but all was very quiet and serious.

Myles riding upon his horse, with Gascoyne holding the bridle-rein, and his attorney walking beside him with his hand upon the stirrups, followed the Constable across the lists to an open space in front of the seat where the King sat. Then, having reached his appointed station, he stopped, and the Constable, advancing to the foot of the stair-way that led to the dais above, announced in a loud voice that the challenger had entered the lists.

"Then call the defendant straightway," said the King, "for noon draweth nigh."

The day was very warm, and the sun, bright and unclouded, shone fiercely down upon the open lists. Perhaps few men nowadays could bear the scorching heat of iron plates such as Myles wore, from which the body was only protected by a leathern jacket and hose. But men's bodies in those days were tougher and more seasoned to hardships of weather than they are in these our times. Myles thought no more of the burning iron plates that incased him than a modern soldier thinks of his dress uniform in warm weather. Nevertheless, he raised the umbril of his helmet to cool his face as he waited the coming of his opponent. He turned his eyes upward to the row of seats on the scaffolding above, and even in the restless, bewildering multitude of strange faces turned towards him recognized those that he knew: the Prince of Wales, his companions of the Scotland Yard household, the Duke of Clarence, the Bishop of Winchester, and some of the noblemen of the Earl of Mackworth's party, who had been buzzing about the Prince for the past month or so. But his glance swept over all these, rather perceiving than seeing them, and then rested upon a square box-like compartment not unlike a prisoner's dock in the courtroom of our day, for in the box sat his father, with the Earl of Mackworth upon one side and Sir James Lee upon the other. The blind man's face was very pale, but still wore its usual expression of calm serenity—the calm serenity of a blind face. The Earl was also very pale, and he kept his eyes fixed steadfastly upon Myles with a keen and searching look, as though to pierce to the very bottom of the young man's heart, and discover if indeed not one little fragment of dry-rot of fear or uncertainty tainted the solid courage of his knighthood.

Then he heard the criers calling the defendant at the four corners of the list: "Oyez! Oyez! Oyez! William Bushy Brookhurst, Earl of Alban, come to this combat, in which you be enterprised this day to discharge your sureties before the King, the Constable, and the Marshal, and to encounter in your defence Myles Falworth, knight, the accepted champion upon behalf of Gilbert Reginald Falworth, the challenger! Oyez! Oyez! Oyez! Let the defendant come!"

So they continued calling, until, by the sudden turning of all faces, Myles knew that his enemy was at hand.

Then presently he saw the Earl and his attendants enter the outer gate at the west end of the barrier; he saw the Constable and Marshal meet him; he saw the formal words of greeting pass; he saw the Constable raise the umbril of the helmet. Then the gate opened, and the Earl of Alban entered, clad *cap-a-pie* in a full suit of magnificent Milan armor without juppon or adornment of any kind. As he approached across the lists, Myles closed the umbril of his helmet, and then sat quite still and motionless, for the time was come.

So he sat, erect and motionless as a statue of

iron, half hearing the reading of the long intri-cately-worded bills, absorbed in many thoughts of past and present things. At last the reading ended, and then he calmly and composedly obeyed, under the direction of his attorney, the several forms and ceremonies that followed; answered the various official questions, took the various oaths. Then Gascoyne, leading the horse by the bridle-rein, conducted him back to his station at the east end of the lists.

As the faithful friend and squire made one last and searching examination of arms and armor, the Marshal and the clerk came to the young champion and administered the final oath by which he swore that he carried no concealed weapons.

The weapons allowed by the High Court were then measured and attested. They consisted of the long sword, the short sword, the dagger, the mace, and a weapon known as the hand-gisarm, or glavelot—a heavy swordlike blade eight palms long, a palm in breadth, and riveted to a stout handle of wood three feet long.

The usual lance had not been included in the list of arms, the hand-gisarm being substituted in its place. It was a fearful and murderous weapon, though cumbersome, unhandy, and ill adapted for quick or dexterous stroke: nevertheless, the

Earl of Alban had petitioned the King to have it included in the list, and in answer to the King's expressed desire the Court had adopted it in the stead of the lance, yielding thus much to the royal wishes. Nor was it a small concession. The hand-gisarm had been a weapon very much in vogue in King Richard's day, and was now nearly if not entirely out of fashion with the younger generation of warriors. The Earl of Alban was, of course, well used to the blade; with Myles it was strange and new, either for attack or in defence.

With the administration of the final oath and the examination of the weapons, the preliminary ceremonies came to an end, and presently Myles heard the criers calling to clear the lists. As those around him moved to withdraw, the young knight drew off his mailed gauntlet, and gave Gascoyne's hand one last final clasp, strong, earnest, and intense with the close friendship of young manhood, and poor Gascoyne looked up at him with a face ghastly white.

Then all were gone; the gates of the principal list and that of the false list were closed clashing, and Myles was alone, face to face, with his mortal enemy.

CHAPTER XXXIII.

THERE was a little while of restless, rustling silence, during which the Constable took his place
in the seat appointed for him directly in front of
and below the King's throne. A moment or two
when even the restlessness and the rustling were
quieted, and then the King leaned forward and
spoke to the Constable, who immediately called
out, in a loud, clear voice,

"Let them go!" Then again, "Let them go!"
Then, for the third and last time, "Let them go
and do their endeavor, in God's name!"

At this third command the combatants, each
of whom had till that moment been sitting as
motionless as a statue of iron, tightened rein,
and rode slowly and deliberately forward without
haste, yet without hesitation, until they met in
the very middle of the lists.

In the battle which followed, Myles fought with
the long sword, the Earl with the hand-gisarm for
which he had asked. The moment they met, the

combat was opened, and for a time nothing was heard but the thunderous clashing and clamor of blows, now and then rising with a ceaseless uproar and din, now and then beating intermittently, now and then pausing. Occasionally, as the combatants spurred together, checked, wheeled, and recovered, they would be hidden for a moment in a misty veil of dust, which, again drifting down the wind, perhaps revealed them drawn a little apart, resting their panting horses. Then, again, they would spur together, striking as they passed, wheeling and striking again.

Upon the scaffolding all was still, only now and then for the buzz of muffled exclamations or applause of those who looked on. Mostly the applause was from Myles's friends, for from the very first he showed and steadily maintained his advantage over the older man. " Hah! well struck! well recovered!" " Look ye! the sword bit that time!" " Nay, look, saw ye him pass the point of the gisarm?" Then, " Falworth! Falworth!" as some more than usually skilful stroke or parry occurred.

Meantime Myles's father sat straining his sightless eyeballs, as though to pierce his body's darkness with one ray of light that would show him how his boy held his own in the fight, and Lord Mackworth, leaning with his lips close to the

w
313

blind man's ear, told him point by point how the battle stood.

"Fear not, Gilbert," said he at each pause in the fight. "He holdeth his own right well." Then, after a while: "God is with us, Gilbert. Alban is twice wounded and his horse faileth. One little while longer and the victory is ours!"

A longer and more continuous interval of combat followed this last assurance, during which Myles drove the assault fiercely and unrelentingly as though to overbear his enemy by the very power and violence of the blows he delivered. The Earl defended himself desperately, but was borne back, back, back, farther and farther. Every nerve of those who looked on was stretched to breathless tensity, when, almost as his enemy was against the barriers, Myles paused and rested.

"Out upon it!" exclaimed the Earl of Mackworth, almost shrilly in his excitement, as the sudden lull followed the crashing of blows. "Why doth the boy spare him? That is thrice he hath given him grace to recover; an he had pushed the battle that time he had driven him back against the barriers."

It was as the Earl had said; Myles had three times given his enemy grace when victory was almost in his very grasp. He had three times spared him, in spite of all he and those dear to him must suffer should his cruel and merciless enemy gain the victory. It was a false and foolish generosity, partly the fault of his impulsive youth—more largely of his romantic training in the artificial code of French chivalry. He felt that the battle was his, and so he gave his enemy these three chances to recover, as some chevalier or knight-errant of romance might have done, instead of pushing the combat to a mercifully speedy end—and his foolish generosity cost him dear.

In the momentary pause that had thus stirred the Earl of Mackworth to a sudden outbreak, the Earl of Alban sat upon his panting, sweating war-horse, facing his powerful young enemy at about twelve paces distant. He sat as still as a rock, holding his gisarm poised in front of him. He had, as the Earl of Mackworth had said, been wounded twice, and each time with the point of the sword, so much more dangerous than a direct cut with the weapon. One wound was beneath his armor, and no one but he knew how serious it might be; the other was under the overlapping of the épaulière, and from it a finger's-breadth of blood ran straight down his side and over the housings of his horse. From without, the still motionless iron figure appeared calm and expressionless; within, who knows what consuming blasts of hate, rage, and despair swept his heart as with a fiery whirlwind.

As Myles looked at the motionless, bleeding figure, his breast swelled with pity. "My Lord," said he, "thou art sore wounded and the fight is against thee; wilt thou not yield thee?"

No one but that other heard the speech, and no one but Myles heard the answer that came back, hollow, cavernous, "Never, thou dog! Never!"

Then in an instant, as quick as a flash, his enemy spurred straight upon Myles, and as he spurred he struck a last desperate, swinging blow, in which he threw in one final effort all the strength of hate, of fury, and of despair. Myles whirled his horse backward, warding the blow with his shield as he did so. The blade glanced from the smooth face of the shield, and, whether by mistake or not, fell straight and true, and with almost undiminished force, upon the neck of Myles's war-horse, and just behind the ears. The animal staggered forward, and then fell upon its knees, and at the same instant the other, as though by the impetus of the rush, dashed full upon it with all the momentum lent by the weight of iron it carried. The shock was irresistible, and the stunned and wounded horse was flung upon the ground, rolling over and over. As his horse fell, Myles wrenched one of his feet out of the stirrup; the other caught for an instant, and he was flung headlong with stunning violence, his armor crashing as he fell. In the cloud of dust that arose no one could see just what happened, but that what was done was done deliberately no one doubted. The Earl, at once checking and spurring his foaming charger, drove the iron-shod war-horse directly over Myles's prostrate body. Then, checking him fiercely with the curb, reined him back, the hoofs clashing and crashing, over the figure beneath. So he had ridden over the father at York, and so he rode over the son at Smithfield.

Myles, as he lay prostrate and half stunned by his fall, had seen his enemy thus driving his rearing horse down upon him, but was not able to defend himself. A fallen knight in full armor was utterly powerless to rise without assistance; Myles lay helpless in the clutch of the very iron that was his defence. He closed his eyes involuntarily, and then horse and rider were upon him. There was a deafening, sparkling crash, a glimmering faintness, then another crash as the horse was reined furiously back again, and then a humming stillness.

In a moment, upon the scaffolding all was a

tumult of uproar and confusion, shouting and gesticulation; only the King sat calm, sullen, impassive. The Earl wheeled his horse and sat for a moment or two as though to make quite sure that he knew the King's mind. The blow that had been given was foul, unknightly, but the King gave no sign either of acquiescence or rebuke; he had willed that Myles was to die.

Then the Earl turned again, and rode deliberately up to his prostrate enemy.

When Myles opened his eyes after that moment of stunning silence, it was to see the other looming above him on his war-horse, swinging his gisarm for one last mortal blow — pitiless, merciless.

The sight of that looming peril brought back Myles's wandering senses like a flash of lightning. He flung up his shield, and met the blow even as it descended, turning it aside. It only protracted the end.

Once more the Earl of Alban raised the gisarm, swinging it twice around his head before he struck. This time, though the shield glanced it, the blow fell upon the shoulder-piece, biting through the steel plate and leathern jack beneath even to the bone. Then Myles covered his head with his shield as a last protecting chance for life.

For the third time the Earl swung the blade flashing, and then it fell, straight and true, upon the defenceless body, just below the left arm, biting deep through the armor plates. For an instant the blade stuck fast, and that instant was Myles's salvation. Under the agony of the blow he gave a muffled cry, and almost instinctively grasped the shaft of the weapon with both hands. Had the Earl let go his end of the weapon, he would have won the battle at his leisure and most easily; as it was, he struggled violently to wrench the gisarm away from Myles. In that short, fierce struggle Myles was dragged to his knees, and then, still holding the weapon with one hand, he clutched the trappings of the Earl's horse with the other. The next moment he was upon his feet. The other struggled to thrust him away, but Myles, letting go the gisarm, which he held with his left hand, clutched him tightly by the sword-belt in the intense, vise-like grip of despair. In vain the Earl strove to beat him loose with the shaft of the gisarm, in vain he spurred and reared his horse to shake him off; Myles held him tight, in spite of all his struggles.

He felt neither the streaming blood nor the throbbing agony of his wounds; every faculty of soul, mind, body, every power of life, was centred in one intense, burning effort. He neither felt, thought, nor reasoned, but clutching, with the blindness of instinct, the heavy, spiked, iron-headed mace that hung at the Earl's saddle-bow, he gave it one tremendous wrench that snapped the plaited leathern thongs that held it as though they were skeins of thread. Then, grinding his teeth as with a spasm, he struck as he had never struck before—once, twice, thrice full upon the front of the helmet. Crash! crash! And then, even as the Earl toppled sidelong, crash! And the iron plates split and crackled under the third blow. Myles had one flashing glimpse of an awful face, and then the saddle was empty.

Then, as he held tight to the horse, panting, dizzy, sick to death, he felt the hot blood gushing from his side, filling his body armor, and staining the ground upon which he stood. Still he held tightly to the saddle-bow of the fallen man's horse until, through his glimmering sight, he saw the Marshal, the Lieutenant, and the attendants gather around him. He heard the Marshal ask him, in a voice that sounded faint and distant, if he was dangerously wounded. He did not answer, and one of the attendants, leaping from his horse, opened the umbril of his helmet, disclosing the dull, hollow eyes, the ashy, colorless lips, and the waxy forehead, upon which stood great beads of sweat.

"He held tightly to the fallen man's horse"

"Water! water!" he cried, hoarsely; "give me to drink!" Then, quitting his hold upon the horse, he started blindly across the lists towards the gate of the barrier. A shadow that chilled his heart seemed to fall upon him. "It is death," he muttered; then he stopped, then swayed for an instant, and then toppled headlong, crashing as he fell.

CONCLUSION.

But Myles was not dead. Those who had seen his face when the umbril of the helmet was raised, and then saw him fall as he tottered across the lists, had at first thought so. But his faintness was more from loss of blood and the sudden unstringing of nerve and sense from the intense furious strain of the last few moments of battle than from the vital nature of the wound. Indeed, after Myles had been carried out of the lists and laid upon the ground in the shade between the barriers, Master Thomas, the Prince's barber-surgeon, having examined the wounds, declared that he might be even carried on a covered litter to Scotland Yard without serious danger. The Prince was extremely desirous of having him under his care, and so the venture was tried. Myles was carried to Scotland Yard, and perhaps was none the worse therefore.

The Prince, the Earl of Mackworth, and two or three others stood silently watching as the worthy shaver and leecher, assisted by his apprentice and Gascoyne, washed and bathed the great gaping wound in the side, and bound it with linen bandages. Myles lay with closed eyelids, still, pallid, weak as a little child. Presently he opened his eyes and turned them, dull and languid, to the Prince.

"What hath happed my father, my Lord?" said he, in a faint, whispering voice.

"Thou hath saved his life and honor, Myles," the Prince answered. "He is here now, and thy mother hath been sent for, and cometh anon with the priest who was with them this morn."

Myles dropped his eyelids again; his lips moved, but he made no sound, and then two bright tears tricked across his white cheek.

"He maketh a woman of me," the Prince muttered through his teeth, and then, swinging on his heel, he stood for a long time looking out of the window into the garden beneath.

"May I see my father?" said Myles, presently, without opening his eyes.

The Prince turned around and looked inquiringly at the surgeon.

The good man shook his head. "Not to-day," said he; "haply to-morrow he may see him and his mother. The bleeding is but new stanched, and such matters as seeing his father and mother may make the heart to swell, and so maybe the wound burst afresh and he die. An he would hope to live, he must rest quiet until to-morrow day."

But though Myles's wound was not mortal, it was very serious. The fever which followed lingered longer than common—perhaps because of the hot weather—and the days stretched to weeks, and the weeks to months, and still he lay there, nursed by his mother and Gascoyne and Prior Edward, and now and again by Sir James Lee.

One day, a little before the good priest returned to Saint Mary's Priory, as he sat by Myles's bedside, his hands folded, and his sight turned inward, the young man suddenly said, " Tell me, holy father, is it always wrong for man to slay man ?"

The good priest sat silent for so long a time that Myles began to think he had not heard the question. But by-and-by he answered, almost with a sigh, " It is a hard question, my son, but I must in truth say, meseems it is not always wrong."

" Sir," said Myles, " I have been in battle when men were slain, but never did I think thereon as I have upon this matter. Did I sin in so slaying my father's enemy ?"

" Nay," said Prior Edwards, quietly, "thou didst

not sin. It was for others thou didst fight, my son, and for others it is pardonable to do battle. Had it been thine own quarrel, it might haply have been more hard to have answered thee."

Who can gainsay, even in these days of light, the truth of this that the good priest said to the sick lad so far away in the past?

One day the Earl of Mackworth came to visit Myles. At that time the young knight was mending, and was sitting propped up with pillows, and was wrapped in Sir James Lee's cloak, for the day was chilly. After a little time of talk, a pause of silence fell.

" My Lord," said Myles, suddenly, " dost thou remember one part of a matter we spoke of when I first came from France?"

The Earl made no pretence of ignorance. " I remember," said he, quietly, looking straight into the young man's thin white face.

" And have I yet won the right to ask for the Lady Alice de Mowbray to wife?" said Myles, the red rising faintly to his cheeks.

" Thou hast won it," said the Earl, with a smile.

Myles's eyes shone and his lips trembled with the pang of sudden joy and triumph, for he was still very weak. " My Lord," said he, presently, "belike thou camest here to see me for this very matter?"

The Earl smiled again without answering, and Myles knew that he had guessed aright. He reached out one of his weak, pallid hands from beneath the cloak. The Earl of Mackworth took it with a firm pressure, then instantly quitting it again, rose, as if ashamed of his emotion, stamped his feet, as though in pretence of being chilled, and then crossed the room to where the fire crackled brightly in the great stone fireplace.

Little else remains to be told; only a few loose strands to tie, and the story is complete.

Though Lord Falworth was saved from death at the block, though his honor was cleansed from stain, he was yet as poor and needy as ever. The King, in spite of all the pressure brought to bear upon him, refused to restore the estates of Falworth and Easterbridge—the latter of which had again reverted to the crown upon the death of the Earl of Alban without issue—upon the grounds that they had been forfeited not because of the attaint of treason, but because of Lord Falworth having refused to respond to the citation of the courts. So the business dragged along for month after month, until in January the King died suddenly in the Jerusalem Chamber at Westminster. Then matters went smoothly enough, and Falworth and Mackworth swam upon the flood-tide of fortune.

So Myles was married, for how else should the story end? And one day he brought his beautiful young wife home to Falworth Castle, which his father had given him for his own, and at the gate-way of which he was met by Sir James Lee and by the newly-knighted Sir Francis Gascoyne.

One day, soon after this home-coming, as he stood with her at an open window into which came blowing the pleasant May-time breeze, he suddenly said, "What didst thou think of me when I first fell almost into thy lap, like an apple from heaven?"

"I thought thou wert a great, good-hearted boy, as I think thou art now," said she, twisting his strong, sinewy fingers in and out.

"If thou thoughtst me so then, what a very fool I must have looked to thee when I so clumsily besought thee for thy favor for my jousting at Devlen. Did I not so?"

"Thou didst look to me the most noble, handsome young knight that did ever live; thou didst look to me Sir Galahad, as they did call thee, withouten taint or stain."

327

Myles did not even smile in answer, but looked at his wife with such a look that she blushed a rosy red. Then, laughing, she slipped from his hold, and before he could catch her again was gone.

I am glad that he was to be rich and happy and honored and beloved after all his hard and noble fighting.